A *Lady* LIKE SARAH

A ROCKY CREEK ROMANCE

MARGARET BROWNLEY

DOUBLEDAY LARGE PRINT HOME LIBRARY EDITION

THOMAS NELSON
Since 1798

NASHVILLE   DALLAS   MEXICO CITY   RIO DE JANEIRO   BEIJING

Published in Nashville, Tennessee. Thomas Nelson is a registered trademark of Thomas Nelson Inc.

Thomas Nelson, Inc. titles may be purchased in bulk for educational, business, fundraising, or sales promotional use. For information, e-mail SpecialMarkets@ThomasNelson.com

Scripture quotations are taken from the King James Version of the Bible. Public domain.

This novel is a work of fiction. Any references to real events, businesses, organizations, and locales are intended only to give the fiction a sense of reality and authenticity. Any resemblance to actual persons, living or dead, is entirely coincidental.

ISBN-13: 978-1-61523-406-6

Printed in the United States of America

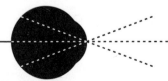

This Large Print Book carries the
Seal of Approval of N.A.V.H.

To George . . .
For the privilege and joy of loving you.

One

1879
Missouri

Vultures signaled trouble ahead.

"Whoa, boy." Reverend Justin Wells tugged on the reins of his horse, bringing his brown gelding to a standstill.

Adjusting the brim of his dusty felt hat, he narrowed his eyes against the bright afternoon sun and peered across the wide, arid plains. Trees grew directly ahead of him, the first he'd seen since leaving St. Louis five days prior. The graceful, tall sycamores suggested the welcome presence of water, perhaps a stream.

He mopped his damp brow with a kerchief, then lifted his eyes upward. They were vultures, all right. No question about it. The scavengers circled overhead on broad, outstretched wings, scanning the ground in waiting silence.

Something or someone was dying. An animal no doubt. He'd passed his share of buffalo skulls and cattle carcasses in recent days, and each had made him ruminate on dying and the meaning of life.

Born and raised in Boston, he never planned to travel across country, never really had a hankering for adventure. Not like most men he knew. Certainly he never expected to leave his hometown in disgrace.

He reached for his canteen, every muscle in his body protesting. He wasn't just saddle sore; his back ached from the restless nights spent on the hard, unyielding ground. Sleep, if it came at all, had been fleeting at best and offered little respite from his troubled thoughts.

He pulled off the cork top of his tin canteen and lifted it to his parched lips. Never one to question God's will in the past, it disturbed him that he questioned it now.

Texas!

What possible reason could God

have for sending him to a rough, untamed town in Texas?

He thought of all the work left undone in Boston. To be separated from the congregation he loved seemed a fate worse than death. Though what choice did he have but to accept God's will?

Behind him, Moses, his pack mule, made a strange whinnying sound that ended in a loud hee-haw. The short, thick head moved from side to side; the long ears twitched.

Having learned to trust the animal's instincts, Justin felt a sense of unease. With increased alertness, he rose in his saddle and scanned the area ahead. A movement in the trees caught his attention. A previously unnoticed horse stood in the shade. At first he thought it was a wild mustang that had strayed away from its herd. Upon closer observation, he realized his mistake. This horse was saddled.

He glanced at the still-circling buzzards and a sense of urgency shot through him. "Let's go, boy." Digging his heels gently into his gelding's ribs, he galloped along the trail, kicking up dust behind him.

Moses followed close behind, the pots and pans tied to the mule's pack clanking like old rusty chains.

Moments later, Justin dismounted, stabbed the ground with a metal picket, and staked his horse. He approached the bay cautiously, his gaze scanning the nearby terrain for its owner.

Tethered to a sapling, the horse pawed the ground and neighed, its long black tail swishing back and forth. Something—a red neckerchief— fluttered from a nearby bush.

Leaving horses and mule behind, he followed a narrow path toward the stream, stopping to pick up the kerchief en route.

Two bodies lay side by side in the grass, and he hurried toward them, searching for signs of life. One man wore a badge on his black vest, identi- fying him as a U.S. Marshal. The other man, judging by the handcuffs, was his prisoner.

Justin kneeled by the lawman's side

and felt for a pulse. The man's eyes flickered open and his parched lips quivered. He had been shot. Blood had seeped through his clothes and trickled to the ground.

"Don't talk," Justin said. "Save your strength. I'll get you some water."

The marshal reached for Justin's arm. "Promise me—" He coughed. "My prisoner . . . promise—" He spoke in a murmur that was almost drowned out by a sudden gust of wind rippling through the tall prairie grass. "Take . . . to . . . Texas—"

Justin sat back on his heels in surprise. "Texas? You want me to take the prisoner to Texas?"

The lawman nodded slightly and closed his eyes, his breathing labored.

Intent upon getting the marshal water, Justin straightened. A moaning sound, soft as a kitten's first mew, made him take a closer look at the prisoner. That's when he saw the man's foot move.

Dropping down on his knees by the prisoner's side, Justin leaned over him. "Take it easy, lad." The prisoner's face was covered in dust, but he appeared to be a young man, clean-shaven, probably still in his teens. The boy's youth would probably account for his ill-chosen bright red boots, which looked all the more garish in full sunlight.

"Just stay put." Justin squeezed the man's slight shoulder. "I'll get you something to drink." There was nothing to be done about the boots.

Returning to his horse, Justin retrieved the canteen tied to his saddle, then hurried to the fast-running stream. Removing the stopper, he dipped the canteen into the cool, clear waters and rushed back to the injured men, chasing away one of the vultures that had landed nearby.

"Here." Lowering himself onto his knee again, he slid one arm beneath the marshal's head and lifted the canteen to the man's swollen lips. The lawman took a sip and then slumped back as if it took all his energy to swallow. His eyes open, he looked worried or distressed, maybe both.

"Tell my . . . f-family—"

Justin tried to reassure him. "You'll be all right," he said. He didn't know anything about bullet wounds. It wasn't the kind of thing taught at Boston Theological Seminary. Still, he couldn't just let the man die. There had to be something he could do.

But first things first. He turned to the prisoner. Slipping his hand beneath the young man's shoulders, he lifted the youth's head. The man's wide-brimmed slouch hat was crushed behind him, the leather strap still beneath his smooth chin. Justin pulled the felt hat off and— much to his surprise—long red hair tumbled out of the crown.

Justin froze. Not sure if he could believe his eyes, he blinked and took a closer look. There was no mistake; the prisoner was a woman!

Two

Even before Sarah Prescott's eyes flickered open, she sensed something had
changed. The sun didn't seem quite
as bright or the heat as unrelenting as
it had been previously. Something or
someone blocked the sunlight, but before she could determine whether friend
or foe she drifted off again.

Now, she saw blue. Or was it green?
Something. She imagined herself running along a sweet-scented meadow,
free as the wind that touched her
fevered brow.

Then it hit her. It wasn't the wind she
felt; it was something else, something
soft and gentle and refreshingly cool.

She tried to sit up, but a weight of some kind held her down. *Hands.* Strong yet gentle hands. She lay back, willing the fog in her head to clear.

A face floated into view, the face of a man—not the lawman, but a stranger. A stranger with clear, blue eyes and a handsome, square face that was all at once strong and kind.

He knelt by her side and, cupping her chin in his hand, sponged her forehead with tender strokes. He then lifted her by the shoulders and held a canteen to her dry lips. The water tasted sweet, but it hurt to swallow and she couldn't take much more than a sip at a time.

He lowered her gently. "How do you feel?"

She gazed up at him, still confused. The sun seemed less bright and she realized she lay beneath the shade of a black willow tree. The stranger must have carried her.

She lifted her hand to her head, surprised to find that her handcuffs had been removed. She tried to sit up.

"Whoa, there," he said, his strong fingers pressing into her shoulder. "Take it easy. Some rest and food and you'll be good as new."

She settled back on the canvas roll that served as a pillow, aware that her hat had been removed and her hair had come loose. "Who . . . who are you?"

"Name's Justin Wells. Reverend Justin Wells."

Surprised, she stared at him. She pictured preachers old and stooped-shouldered, lacking in humor. This one stood straight and tall, his broad shoulders straining against his white shirt, rolled up at the sleeves.

"A preacher, eh?"

"That I am." Her surprise seemed to amuse him, and a glint of humor danced in his eyes. His mouth turned up in a grin.

"Talk about dumb luck."

The grin left his face and his dark eyebrows arched upward. "Is there a problem?"

"No," she muttered. "No problem." She lowered her lashes. *Of all things, a preacher.*

"And your name is . . . ?"

She opened one eye and studied him.

The wind ruffled his thick black hair, but his gaze never wavered. "My name's Sarah."

"Sarah, huh?"

Something in his voice made her open the other eye and regard him with suspicion. "You have a problem with my name?"

"Not at all. I think it's a beautiful name. A biblical name."

He didn't look like a preacher, but he sure sounded like one. "You're joshin' me, right?"

"No, honest. Sarah's in the Bible."

She considered this for a moment. If what he said was true, why hadn't she heard about it before now? Thinking he might be poking fun at her, she glared at him. But he looked solemn as soap.

He drew the tip of his finger along his upper lip. Unlike most men, he was clean-shaven, and this gave him an open, honest appearance that made her regret having to be secretive.

"Did you know that 'Sarah' originally meant contentious?"

"Contentious?" She repeated the

word slowly, trying to think if she ever heard it before.

"Quick-tempered," he offered.

"You don't have to tell me what it means," she snapped. Sooner or later she would have figured it out for herself.

"It wasn't until she turned eighty and gave birth to a prince that she became known as Sarah, the princess," he added.

Sarah had never heard of anything so ridiculous in all her born days. "This Sarah woman had a baby when she was eighty?"

He nodded.

"If that don't beat all."

"It was a miracle," the preacher said gently.

"You call it what you want, mister. But any woman who has a baby at that age ain't got both oars in the water."

"I guess that's one way to look at it." He studied her for a moment. "What's the rest? Sarah what?"

"I ain't got no rest," she said. She wasn't about to tell him she was a Prescott. Just 'cuz he was a preacher was no reason to think he wouldn't recognize her name.

"What should I call you?"

Her eyes met his. "Call me Sarah."

"It's customary for a man to address a woman by her surname. Miss—?" He waited.

"I never did cotton much to being called miss," she said. "Makes it sound like I'm missin' out on somethin' just 'cuz I ain't got me no husband. Just call me Sarah."

He grinned. "You sure do have a different way of looking at things."

She wondered if he meant that as a compliment or criticism. It was hard to tell if he was serious. He didn't speak like anyone she knew. He pronounced each word fully with no clipped vowels or lazy drawls, and she wondered if perhaps he was part Irish.

"Where you from?" she asked.

"Boston," he said. "And you?"

She shrugged. "Here and there."

He accepted her answer without question. "So what happened?" he prodded. "Who shot the marshal?"

"Never saw the scoundrel before in

my life," she replied. She gave an indignant toss of her head, and the world spun circles around her.

He placed a steadying hand on her shoulder. "Take it easy."

Not one to pay much heed to physical ailments, she pushed his hand away. "The fool man ambushed us and then done stole my horse."

The preacher sat back on his haunches and regarded her thoughtfully. "You better rest for a while." He turned his attention to the marshal, dabbing the man's feverish face with a cool, wet cloth.

"He ain't lookin' so good," she said.

She glanced at the two horses grazing a short distance away, thinking about the attack. She had pleaded with the marshal to stop so she could rest her weary bones. He cuff-linked her to himself and tucked the key into his saddlebags before letting her dangle her feet in the fresh, cool waters of the stream. As she and the marshal returned to the horses, they were ambushed without so much as a warning.

"If I ever get my hands on that no-good thief, he'll be cold as a wagon wheel," she vowed. She glanced at the preacher for a sign of objection, but his face was oddly expressionless. Whatever he was thinking, he kept it to himself.

Not that she cared what he thought. That scoundrel shot Marshal Owen in cold blood and left them both to die. What was she supposed to do? Forgive and forget?

"So why is the marshal holding you prisoner?" the preacher asked.

She stiffened at his question. "I reckon that's my bus'ness."

He studied her intently but didn't pursue the matter further. "Here, have some more water."

This time he watched her drink from his canteen, unassisted. Then he carefully unwrapped a small wedge of cheese and a generous portion of hard bread and handed it to her.

"Since you haven't eaten in a while, I think you should take it nice and easy," he cautioned.

Ignoring his warning, she stuffed the food into her mouth.

His dark brows slanted in a worried frown, but he said nothing until she had finished every last crumb. "That should tide you over for a while."

He handed her the canteen. After taking another sip, she tried to stand, fighting off the dizziness. The preacher held her down with a firm hand, and she glared up at him. "You ain't keepin' me here ag'inst my will."

"I think the marshal has something to say about that," he said, releasing her. "It would save us both a lot of trouble if you just sat back and concentrated on getting your strength back."

"My strength is back," she argued. She tried standing, again, this time more slowly. A wave of dizziness washed over her, but she stubbornly remained on her feet.

"I'm not stayin' here," she added when her head stopped spinning. Though still light-headed, she started toward the horses, but in her present state she was no match for him. In one easy movement, he clamped his hand around her arm, surprising her with his strength. He might be a city-born preacher, but he was no weakling.

"I'm not going to hurt you," he said in a low, soothing voice, his fingers wrapped tightly around her wrist. He waited for her to stop struggling, then he calmly snapped the marshal's hand-cuffs in place.

Furious, she pulled away and lashed out at him. "You have no right to do that! You ain't no lawman."

"Sorry," he said, and he actually sounded sincere. "It's for your own good. I don't want you taking off in your condition."

"My condition?" She studied him from the corner of her eye. "You make it sound like I'm gonna have me a baby."

The preacher's face turned red. Obviously, he wasn't used to plain talk. "I-I didn't mean to suggest you were in a . . . f-family way," he stammered.

He looked so uncomfortable, Sarah almost felt sorry for him. "Now don't go getting yourself all in a powder," she said. "Take these things off me and I won't give it another thought."

"I'm sorry," he said, "but I can't do

that. I need you to stay in place while I take the bullet out of the marshal's shoulder." Turning his back on her, he set about stacking rocks in a circle for a fire pit.

Exasperated, she flopped down on the ground and quietly seethed. She decided her only option was to watch the preacher's every move until she figured out a plan. "Know your enemies" was one rule she had learned early in life. Though, she had to admit, never before had she met a foe more pleasing to the eyes.

It wasn't often that she saw a man whose face wasn't scarred and whose nose was straight as the day he was born. Nor could she remember the last time she'd met a man who didn't smell of whisky and tobacco. Instead, the preacher smelled of sunshine and something else that filled her with a strange and unfamiliar longing.

Trying not to appear obvious, she kept a wary eye on him. He made several futile attempts to build a fire, and she shook her head in disbelief. The man knew about the Bible, but didn't

know horsefeathers about the funda-
mentals of plain old livin'. He was as
useless as a sundial in the shade. If she
had to depend on him for survival, she
was in worse shape than she thought.

Her disbelief grew as he heaped dry
grass onto a mound, tossed in a small
piece of green wood, and struck a
safety match. As would be expected,
the grass burned bright for a moment or
two before the flames died in a cloud of
gray smoke.

She coughed and turned her head
against the haze that drifted her way.
"You might try buffalo chips." She nodded toward the trail. He gave her a dubious frown.

"The chips make a nice hot fire, with
no stink," she added.

"Is that so?" He sounded like he'd
never heard of such a thing, and she
could only shake her head in wonder.
He tossed the last of the green wood
and started toward the area she indicated.

"Be sure you pick out the dry
ones," she called after him, though she
couldn't imagine anyone doing other-

wise. "And don't forget to give 'em a good kick before pickin' 'em up."

He turned to stare at her, his brows raised in question. "You want me to kick them?"

"You'd be amazed at how many critters live under a chip. If you don't want to end up in a terr'torial dispute with a scorpion, you best pay heed."

He acknowledged her warning with a tip of his hat and continued on his way.

He returned a short while later, his arms full. He dropped the chips in a pile and started tossing them one by one into the pit. In no time flat, hot flames licked the air.

"See? What did I tell you?" she said. "Simple as sin." She immediately regretted her words. Mentioning sin in front of a preacher was askin' for trouble. "I mean—"

"I know what you mean," he said.

That was it? No lecture? No sermon? Curious, she studied him, noting the warm glow of leaping flames reflected in his eyes.

He looked straight at her and she

quickly turned away, irritated at herself for being caught staring.

"Have you done much camping out in the wilderness, like this?" he asked.

Thinking he was mocking her, she stiffened, ready to defend herself. Seeing nothing derisive on his face, she bit back her angry retort.

"This ain't campin' out. This is plain old livin'."

His mouth dipped in a frown. "Don't you have a home? A family?"

"Like I told you before, I ain't got no husband."

"What about parents?" he persisted. "Or brothers and sisters?"

"I reckon I come down on the short side of family," she said, purposely keeping her answers vague. "But I don't let myself worry about it none. You have to play the fiddle you have." She watched him with keen interest. "What about you? Are you hitched?"

"No, I'm not married," he replied, and she detected a tightness in his voice.

"You have something ag'inst gittin' hitched?" she asked.

"No, nothing like that. My church

work takes up all my time." He studied her a moment. "What's your excuse?"

"I don't reckon there's a man alive who would want me for his wife." She shrugged. "Maybe when I'm eighty."

He surprised her with his laughter, a full-hearted resonance both deep and rich, and more than anything, catching.

She grinned at him. What do you know? She done found a preacher with a sense of humor.

The smile died abruptly as he kneeled beside the lawman and carefully re-moved his bloodied shirt. Next, he pulled a knife out of his boot and low-ered the blade into the bright orange flames.

She regarded him with suspicion. "Have you ever removed a bullet?"

"Never."

"Figures."

He glanced at her. "I suppose you have."

"I've removed my share," she said.

It was obvious by his dubious expres-sion that he didn't believe her. As if she cared what he believed.

Knife in hand, he bowed his head and

closed his eyes in prayer. "Dear heavenly Father, Almighty God, Creator of heaven and earth . . ."

On and on he went. Not one to sit still for long, she shifted her body impatiently. If the marshal didn't die before the end of the prayer, that in itself would be a miracle.

"Oh, God, my strength and my salvation . . ."

Growing even more restless, Sarah opened her eyes, though she kept her head bent low. She thought about the simple prayers she'd uttered all those years ago—prayers to save her papa, prayers to save her ma.

All these years she'd blamed God for not answering them. Maybe she had only herself to blame for not using the right words. Or for not addressing God with all those highfalutin' names. Feeling guilty, she forced herself to concentrate on the preacher's every word.

"Amen."

She breathed a sigh of relief but said nothing.

Justin leaned over the lawman and gently lowered the knife. Owen squirmed and let out a bloodcurdling scream. The preacher fell back, the knife still in his hand.

She rolled her eyes. "You better let me do it," she said. Judging by his pinched white face, the preacher was about to faint and that's all they needed.

"You serious?" he asked. "Can you really remove a bullet?" He gave her a long, penetrating look. "This isn't a trick, is it? So you can get away?"

"Where's your faith?" she asked evenly.

The question clearly startled him. He stepped back as if punched in the face, a shadow of indecision on his forehead. "Why would you want to help a man who's holding you prisoner?"

"Owen, here, has three young'uns," she said. "And I don't aim to sit and watch you make orphans out of 'em."

The preacher's expression softened. "That's mighty nice of you to be concerned about his welfare."

"I told you, I'm doin' it for his young'uns. No child deserves to be an orphan." Hoping he hadn't noticed the telltale bitterness that had crept unbidden into her voice, she watched him with a sinking feeling. She knew from his furrowed brow that he hadn't missed the rancor, but it was the softness in his eyes that told her he'd guessed from where it came.

Alarmed by the compassion she saw on his face and the way it made her feel all warm and soft inside, she lifted her chin in open defiance.

She was used to people whispering behind her back or staring at her with accusations. But never before had anyone treated her like she was a real person, maybe even a good person, and she wasn't sure how to handle it.

"Don't go looking at me like that, you hear?" she said irritably.

"Like what?" he asked, sounding genuinely confused.

"Like I'm some sort of—" She glared at him. "We're wastin' time. If we don't get that bullet out soon, it'll be too late."

He reached into his pocket for the key to the handcuffs.

After the cuffs fell away, she rubbed the circulation back into her wrists before taking the knife from him.

She held the shiny dagger in a flame, turning the staghorn hilt slowly in her hand until the blade turned red. It was the sorriest looking knife she'd ever laid eyes on, the serrated cutting edge ill-equipped for the task at hand. Still, it was all she had to work with.

Waving the knife in the air to cool, she knelt by the marshal's side. "You better hold him down," she said.

She waited for the preacher to position himself opposite her. With one hand on Owen's uninjured shoulder and the other on his thighs, the preacher pressed down.

She pulled off a piece of the dark brown bark from a nearby willow and pushed it into the marshal's mouth. "Bite down hard," she said. "You hear?"

Owen stared up at her, his glazed eyes round, but said nothing.

"Alcohol would help," Sarah said.

"So would a doctor," the preacher replied.

As she attempted to dislodge the bullet, the marshal started to bleed profusely. Fortunately, the bullet wasn't embedded in bone. Not having any tongs in which to grab it, she tried to work the tip of the knife beneath the slug.

The marshal cried out and she drew back.

"Hold on," the preacher said, softly, repositioning his hands on the patient. "It'll soon be over."

He signaled his readiness with a nod of his head.

Taking a deep breath, she pushed the knife into the fleshy wound. She couldn't see anything for all the blood. The marshal squirmed and yelled whenever her knife touched bone, and it was only after he passed out that she was able to probe deeper.

Finding the bullet, she gently worked the tip of her knife under the lead and flipped it upward. The slug flew up and landed on the ground nearby.

She glanced up at the preacher, whose head was turned away. "You can look now," she said. "Have you got a clean rag?"

The preacher handed her a clean kerchief from his saddlebag, and she used it to press down on the open wound. "I

need you to fetch me some tumbleweed." She pointed into the distance.

The preacher frowned. "Tumbleweed?"

"A trick I learned from an old medicine man. You pour tumbleweed tea into
the wound to prevent infection."

The preacher nodded and walked
away. His step faltered as he glanced
back over his shoulder and his eyes met
hers. Apparently, he thought she was
going to take off—and if she had the
brain of a bird, she would.

"Stop gawkin' and hurry!" she called
after him. "He's gonna bleed to death."

He returned moments later, carrying a
ball of the thorny weed on the end of a
long stick.

While she pressed on the wound to
slow the bleeding, she told him how
to brew two different types of tea, one
for flushing out the wound and one for
drinking.

Following her directions, he took two
tin cups from the marshal's saddlebags
and dropped pieces of tumbleweed into
one and chunks of willow bark into the
other, adding hot water to both.

After the tumbleweed brew had cooled, Sarah flushed the marshal's wound with it and tied a strip of fabric torn from one of the preacher's clean spare shirts around it.

Then she carefully spooned warm willow bark tea into the injured marshal's mouth. The bitter taste shocked him into consciousness, and he sputtered and groaned.

"This will help with the swellin' and fever," she explained. She shoved another spoonful into the marshal's mouth. His eyes grew round in protest, but he swallowed it, then gasped.

She handed the preacher the cup. "Make him drink some every hour or so."

The preacher glanced at the lawman with uncertainty, but he nodded and set the cup down. He walked with her to the fast-running stream and waited while she washed her hands. She felt grimy and longed to bathe. She glanced over her shoulder and found him watching her every move. Sighing, she dried her hands on her shirt and straightened. When they returned to camp, he pulled out the handcuffs, his face shadowed with regret.

He continued to stare at the metal bracelets in his hand, refusing to meet her gaze. "I'm sorry, Miss—" He caught himself. "I mean, Sarah . . . but I promised him . . ."

He looked so genuinely upset that she felt sorry for the man and didn't have the heart to fight him. Or maybe she simply didn't have the strength. The surgery had taken a lot out of her, and all she wanted to do was lie down and sleep. Sighing, she pressed her hands together and held them out to him. Without another word, he snapped on the cuffs.

He placed his hat on his head. "Sarah, this problem you have with the law . . . If you let me, I know I can help you. In fact, I'm sure of it."

She shrugged. "There ain't nothin' that's a sure thing, 'cept death and trouble."

"That's why we need God," he said.

She frowned but said nothing.

"Anything you tell me will be held in strictest confidence," he said gently.

She glared up at him. "I ain't airin' out my wash to you or anyone else."

He stared at her like he could see right through her, and she feared he could read her mind. She knew such a feat was impossible, of course, but she clamped down on any untoward musings, just the same.

"All right, Sarah. I can't force you to confide in me. I just want you to know that I'll do anything I can to help you, if you'll let me."

"If you want to help, then let me go." She held up her handcuffed wrists, but he made no move toward her.

Grimacing, she twisted her hands back and forth, but the metal cuffs held tight. First she was stuck with Marshal Owen, and now she had a preacher to contend with. If it wasn't chickens, it was feathers.

Plunking down on the ground, she laid her head against a tree and tried to look at the bright side. The preacher wasn't armed, except for that poor excuse for a knife, and he obviously had no stomach for violence. Getting away shouldn't be all that difficult, as long as she did it before the marshal regained his strength.

It was an encouraging thought, and despite her somewhat precarious pre-dicament, her spirits rose. By cracky, that preacher would be eatin' out of her hand in no time, or she ain't no Prescott.

Three

Justin finished making camp, stopping periodically to coax Marshal Owen into drinking more willow tea—no easy task. Out of curiosity, he tasted the brew himself, only to spit it out. If medicinal qualities were based on how bad a tonic tasted, then Sarah's willow bark tea would cure even the most serious of ailments.

A short distance away, Sarah slept in the shade, her flame red hair touched by the waning sunlight.

That Sarah—she was something, all right. She spoke her mind and didn't seem the least bit fazed by his profession. That was a switch. Most people, even hardened criminals, took to watching what they said whenever a preacher was in hearing range. At times he felt like he lived in a world separate from everyone else. He seldom saw people except for when they were on their best behavior.

He wondered if what he saw of Sarah was her best. Or her worst.

She was unlike any other woman he'd ever known. He could barely make out her dainty frame in the shapeless cotton shirt she wore and men's brown canvas pants, rolled at the cuffs to accommodate her womanly height.

With her bright red hair, her big blue eyes, and her generous sprinkling of freckles, she wasn't what you could call beautiful, at least not in the conventional sense. But though she spoke with a toughness generally heard only in Boston's less desirable neighborhoods, something about her—a childlike earnestness, perhaps, a vulnerability she tried to hide—touched a part of him that had been mostly untouchable.

The question was, what had she done

to warrant the attention of a U.S. Marshal?

Not that he was worried. He'd counseled his share of unlawful citizens, and he supposed—with God's help—he could handle the likes of the strange, unpredictable, yet oddly appealing, woman named Sarah. No last name.

⌇

Sarah woke with a start and glanced around. Already, the sun had started to set, bleeding like a wounded warrior across the pale blue sky. A welcome cool breeze whispered through the trees and ruffled the sun-scorched grass.

A short distance away, the preacher watered the horses and mule and led them to where the grass grew sweet and tall. He chatted to the animals, talking in that smooth, deep voice of his. He returned to camp carrying cans of tinned food.

She struggled to sit up, leaned her back against the tree and rested her cuffed hands on her lap. "Did I hear you call your horse Noah?" she asked.

The preacher nodded. "That's his

name. Noah. I bought him on the rainiest day of the year. The streets of Boston were thick with mud and water, but Noah got me home safely."

"That name's in the Bible," she said simply. She remembered her papa reading the story of Noah's ark to her all those years ago—before her childhood had been cruelly snatched away.

"Yes, Noah's in the Bible."

"I guess you could say that ol' Noah and me are swingin' from the same gate."

"I guess you could say that."

"What about the other? The mule?"

"His name is Moses."

"Figures," she said, rolling her eyes.

The preacher studied her for a moment. "I'm not sure what the problem is with Moses. Sometimes when we're on the trail, he refuses to drink."

"Mules are smart," she said. "They're a whole lot smarter than horses. They won't drink if they're too hot. Gives 'em colic."

"Is that so?"

"You best wait till he cools down."

She watched the preacher dump an

entire tin of beans into a hot iron skillet. She decided that she would have to play in his pasture first before she could win him over to her side so that he would let her go.

"I know a thing or two about the Good Book," she declared. "So don't you go thinkin' you've got somethin' over me, you hear?"

"The thought never occurred to me."

"Yeah, well, I know how you preachers think." She tossed her head. "I heard about that golden rule," she persisted. "You know the one? Always dish out the same medicine that other folks dish out to you."

"Actually it's something more along the lines of 'Whatever you want men to do to you, you should also do to them.'"

"Just like I said. And I want you to know that I'm prepared to abide by the rule," she said solemnly. "You take these cuffs off me, and I'll fix supper for you. Now if that ain't dishin' out the same medicine, I don't know what is."

He considered her request carefully before reaching in his pocket for the key. Obviously, he was a man who never did anything without giving it a lot of thought, and she tried to think how to best use this to her own advantage.

"I'll free you, but I'll take care of supper. You've had a rough time of it. You need all the rest you can get before we hit the trail." He dropped down on one knee and fit the tiny key into the rusty hole, and the handcuffs fell away.

Rubbing her sore wrists, she clamped her jaw tight and said nothing. The only way she planned to ride out with him was over her dead body.

"You're on your honor." He stood and pocketed the cuffs.

She absently picked up a leaf that had fallen onto the blanket and tossed it aside. If he believed that, he didn't have enough brains to grease a skillet. Still, the trusting expression on his face filled her with guilt.

"What's a preacher like you doin' out here, anyhow?" she asked, anxious to change the subject.

"I'm on my way to Texas," he replied.

She swallowed hard. "T-Texas?"

"Rocky Creek."

She snapped her mouth shut and

stared at him, her heart pounding. Just hearing the name of the town felt like someone had kicked her in the stomach. Leaning forward, she pressed her crossed arms against her middle.

Sensing her discomfort, his eyes bored into her. "Do you know the town?" he asked.

Taking a deep, unsteady breath, she tried to conceal her anxiety beneath a veil of indifference. "I reckon everyone knows the town."

His gaze locked with hers, and she felt like a butterfly pinned to a board.

"I gather it's not your favorite place," he said.

Irritated, she chewed a fingernail. Just 'cuz he was a preacher was no reason to go 'round reading minds. "It ain't nobody's favorite place," she said. "And if you know what's good for you, you'll turn around and head back to Boston."

Not wanting to answer the question so plainly written on his face, she jumped to her feet and grabbed the woolen blanket off the ground.

"I'm gonna wash up," she said. "And

I don't need anyone watchin' me, you hear?"

He tossed her one of his clean shirts but made no move to follow her.

As anxious to bathe as she was to forget Rocky Creek, she all but ran to the water's edge.

Standing behind the overgrown bushes, she pulled off her clothes. The stream ran only ankle-high, but the water was fresh and clean and, next to the still-warm air, cold enough to freeze the fur off a bear. But not cold enough to erase the memory of Rocky Creek and all that had happened there.

Teeth chattering, she quickly washed off the prairie dust and pulled out the pins that still remained in her unruly mane. Bent at the waist, she rinsed her hair off, wishing for the luxury of soap.

She shuddered as the memory of the night she'd been captured came back to haunt her. Her brothers had left instructions for her to stay hidden in Logan, Missouri, until their return. For days on end she had done exactly as they said, despite her restless nature. Everything would have been fine had that fool merchant not insisted upon charging her double for bonbons. The ensuing argument blew her cover, and she spent the next couple of weeks cooling her heels in the town's flea-ridden jailhouse. The next thing she knew, she and the marshal were heading for Texas.

Pushing her thoughts aside, she waded to the bank and wrapped herself in the blanket. She then piled three rocks, one on top of the other. She found a stick and scratched out the letters KC for Kansas City on the biggest rock.

Satisfied, she stepped back and surveyed the stack from a distance. A casual traveler could easily miss the sign, but not George. Nothin' escaped her brother's attention.

Her three brothers had surely returned to Logan by now, and the moment they found her missing and heard about her capture, they would pound the trail after her.

It was dark by the time she returned to camp, her hair falling loosely down her back. The preacher's shirt was too big for her, but it was clean. She tied the tails together and rolled up the sleeves until she had somewhat contained the volumes of fabric.

She caught the preacher changing his shirt. The unexpected glimpse of his broad shoulders and bare chest made her heart race like a runaway horse. She waited until he was dressed before stepping into the light of the fire and re-vealing her presence.

The preacher's gaze traveled the length of her. Thinking she saw amuse-ment on his face, she was about ready to tell him to keep his eyes to himself when he scooped a spoonful of beans onto a tin plate and handed it to her.

Her stomach turned over in hunger, and she immediately began to shovel the food into her mouth. Somehow, he had managed to burn the beans, but she didn't care. She hadn't had a de-cent meal in days and, by gummy, she'd eaten worse, though not much worse.

He sat on the opposite side of the fire, watching her, his own plate in hand.

"What are you gawkin' at?" she asked.

"Nothing," he said. He lowered his

head and waited for her to do likewise before he proceeded to give thanks to God for their supper.

"Dear heavenly Father, Almighty God, Creator of heaven and earth . . ."

She doubted that God wanted credit for the burned beans, but she lowered her fork and didn't move until the long-winded preacher finally finished the prayer with a hearty amen.

She shoveled another forkful of beans into her mouth and grimaced. "It still tastes burned," she said, "even with the blessin'." To make matters worse, the beans were now cold. "I reckon it would take a miracle to improve your cookin'."

The preacher's mouth curved in a half-smile. "You surprise me, Sarah. I didn't think you'd be the kind to believe in miracles."

"I don't," she muttered, staring down at her plate. "I never saw a miracle in my life." She glanced at him from beneath lowered lashes. "Nor did I ever have a prayer answered."

"You probably had lots of prayers answered. You just didn't know it."

She glowered at him. "A person

would have to be mighty dumb not to recognize an answered prayer when they see it."

She waited for the preacher to argue the point and didn't have to wait long. He leaned forward, the fire turning his handsome face to bronze.

"It seems to me that my finding you and the marshal was an answer to a prayer," he said.

"Not if you're plannin' to take me to Texas, it's not," she snapped.

He drew back and regarded her in that searching way of his that was beginning to get on her nerves.

Doing her best to ignore him, she finished her meal without comment, then she lifted a canteen to her lips in an effort to get rid of the acrid taste in her mouth.

After dinner she sat crossed-legged next to the marshal to keep an eye on him. The buffalo chips burned brightly, keeping the shadows at bay.

The lawman lay on the preacher's bedroll. He lay so still that the slight rattling sound in his chest was the only sign he was still alive.

From time to time the preacher held Owen's head upright while she spooned willow bark tea into his mouth to ease his pain and guard against fever.

Convinced that she'd done all she could do for the lawman, she was anxious to make her escape. She eyed the horses. Owen's horse was fast, and she was an expert rider. With a little luck, she would be miles away before the preacher even knew she was gone.

She decided against chasing off the other horse, Noah. The preacher had saved her life, and she didn't have the heart to put him and the injured lawman in any more danger than they already were.

And they were in danger, all right. Two men on a single horse wouldn't have much chance of outrunning trouble. As far as she could tell, the preacher didn't even own a gun. Who ever heard of anyone traveling across country with nothing more than a knife—and a sorry one at that?

That no-good scoundrel who stole her horse also stole the marshal's weapons. Not that a gun would do much good should Indians or outlaws attack, but it never hurt to put up a decent fight, and sometimes it even helped.

The preacher checked on Owen and sat down by the fire opposite her. He assessed her with thoughtful, questioning eyes.

"So tell me what you know about Rocky Creek," he said.

She didn't want to talk about Rocky Creek or anything else for that matter. What she wanted was for the preacher to get some shut-eye so she could make her escape.

"What do you want to know?" she asked, her voice tight.

He shrugged. "What the town's like? What to expect?"

"You can expect trouble and a lot of it," she answered quickly. She could tell by his knitted brow that it wasn't what he wanted to hear, and she regretted her hasty reply.

He gave her a questioning look. "I was told that Rocky Creek is one of the best towns in Texas."

She pursed her lips and tried to think

of something positive to say about the town. "It has the basic necess'ties. Seven saloons, one street lamp, a dem'-cratic street sprinkler, and the fastest-growin' cemetery in Texas."

Not wanting to discourage him entirely, she'd chosen her words carefully, something she rarely—if ever—did. But if the dismay on his face was any indication, she could have saved herself the trouble and spoken plainly.

"Only one street lamp?" he asked after a while.

She eyed him curiously. "How many lamps do you want?" she asked. "How many does your town have?"

"Boston? I don't know. Hundreds."

"Kind of like St. Louis," she said. "I don't know how a body can get any sleep with all those lights ablazin'."

"What is the church like?"

"I don't know nothin' about no church," she said truthfully.

For a long while he stared into the fire and said nothing. Finally he asked, "What else?"

She thought for a moment. "It has an independent newspaper, which means it comes out whenever it feels like it. Last time I heard, there were fifteen fellows in jail, not countin' the ones scheduled for hangin'."

His eyes filled with dismay. "They hang a lot of people, do they?"

"Not as many as they hang in Judge Parker's territory," she said. Noting the horror on his face, she hastened to add, "Don't you worry none, you hear? Far as I know, they ain't never hung a preacher."

Rather than looking relieved at the news, his expression turned grim. After a while, he asked, "What's the story of the boots?"

"What?"

"Your boots. I've never seen anyone wear red boots before."

Sarah stared down at the scuffed red leather toes peering from beneath her pant legs. "My papa gave me a pair of red boots when I was six. He said the bottom of me should match the top of me, and I ain't never seen fit to change colors. My brother George says you can't tell if I'm right side up or not, bein' that my hair and boots are both red."

He chuckled. "Is your father still alive?"

She shook her head. "He's dead," she said, her voice terse enough to forbid further questions. She knew better than to reveal anything about her family or background, and it shocked her that some of her carefully guarded secrets had slipped out so effortlessly.

"I'm sorry," the preacher said. Though he continued to scrutinize her, he asked nothing more.

She covered a yawn with her hand. Much to her relief, he took the hint. He stood, checked the marshal again, and then settled down on his bedroll next to the lawman's side.

"Good night, Sarah."

Finally! Making a show of pulling off her boots, she settled into her own bedroll. "It's a good night," she muttered, her voice so low she doubted he could hear her. Just the kind of night for making a quick getaway.

After a while, the preacher called to her. "Don't forget now, Sarah. You're on your honor. I expect you to find you here in the morning."

Not on your tintype! she thought. When she didn't respond to him, he repeated his warning.

Pretending to be asleep, she clamped her mouth shut and kept the blanket drawn up to her brow. She had no intention of telling him a thing. Nor did she want to be on her honor. She had enough problems.

The fire died down, and only a few hot embers remained. In the cover of night, she rolled on her back, placed her hands behind her head, and didn't move.

Overhead the stars burned bright, and she imagined herself escaping along the Milky Way.

No doubt her brothers were already hot on her trail. Her oldest brother, George, would be furious at her for getting into yet another scrape. Maybe the messages she left along the trail telling them to meet her in Kansas City would put her back in George's good graces. Then again, maybe not.

It was late before the preacher stopped twisting and turning. The position of the stars told her it was close to midnight. That gave her several hours before dawn. She would be miles away before he even knew she was gone.

She sat up and reached for her boots. The flapping wings of an owl, followed by a low hoot, made her glance anxiously at the preacher. He didn't move.

Fortunately, the night was moonless, though she didn't particularly look forward to making her way along the trail in total darkness. There was a real danger of her horse stepping into a prairie dog burrow or stumbling into a hole dug out by badgers searching for gopher nests.

Not that she had a choice. The preacher was determined to take her to Texas. She'd just as soon die out here than step foot in that state again.

She rose, grabbed the lawman's saddle, then followed the sound of water to the horses.

Marshal Owen's horse neighed softly and pressed its velvet soft nose next to her neck. The lawman called the bay Blizzard, though no white could be found anywhere on its reddish-brown hide.

Not far away, Noah nickered. "You

stay quiet now, you hear?" she whispered. Moses, the mule, remained silent.

Saddling the bay in the dark was no easy task, but she managed. Taking Blizzard's reins, she eased the horse forward. She had no intention of mounting him until she was out of hearing range.

She was just about ready to jab her foot into the stirrup when a voice floated out of the darkness. "Don't forget, Sarah, you're on your honor."

Stopping dead in her tracks, her mind raced. She would have sworn the preacher was asleep. Still, it was no time to panic. Now that she'd recovered some of her strength, he'd have a hard time holding her back.

Knowing him, he was probably already praying to keep her from leaving. If the beans were any indication of the power of prayer, she had nothing to worry about. He could pray all he wanted for all she cared.

Once she'd made up her mind to do something, nothing or no one could stop her. She glanced up just as a

shooting star blazed a fiery path overhead.

"Not even You, God."

She hated to take advantage of the
preacher's foibles, but it couldn't be
helped. She felt for the stirrups with her
foot and mounted the horse with one
fluid motion.

"Sorry, Preacher," she called into the
darkness. "But when it comes to choosing 'twixt honor and savin' my neck, it
ain't no contest."

Four

Justin stood in the darkness and didn't move. The sound of galloping hooves had faded away, leaving behind an empty silence that had a chilling effect on him.

He knew she'd run, of course, but he didn't think she'd try to escape before daybreak.

What a foolhardy thing for her to do. Who in their right mind would take off in the middle of the night? She could fall prey to Indians, outlaws, or even wild animals. Anything could happen.

But even as he worried about the dangers that could befall her, he heaved a sigh of relief. The last thing he wanted was to help put a woman in jail. He didn't know who she was or even what criminal act she'd committed. For all he knew, she could be an innocent by-stander, though somehow he doubted it.

What he did know was that she'd saved the marshal's life. The lawman wouldn't have made it this long without Sarah's help. For all her toughness, he sensed something soft and pure in her. Something that brought out some need within him to protect her.

He hated not keeping his word to Owen, but how could he? What did he know about holding a prisoner captive? Nothing in his experience prepared him for this. He had enough problems taking care of the lawman.

He debated what to do. He could ride after her, chase her down, make her wait till morning before taking off, but he discounted each idea in turn. Judging by the way she tore away from camp, she could outride him by far. And he had no way of following her trail in the dark.

He glanced upward. During the long, hard weeks of travel, he'd learned a lot about the sky. Enough to know it was still several hours before dawn.

He walked back to the campsite, surprised at how lonely it seemed now that Sarah had gone. He'd been traveling for weeks. Sometimes days would pass before he saw another living soul. But he welcomed his solitary journey. Had in fact chosen to travel by horseback rather than hassle the unpredictable train and stage schedules. He wanted—desperately needed—time to think, to talk to God and ask for help in preparing for the challenges ahead.

Tonight, however, the silence offered him no such solace.

He checked on Owen. The lawman's head still felt cool to the touch.

He lay on his bedroll, his heart heavy as a new molded brick. Even though he'd allowed her to escape, he couldn't shake the feeling that he had let her down. He'd been doing that a lot lately. Letting people down.

When he was first ordained as a minister, eight years ago, things had seemed so simple. He had a sense of God's purpose for his life. But now, at the age of thirty-two, confusion had chipped away at his resolve until he was no longer certain if his heavenly Father even had a plan for him.

How could he know what God wanted when he couldn't even trust his own judgment? He'd been wrong about a lot of things. About his life. About his church.

His faith had burned like a steady light inside him all these years, but even that had been shaken in recent months.

Who knows? Maybe he was even wrong about Sarah. Maybe he only imagined the goodness he saw in her, the vulnerability.

From the distance came the howling of wolves. It was a lonely sound that seemed to echo the very loneliness inside him.

"Dear heavenly Father, Almighty God, Creator of heaven and earth . . . Keep her safe, God. Keep her safe."

The hours dragged on until, at last, a silver thread of light on the distant horizon announced the near arrival of dawn. Stumbling around in the darkness, Justin packed up his belongings and loaded them on to Moses, careful to balance the load so as not to add undue stress to the animal's back.

He'd not slept a wink since Sarah left. He rubbed his neck and stretched the muscles in his back. He wondered if a body ever got used to sleeping on the cold, hard ground.

However, his low spirits had little if anything to do with his physical complaints. He couldn't stop thinking about Sarah, praying for her safety, wondering whether he'd made a mistake in not keeping better watch over her. The truth was, he detested the idea of handcuffing her. Holding her against her will went against his very nature.

Even if his chances of catching up to her were slim or altogether impossible, he should have gone after her. If for no other reason but to make her wait till daylight to escape.

Why hadn't he?

And why, for that matter, hadn't he stayed in Boston and faced his accusers? Why did he always take the path of least resistance? It was a question very much on his mind that morning as he wandered about in the dawn's early light.

Marshal Owen woke at his touch. His skin sallow and parched, his cheeks hollow, he gazed at Justin from sunken eyes.

"How are you feeling?" Justin asked.

"Like I was run over by an iron horse," Owen replied, his voice weak.

Justin debated what to do. "Do you think you're well enough to travel? There's a town about thirty miles away." Normally, he would have easily made it there in less than a day, but with two men on a single horse, he wasn't sure how long it would take. "We might find a doctor there."

The response was slow in coming. "I can try."

"We only have one horse," Justin said.

"The prisoner—"

"Shh. Don't try to talk. You need to conserve your strength."

"Just don't make me drink any more of that ghastly tea," Owen pleaded.

The silvery sky gradually turned blue with not a cloud in sight. North and west of him, the Missouri prairie seemed to go on forever. To the far south, the Ozarks rose like ghostly ships sailing across the sealike plains.

The lawman slumped on the saddle in front of him, Justin made his way along a rutted trail. Travel was slow, but it couldn't be helped.

Spotting fresh horse tracks, he stopped for a closer look. He felt certain the tracks belonged to Sarah, and the way the hoofs sank into the ground indicated she'd been traveling fast. She was probably miles away by now.

It was still only May, but already the temperatures began to soar. He studied the landscape ahead for even the slightest motion, but nothing, not even a blade of grass, moved beneath the shimmering, hot sun.

He rode for the better part of the morning, stopping only long enough to water his horse and pack mule in one of the many natural springs that dotted the area, and to check Owen's bandage and make him drink.

The red, swollen skin around the jagged wound worried him. If only Sarah were here, she'd know what to do, he was certain of it.

He rode past herds of wild horses and graceful antelope. A lone buffalo bull bellowed, then walked away on legs that seemed too short and thin for such a large, cumbersome body. The sound woke Owen. "Mating season," he muttered before closing his eyes again.

Never having seen such an odd animal, Justin stopped to watch it. He'd heard that the plains were once filled with the woolly beasts, but he had always assumed the reports were exaggerated. That was before he'd witnessed for himself the unbelievable number of bleached bones strewn across the land. Feeling a sense of sadness, Justin watched the magnificent creature until it moved away.

Around noon, the ground grew muddy. Shallow pools of water made travel increasingly difficult.

Something caught his eye—a horse. *Sarah's horse.* He anxiously scanned the marshy bogs. Her untethered bay stood a short distance away, grazing, but there was no sign of Sarah.

Fearing the worst, he urged Noah on. The horse gingerly picked his way around the soggy ground with Moses plodding behind.

Birds took flight as he drew near. Ducks, geese, and loons rose to the sky and scattered like feathers in the wind. Striped frogs jumped out of the way, splash-landing into sodden swales. Dragonflies hovered close to the water's surface, their blue bodies gleaming in the sun. The air was abuzz with dark clouds of bugs that flittered back and forth in a graceless dance.

He found a relatively dry spot next to Blizzard and tethered both horses together. Fearing the marshal would fall out of the saddle if left unsupervised, he helped Owen to the ground and settled him on a blanket in the skimpy shade of a low-growing willow.

As quickly as he dared, he circled the marshy bog on foot, his sense of dread increasing with each hurried step. He cupped his hands around his mouth and called her name. "Sarah!"

"It's 'bout time you got here!"

His heart leaped at the sound of her

voice. Unable to discern where her voice came from, he squinted against the sun. "Where are you?"

"Over here!"

He spotted her, at last, in the middle of a murky pool. Alarm shot through him. "What in the world . . .!"

"Don't come any closer," she warned. "If you get stuck, neither of us has got a prayer of gettin' out. This stuff holds on tighter than a corset."

"A corset, eh?" He couldn't help but laugh. He was so relieved to see her he almost jumped with joy. "You don't strike me as the type to have firsthand knowledge of such a garment."

"You don't have to wear them to know how they fit," she snapped. "Now get off the stick and get me outta here!"

Without another word he backed away, watching his every step until he reached hard ground again. "Don't move," he called. He then raced back to the horses. A coil of rope hung from the skirts of the marshal's saddlebags. He hoped it was long enough to do the job.

Rope in hand, he started back. Moving as close to Sarah as he dared, he uncoiled the rope. "Grab hold of this," he called. "I'll haul you in."

He tossed one end of the rope to her, and it fell a distance away.

"You throw like you build a fire," she complained.

Pulling the rope back in, he grinned. "I'm glad to see you've retained your usual sweet disposition."

"Don't go gettin' your hopes up high, Preacher," she said. Although her fate was in his hands, she made no attempt to agree with him or even placate him. "I might have one foot in the grave, but I ain't about to mend my ways."

"That's two feet you have in the grave," he teased. "And if you mended your ways, I wouldn't have to keep rescuing you." He tossed the end of the rope again, this time hitting his mark.

She grabbed hold of it, and he slowly reeled her in. When she was close enough to reach, he held out his hand and yanked her out of the mire.

She followed him back to the horses with her arms straight out like a scarecrow's, complaining all the way. "Did you ever see such a mess in all your born days?" she cried.

"We'll find a safe place for you to clean off," he said. "While you're doing that, I'll fix us something to eat."

"I'll eat with you. But I ain't goin' to Texas with you," she said. "So you can just forget that notion, you hear?"

By the time they had moved to dry land and found clean water, she was in an even worse mood than before. Her pants, shirt, boots—everything—were caked with sand and she walked like a stiff board.

Apparently, it wasn't in Sarah's nature to suffer in silence. She voiced her complaints nonstop till his ears began to ring.

He pulled a blanket off the horse and handed her a pair of clean pants and a shirt. He then pulled out a bar of Blue India soap he had tucked away in his saddlebags and tossed it to her. She stared down at the soap in her hand, and her face softened.

Without a word, she turned and disappeared behind a clump of trees.

She was in a considerably better

mood when she returned. Her damp hair fell to her shoulders in tangled curls. His clothes were too large for her, and she had rolled up the legs of his pants and the sleeves of his shirt. She flung her newly washed clothes over Moses' saddle to dry.

He offered her a strip of dried meat and hard tack bread, and she sat down and ate with great relish. Her hearty appetite and the way she devoured whatever he placed in front of her would be deemed scandalous by Boston standards. He wondered what Sarah would think of the dainty portions and timid eating habits of Boston's female population. The thought amused him.

On the ground nearby, Owen slept, his chest rising and falling visibly with each labored breath.

Sarah watched the marshal from beneath a furrowed brow. "He don't sound so good," she said.

Justin leaned against a tree, his arms crossed in front. "I figure there must be a reason why you didn't get away," he said. He expected a reaction and she didn't disappoint him.

She glanced up quickly, her face etched in confusion. "You ain't thinkin' that bog was some sort of . . . you know?"

"Divine intervention?"

She shrugged. "Somethin' like that."

"Can you think of a better explanation?" he asked.

"Yeah, I can. It was dark. I couldn't see farther than a blindfolded hog. So I decided to wait till mornin'. I got off my horse and took a tumble. It was my own stupid fault."

"And you're not even willing to consider the possibility that maybe this is all part of a plan? That God has something up His divine sleeve?"

"No one makes plans for me, you hear?" The sharp tone of her voice was at odds with the uncertainty in her voice. As if to explain the discrepancy, she added, "Not without my say-so."

"Maybe He brought you back for Owen," Justin said.

"If God wanted to help Owen, I reckon He would have sent a doctor."

Later, as they prepared to hit the trail again, Justin checked his saddle. As far as he could determine, the extra burden of Owen's weight didn't create any problems for his horse.

He rubbed the gelding's forehead. "What do you say, Noah? Was that or was that not divine intervention?"

~

It was hot and humid that afternoon, and Sarah felt utterly miserable. Her canteen was empty, her mouth dry as cotton, and her head felt like someone was hammering inside, trying to get out. She was beginning to think they would never reach the town of Stonewell.

She coaxed Blizzard to go faster until she reached the preacher's side. Owen was slumped over, his head bopping with each jolting step.

"How's he doin'?"

"Not too good," the preacher replied. "I only hope we reach Stonewell in time."

"If we don't rest our horses, we ain't gonna make it to the next stump."

He frowned in protest but nodded in agreement. "Looks like some trees about a mile ahead."

They rode side by side in silence for several moments.

She stole a glance at the preacher's profile. He looked tired but no less determined. Moisture glistened on his sun-darkened skin. For no good reason, she felt a sense of guilt for causing him so much trouble.

"Don't you go thinkin' I'm not grateful for what you've done for me," she said.

He turned to look at her, his face shadowed by his hat.

She took a deep breath and continued. "I've been buzzards' bait twice, and both times you saved my carcass." She stared at the trail ahead. "I ain't used to people being nice to me."

"Maybe you don't give them a chance to be nice to you."

Her eyes locked with his. "The last time I gave someone a chance to be nice, he held me up at gunpoint. Stole all my money, he did."

"I won't steal anything from you, Sarah."

Something in his voice touched her and made it harder to fight the battle inside. Part of her wanted to trust him, but to do so would only add to his own burdens without relieving any of hers. Still, she was tempted—and it practically scared the life out of her.

"Let me help you," he beseeched her in a soft, clear voice.

She tossed her head and lifted her chin. "I can tote my own skillet, and don't think I can't." With that she snapped the reins, forcing Blizzard to pull ahead.

Later, as she sat around the campfire, the marshal asleep nearby, the preacher settled next to her. "Sarah . . . Everyone can use a friend, and I want to be yours. But I can't help you if you don't tell me what kind of trouble you're in. Why were you handcuffed to the marshal? What crime have you been accused of? What is it about Texas . . . specifically, Rocky Creek, that has you running scared? Come on, Sarah. I can't be your friend if you don't trust me."

She stared at the blazing hot fire. She'd never had a friend. Never knew anyone she could trust except her brothers. Her first instinct was to push him away as she had done earlier, but the cautionary voice inside didn't have a chance next to his gentle and persuasive voice. Maybe it was the harrowing night spent in that bog or just plain exhaustion, but she could no longer fight the friendship he offered her.

She watched him through lowered lashes. "That old marshal . . . Owens . . . was escortin' me back to Texas."

The preacher nodded. "To jail."

"No." She lifted her head and searched his face, studying every nuance for signs of censure. She was about to find out just what kind of friend he was.

"To the gallows."

Five

Justin turned gray, his eyes round as two pie plates. His shock radiated outward until even the very fire seemed to dim in the aftermath of her revelation. "But . . . but you're a woman!" he said, horror written all over his face.

She gave him a curious look. "Don't they hang women in Boston?'

"Maybe a hundred years ago," he said. "But not anymore."

For several moments the only sounds that could be heard was Owen's labored breathing and a chorus of noisy crickets in the nearby grass.

She studied his face and wondered if it had been a mistake to trust him. From earliest childhood, she'd been taught by her brothers to reveal nothing and admit to even less, and that advice had served her well through the years.

But it was hard to resist this preacher, whose soft-spoken words and kind demeanor lulled her into believing she could trust him. She only hoped she wouldn't live to regret confiding in him.

"The g-gallows—" he muttered as if he still couldn't believe it. His voice sounded like gravel rattling in an old wooden bucket. "I knew you were in trouble, Sarah, but . . . never did I imagine anything so . . . like this."

Sensing no reproach, she allowed herself to breathe. "You still want to be my friend?" It was more of a plea than a request.

"I said I did, and I mean it. But this . . . this is too serious to handle by yourself. Let me talk to the authorities. I'm a man of God. They'll listen to me."

She pursed her lips. She could only imagine the look on her brothers' faces upon hearing that a preacher offered to put in a good word for her. "Have you

ever talked anyone out of a hangin' before?"

The question seemed to surprise him.
"Uh . . . no. But that doesn't mean I
can't." He thought for a moment.
"First . . . first, I have to know . . ." He
rubbed his chin as if he dreaded even
having to ask the question. "What did
you do?"

"I ain't done nothin'. Except that
golden rule stuff. You know the one
'bout dishin' out the same medicine that
other folks dish out to you."

Sarah had hoped this would set the
preacher's mind at rest, but the worry
lines on his forehead only deepened.

"Since you're still very much alive, I'm
assuming you didn't kill anyone?"

"Never killed anyone in my life, but I
sure have been tempted."

He frowned. "Did you steal?"

This question was a bit trickier.
"Never stole a thing that wasn't mine,"
she replied, after a while.

"You can't steal what's yours."

"Really?" *Now, if that ain't the bird's
twitter.* She wondered if her brothers

knew about that one. "Well, then, I'm as innocent as a newborn babe."

The ridge between his eyebrows grew another notch deeper. "I seriously doubt that. Tell me, why do they want to hang you? And I want the truth, Sarah."

"The truth?"

"You know, the facts as they really happened, with no embellishments or omissions."

"There ain't much to tell," she said. "My brothers and I were ridin' out of town—"

"Would that be Rocky Creek?" he asked.

She nodded. "Like I was saying, we were hitting the grit when I spotted this stray dog hung up on a fence. If I hadn't stopped to help it, the dog would have been wolf bait sure as shootin'. The next thing I knew, the marshal was on top of me and I was eatin' dirt."

He looked perplexed. "I don't understand. The marshal arrested you for helping a dog?"

She bit down on her lower lip. "The dog ain't got nothin' to do with it," she said. "It was because my brothers stopped a stage."

"Why did they do that? Stop a stage?"

She stared at him in disbelief. Even a preacher couldn't be *that* dense, even if he was from Boston. "It's the easiest way to rob it," she said, matter-of-factly.

His eyes widened in astonishment before he caught himself. She had to give him credit; he was obviously trying not to pass judgment. But if the swollen veins in his neck were an indication, his efforts to remain impartial didn't come easy.

"So . . . so how did you get away?" he asked, his voice strained.

"I didn't. Not until after they tried me in mustang court," she said, using the Texas phrase for mock justice. "The old pros'cutor blamed me and my brothers for things we ain't done."

His face brightened. "Are you saying you don't rob stages?"

"Oh, we rob them all right. But we ain't killed no one like he said we did."

A muscle flickered at his jaw, but

whether in relief or disapproval, she couldn't say. "So how *did* you escape?"

"My brothers finally showed up and blowed a hole in the wall of the jailhouse. You never saw such a mess in all your born days. But don't you go worryin' none, you hear? No one got hurt or anythin'."

"That should go in your favor," he said slowly. "And when the town marshal hears how you saved Owen . . . how you took care of his bullet wound, he's bound to take your side."

She frowned. "I'd sooner have a rattler in my bedroll." Hating what she saw in his eyes, she protested, "Don't look at me like that. Wells Fargo deserves to be robbed. They took our papa away."

His gaze softened. "How?" he asked. "What happened to your father?"

Words rushed from her. She told him how the bank had threatened to take her parents' farm away following tough times. "Papa pleaded with the bank president, and they got into an argument. Next day, the president was dead with a knife in his back. They strung

Papa up before they found the real culprit. By then, it was too late."

He shook his head in disbelief. "I'm so sorry, Sarah. How old were you when this happened?"

"Six," she said.

His voice soft with sympathy, he asked, "What about your mother?"

She took a deep breath. "She died six months later. Some say she died of a broken heart." She lifted her eyes to his. "Now do you see why my brothers rob stages? Wells Fargo took everything from us."

For the longest while, he didn't speak. Finally, he said, "I'll do everything possible to help." He sounded oddly distant and so unlike himself.

"What does that mean, everythin'?" She studied his profile. "Does that mean you'll let me go?"

His face was without expression as if an inner door had closed, creating a barrier between them. "If I let you go, you'll live a life on the run. Is that what you want? Don't you think it would be better to face your accusers and demand a fair and just trial?"

She considered his suggestion for all of a second. "Fair and just? If the last trial was any ind'cation, I druther take my chances runnin'."

"And spend the rest of your life looking over your shoulder? Facing your accusers is better. I know it is." After a moment, he added, "Maybe we can get your sentence commuted to prison time."

She wrinkled her nose. "I ain't sittin' in no prison makin' horsehair saddles for something I ain't done."

He tilted his head toward her. "Maybe you won't have to. You're a woman, and that's bound to work in your favor."

She gave him a sidelong glance. "It's never worked in my favor before."

"Really?" His gaze traveled the length of her. "Maybe they'd be less inclined to hang you if you . . . uh . . . dressed more . . . you know, like other women . . . if you emphasized the fact that you're a—a . . . lady."

"E-emphasize?" she stammered, surprised to feel her cheeks grow warm. Nobody had ever accused her of being a lady before, but knowin' the preacher, he probably meant it as a compliment.

A look of horror crossed his face. "I didn't mean to suggest—" He cleared his throat and glanced away.

He looked so uncomfortable that she almost felt sorry for him. "What . . . what *are* you suggestin'?"

His eyes met hers. "Only that it might be to your advantage to wear a frock instead of men's clothes."

She glanced down at her canvas pants.

"And the way you talk."

She looked up. "What's wrong with the way I talk?"

He peered at her intently. "I think you could probably tone down your speech here and there."

She wrinkled her forehead. "Are you saying you want me to act like one of those spoiled society ladies who don't know the difference between a Henry and a Winchester rifle?"

His face shadowed in confusion, he nonetheless gave a quick nod of his head. "That would be a start."

She chewed on a fingernail. "I don't

know. Being a lady ain't gonna come easy for the likes of me."

"I'm only thinking of your welfare. It would be to your advantage once we arrive in Texas to face your accusers."

She glanced at the marshal asleep nearby. The man hadn't moved since Justin settled him on bedroll. "So you're sayin' that wearin' a dress and talkin' like a lady will save my neck?"

He hesitated. "I can't make any promises. Prosecutors in Boston tend to be more lenient with . . . ladies. I imagine it's the same in Texas."

She sat back, hand on her chest. "Now if that don't take the rag off the bush. How come no one ever told me this before?"

"It's probably not something that comes up in general conversation."

It was a comforting thought, but she couldn't imagine a Texas judge being swayed by a woman's speech or dress.

After a beat, he added, "I think we better get some shut-eye. I want to get an early start. We can't be too far from Stonewell."

He reached into his pocket and pulled

out the handcuffs. He stared down at them for a moment. "I'm sorry, Sarah. I don't want you taking off in the middle of the night again. It's too risky."

She stared at the manacles in his hands and wondered what he saw when he looked at her. Did he see an outlaw or someone else—the woman whose heart suddenly yearned to be held by a man? By him? Cheeks aflame, she looked up.

Head lowered, he reached for her hand, but before cuffing her, he hesitated.

She searched his face and he met her gaze. She wanted him to look at her like she had seen her brothers look at other women. But anything would be better than the pity she saw in his eyes.

Look at *me*, she wanted to cry. *Look at me*. Without thinking, she threw her arms around his neck. If he was surprised, she couldn't tell. For his lips melted against hers, sending waves of heat down her body. His mouth on hers was both gentle and demanding, sweet and warm, and more than anything, persuasive. She drank in the moment, wishing it would last forever.

Great sand and sagebrush! How come no one ever told her that kissin' a man was even more fun than fightin' a bear? She'd heard tell about this man and woman stuff, but no one ever said it felt this good, felt so completely and utterly right.

The kiss ended far too soon. One hand on her shoulder, he firmly pushed her away. The mouth that moments earlier had been soft and yielding was now hard and unrelenting. No pity showed in his eyes now. Only rejection . . . and, somehow, that was even worse.

Her senses in turmoil, she didn't know what to think. She wondered if she had only imagined his response, imagined that he'd welcomed her kiss.

Confused as much by her own actions as his, she stared up at him.

"I'm sorry, Sarah."

She couldn't have felt more humiliated had she been thrown from a horse. For the longest while, they stared at each other like two wild animals meeting by chance.

"Forgive me," he pleaded. "I can't do this."

Had he thrust a knife in her heart, he couldn't have hurt her more. "Because of who I am?" she lashed out at him. "Because I'm a wanted woman and not fit to wipe your feet?"

He shook his head sadly. "No, Sarah. Because of who *I* am."

No sooner had he cuffed her than he walked away, leaving her and the sleeping marshal alone. Unable to settle down, she paced a circle around the fire pit.

There was no denying it; she had thrown herself at a man—and a preacher at that—and even she couldn't think of a way to excuse such a brazen act.

All her life she'd been accused of being impulsive. Of acting without thinkin'. Of runnin' headlong into trouble. But kissin' the preacher was far and beyond anything she had ever done before.

True, the preacher had offered to help her and for that she was grateful. But gratitude don't excuse brash behavior.

She would definitely have to keep a tight rein on her impulses in the future.

Still, recalling the feel of his lips on hers, she couldn't help but smile. She pressed her fingers against her still burning mouth. The memory made her cheeks grow warm again, and she felt a strange excitement unlike any she had ever known.

She might not be a lady, but for all his talk of proper behavior, there was no denying that Justin Wells had, for one short but magical moment, kissed her back.

Six

That night, Justin lay awake for hours, staring at the sky. Stars spilled across the heavens like polished diamonds, but he hardly noticed. He squeezed his eyes shut in an attempt to block out the memory of Sarah's lips on his, but it was nearly impossible to do. Even with his eyes closed, he could still see her, feel her. To make matters worse, her slightest movement and softest sigh played on his senses, keeping him on edge.

With a heavy heart, he opened his eyes and resisted the urge to glance her way. Had she told him the truth? All that business about robbing a stage? Being tried for murder? It was hard to believe. He didn't want to believe it.

Why had God brought this woman, this outlaw, into his life? Was it to test him? To punish him? Or to tempt him?

Sarah, Sarah, Sarah. Her very name seemed to nestle into some secret part of him. She might be tough as old leather, but her lips had felt soft as fine silk. The unbidden memory added still more weight to his already troubled thoughts.

He'd had his share of women in the past, but that was before he realized his calling and was ordained as a minister. Since that time eight years ago, he'd immersed himself fully into church work, giving little if any attention to his own physical needs.

There were, of course, many single women in the church, some who would make fine wives. But none interested or even tempted him, and it was an effort not to look bored when they prattled on about the latest Parisian fashions or current opera season.

Through the years he'd learned to cultivate a certain demeanor that effec-

tively warded off overzealous mothers
eager to marry off their daughters. He
was never without his frock coat and
collar, except when traveling, and carried a Bible with him at all times. However, he was convinced that none of his
carefully crafted barriers would have
worked with Sarah, whose unconven-
tional and unpredictable ways had simply and effectively caught him off-guard.

No more. From this moment on he
would watch his every step. He would
keep his distance and never again think
about her pretty pink lips or those big
blue eyes.

To that end, he forced himself to concentrate on her legal problems. Though
the crimes she described were serious,
he was convinced of her innocence. He
just couldn't believe that the woman
who worked so hard to save Marshal
Owen's life and risked capture to save
a dog was capable of a serious felony.
She said her brothers had stopped the
stage. Did that mean she wasn't there?
That she had nothing to do with the actual robbery?

He knew what it was like to be wrongfully accused. His work in Boston came to an abrupt halt when a wealthy widow accused him of taking advantage of her. Nothing could be further from the truth.

Mrs. Geoffrey Thornhill, an active member of the church, called one day asking for him. She sounded desperate. He hurried to her home to offer counsel and was stunned when she made her true intentions known. He turned her down as kindly as he could, of course, but whether out of anger or spite, she reported him. It was his word against hers. When she threatened to withhold a substantial amount of money from the church if he wasn't reprimanded, Justin was asked to leave.

It was only because one of his superiors believed in his innocence that he was given a second chance—not to clear his name, but to continue to carry out the Lord's work, this time in a little church in the small Texas town of Rocky Creek.

But the second chance came with a severe warning: he was told to stay away from trouble—and there lay the problem. There wasn't a doubt in his mind that Sarah was trouble, whether or not she actually had a hand in robbing that stage.

Yet he couldn't just turn his back on her. What kind of preacher would just walk away? What kind of man? These questions kept him tossing and turning for the remainder of the night.

The next day Justin was in the worst possible mood. His head ached, partly from lack of sleep, but mostly because he had made the decision to fulfill his promise to Owen and take Sarah to Texas. It was the hardest decision he ever had to make. It meant he would have to fight to save her.

He didn't know if he could or even if it were possible, but he had to try.

What choice did he have? Now that he knew the extent of her problems, he could no longer justify letting her go. When he was ordained, he had taken an oath to obey God's commandments, and that included the one about obeying the laws of the land.

He knew many preachers who struggled with this very commandment, especially during the War Between the

States, when conscience was often at odds with the law. There was no way he could justify letting Sarah go under these circumstances. The Bible was clear on that account.

He would fulfill his promise to the marshal, take her to Texas, and demand that she be tried in front of a lawful court. If she was innocent as she claimed, all they'd have to do was prove it. Yet making the decision brought him no peace of mind.

Aligning himself with an outlaw against an entire town could have grave consequences for him as a preacher, and he could well lose his ministerial rights. The thought of not being allowed to preach God's Word again was more than he could bear.

Why, God? he asked in tortured silence. *Why are You doing this to me?* He'd never questioned God's will in the past. Why, then, did he question it now?

To make matters worse, it was already hot and the air heavy with dust. Every step felt like walking uphill.

Owen had slept fitfully through the night, and it was obvious that the lawman had taken a turn for the worse. His skin was hot and clammy; the wound on his shoulder appeared even more red and swollen than it had the day before.

Owen needed medical help, and he needed it now.

As far as Justin could figure, they were still fifteen or more miles away from the closest town. With a wounded man and handcuffed woman in tow, he'd be lucky if he got there by late afternoon.

He only hoped there was a doctor in residence. If not, at least they should be able to obtain clean bandages and maybe even find a decent bed.

If things weren't dismal enough, Sarah was at her combative worst. She begged him to free her, and when he refused she became even more difficult to handle, forcing him to pick her up, haul her over his shoulder, and set her on her horse.

Until he could figure out a plan, he had no choice but to keep her handcuffed, and he was sorely tempted to gag her as well.

"I'm not going to Texas!" she yelled at him.

"You're going," he insisted.

"Over my dead body."

"God's commandments make that option unfeasible."

She leveled cold blue eyes at him. "If they hang me, my blood will be on your hands for the rest of your born days. Is that what you want?"

"What I want is to make sure that no noose ever touches that pretty neck of yours."

A light like a candle flared in her eyes, and she looked ready to retort, but instead she clamped her mouth shut. Her hands still handcuffed together, she took hold of the reins.

He roused Owen. It was a struggle to help Owen onto Noah. Owen could barely stay awake and he slumped over the horse's neck. Justin kept a steady hand on the man while mounting the saddle behind. His arms around Owen, he tightened his hold on the reins.

He glanced at Sarah, who sat on her horse looking remarkably obstinate given her circumstances. Smiling to himself, he clicked his tongue and started along the trail.

For the most part, Sarah remained silent for the rest of the morning, which suited him just fine. He had enough to worry about.

The farther south they traveled across Missouri toward the Ozarks, the more available water they found. Flat grass-lands gradually gave way to rocky in-clines and deep ravines surrounded by loose soil. He soon gave up any hope of reaching the town until nightfall, if then.

Justin didn't know how much longer Owen could survive.

With each cautious step, the hooves of their horses slipped dangerously, sending rocks and soil tumbling into the valley below. An unexpected clearing al-lowed him to put Moses in front, and this turned out to be a wise decision. Whereas Noah grew ever more skittish and confused, the mule showed no such hesitation, leading the way with sure-footed confidence.

On occasion, they were forced to cross a fast-flowing stream or detour around a tangled thicket. Upon circling one such dense growth, they roused several deer from a hidden lair, sending the frightened animals bounding away in alarm. A spotted fawn wobbled after them.

The relentless glare of the sun began to take its toll. Justin mopped his wet forehead and glanced back at Sarah, but she avoided his eyes. He could see she was tired. Her face was flushed and less lively than usual, but she looked no less stubborn. Even so, he felt sorry for her.

He wondered if somehow they had missed the town. He searched the trail ahead for a shady place to rest, but it was another hour before they actually found a suitable spot next to a sparkling stream and grove of sturdy cotton-woods.

After helping Owen off the horse, Justin settled the feverish man down on a soft patch of grass. He turned to give Sarah a hand, but she had managed to slip off her mount without his help. He took off her cuffs so she could cool herself in the water.

Justin knelt at the stream and doused

himself with water before rinsing off his neckerchief. He then removed Owen's hat and gently dabbed his face with the wet cloth. Owen's skin was flushed red, and he was breathing hard.

Fearing for the man's life, Justin stared at the rocky trail ahead. "Traveling is taking a lot out of him. At the rate we're going, we won't make it to the next town till after nightfall," he said. Lowering himself onto a fallen log, he held his weary head with both hands and said a silent prayer.

He felt her hand on his back, her head on his shoulder.

Startled by the way her touch made his heart leap, he jumped to his feet.

The initial surprise on her face turned to hurt. "I was only tryin' to be a friend," she said.

Feeling utterly foolish, he raked his hand through his hair. "I apologize."

Her eyes blazed into his. "Don't go gettin' yourself all worked up. I ain't that desperate, and you ain't that—"

"Irresistible?" he asked, hoping to break the tension with a little humor.

She bit her lip and lowered her eyes. "It's the first time I ever done that, you know," she said, her voice barely more than a whisper.

"First time you did what? Try to be a friend?"

"I ain't talking about no friends. You're the first man I ever kissed."

Hands on his hips, he stared at the ground. "I think it would be best if we don't talk about it."

"Really?" She sounded surprised. "Is that one of those subjects that ladies can't discuss?"

He looked up. "I suppose it's all right if you're married," he said gently, not wanting to hurt her feelings any more than he already had. "But unmarried ladies aren't supposed to talk about kissing . . . and things." *He* couldn't talk about such things. Not with her so close and looking so fetching.

Sarah shook her head. "If that don't beat all." She frowned. "Is that one of those rules in the Good Book?"

"Rules? Oh, you mean the Ten Commandments. The Bible is clear on the importance of remaining honorable until marriage."

She chewed on her lip. "By 'honorable,' you mean—"

"Yes," he said quickly, his terse voice meant to discourage further discussion.

Much to his dismay, she persisted. "What about kissin'?"

He cleared his throat. "There's nothing in the Bible that specifically addresses the subject of . . . kissing. It's just something that polite society expects."

"So what you're sayin' is that it's okay with God if I talk about kissin', but it ain't okay with society?"

"I suppose."

She glanced around. "I don't see no society here, do you?"

"Well—"

"It's just you, me, and God." She glanced at Owen as if trying to decide if his presence counted. "So that means that I can talk about kissin'."

He stared at her, not knowing how to handle such logic. "I don't really see what there is to talk about. I mean . . ." Needing all the defenses he could muster, he slipped into his role as pastor as easily as he donned a coat.

He continued, "Sometimes people do things when they're carrying a burden that they wouldn't normally do. In view of your troubles, it's perfectly understandable that you might do something you'd later regret."

"I ain't regrettin' nothin'," she said with a frown.

Not knowing how to respond, he looked away and remained silent. Most people were quick to admit their transgressions in his presence and were enormously relieved when he told them of God's forgiveness. But Sarah wasn't like anyone he'd ever met. He wondered if she were one of a kind or if people in these parts had their own way of looking at things. If that were the case, he was in trouble, for he couldn't begin to think like she did.

Sarah made him feel like he was in a foreign country. She didn't even speak the same language. It came as a shock to think how limited his pastoral work in Boston had been. He felt totally unprepared for the challenges of the West. Nor did he have a clue how to deal with people like Sarah, whose plain-talking ways were both refreshing and alarming.

After a long silence, she said, "I just want to know if I done it right."

Feeling a flicker of hope, he cleared his throat. Maybe if he put her mind at ease, she would abandon the subject. "Other than the fact that you threw your-self at me," he began slowly, "I'd say you did everything else . . . very well."

"Is that so?" She smiled and her whole face lit up. It was the first real smile she'd given him all day.

"It must come nat'ral, being that I lack experience and all," she said.

As much as her boldness disarmed him he was also intrigued, and he re-gretted having to discourage such frank talk. "It might help you to know that it's the man who does the initiating, not the woman." If she would keep her dis-tance, then surely he could keep his.

"Don't tell me," she said. "It's one of those society rules, right?"

"Right."

"So if it's just God watchin'—"

He quickly stepped back, putting more distance between them. "Same rules apply," he said firmly.

Seven

"Where's the prisoner?"

Startled by the man's gravelly voice, Justin spun around to find the marshal's eyes open.

"You're awake." Justin scraped off the last of his whiskers with a hoe-shaped razor and swished it in a cup of hot water. The new-type razor had been developed so men could shave safely aboard a moving train, but Justin preferred the old blade type, which was easier to strop.

Owen shifted his legs and tried to sit up. "I'm awake," he mumbled.

"Hold on." Justin quickly wiped the remaining soap away from his freshly shaven chin, then moved to the marshal's side.

Owen's breath rattled in his chest, his lips tinged in blue.

Kneeling down on one knee, Justin slipped his hands beneath Owen's armpits and lifted the man into a sitting position.

"Thank you," Owen wheezed. He leaned his head back against a tree. Groaning, he pressed his hand gently on the wad of fabric protecting the wound at his shoulder.

"You got a name?" he asked, his voice barely above a whisper.

"My name's Wells. Reverend Justin Wells."

"A preacher, huh? What do you know?" He took a moment to catch his breath before adding, "This is the last place I'd expect to run into a fire escape."

Justin chuckled. As a preacher, he'd been called a "sin twister" and other such names, but "fire escape" was a new one on him. "It's the last place I expected to be," Justin said. "Would you like some Arbuckle's?"

"Only if it tastes better than that tea you keep forcing down my throat," Owen rasped.

Justin smiled to himself. Sarah had a few choice words to say about his coffee—none of them good—but he wasn't about to repeat her sentiments.

He poured the steaming coffee into a tin cup and, stooping low, held the cup next to Owen's lips.

Owen blew on the hot liquid, took a sip, and grimaced. "Sure hope your sermons are better than your coffee."

"There are some who would argue in favor of the coffee," Justin said.

Owen leaned his head against the tree. His gaunt, ash-colored face hardly seemed able to support his dark, drooping mustache and stubbly beard. His sunken eyes looked like two black holes. "You still haven't told me where the prisoner is."

Justin tossed a nod in the direction she'd gone. "She's down by the stream, bathing."

Owen grimaced, but whether from pain or disapproval, Justin couldn't tell.

"I'll wager the last breath in me that she skips, if she hasn't already."

"Then you'd be one sorry man," Justin said.

Owen coughed. "If you knew what awaited her in Texas . . ."

"She told me about the hanging."

Owen's eyebrows arched in surprise. "You know, and you still think she won't escape? She's no fool." He coughed and then continued, his voice fading with each spoken word. "She's . . . she's not about to stay around . . . for her own lynching party."

"I made her leave her boots here at camp. Without boots and a horse, she won't get very far."

"She escaped once . . ." Owen cleared his voice and started again. "Rocky Creek's town marshal made the mistake of underestimating her. Don't you make the same mistake."

Not about to admit it was a mistake he'd already made, Justin tossed the dregs of his coffee on the ground and set the tin cup down on a flat rock. He rose and reached for the spare shirt used for bandages. One sleeve and half the back was all that was left. He tore a strip of cotton, dampened it, and squeezed out the excess water. Kneeling by Owen's side, he laid the cool damp cloth on the marshal's forehead.

"She told me she and her brothers were wrongly accused of murder."

"It's not my job to determine guilt or innocence. It's not yours either."

"She saved your life," Justin said.

Owen looked at him with clouded eyes. "And you want me to save hers." It was a statement more than a question.

"She's a woman."

"The judge found her guilty."

"She didn't kill anyone," Justin said firmly.

"Maybe not. But she and her brothers are guilty of other crimes," Owen wheezed. "Robberies."

"They don't hang people for robberies," Justin argued, then caught himself. He had no right to quarrel with a wounded man. "I'm sorry," he said, his tone beseeching. "It's just . . . not right."

"It's not our . . . decision." Owen's voice faded away.

Justin sighed and let his gaze travel toward the stream. The trees hid Sarah from view, but there was no hiding from the fate that awaited her.

"What happens if you don't bring her in?"

"A U.S Marshal doesn't get paid until he delivers the goods." Owen's voice was barely more than a whisper, each word sounding more strained than the one before it. He coughed so hard that his whole body shook. Catching his breath, he gasped for air and closed his eyes.

Justin laid a hand on top of Owen's and said a silent prayer. *Dear heavenly Father, Almighty God, Creator of heaven and earth . . .*

He finished the prayer, but even after asking for God's help, he felt no peace. He felt . . . nothing. Here in the wilderness God's handiwork was everywhere, from the magnificent sky to the tiniest blade of grass beneath his feet. Yet, never had he felt more distant from God, more alone. He stared across the endless Missouri plains and thought about the Israelites wandering the desert. God had tested them as He now appeared to be testing Justin.

He lifted his eyes to the heavens. "I sure do hope it doesn't take me forty years to pass Your test, God," he said. He sighed and reached for the cloth on Owen's forehead. The man was still burning with fever.

Owen stirred and regarded Justin through half-shut eyes. "You . . . you promised to take her to Texas. If you can't trust a man of God—"

"She took the bullet out of your shoulder. She saved your life."

Owen said something, but his voice was so weak, his words were nothing more than a wisp of air. Justin leaned over until his ear was mere few inches from Owen's quivering lips. "What did you say?"

"I said . . . There's a generous reward for her capture." He gasped before continuing. "A . . . A fire escape like you could do a lot of good with that kind of money."

Justin shook his head. "That's blood money. I don't want any part of it."

"Then maybe you'd be good

enough"—Owen coughed—"to . . . to see that my wife gets it. Raising three young'uns by herself . . . she'll need all the help she can get."

Justin pulled back and regarded Owen with grave concern. He wanted to say something, anything, to put the man's mind at ease, his worries to rest. He wanted to tell him he wasn't going to die, that he would see his children reach adulthood. But Justin had sat by enough deathbeds to recognize the near-end of life. To lie would deny Owen the chance to put his worldly concerns aside and prepare himself to meet his Maker.

He squeezed the lawman's hand. "Where can I find your family?"

"About . . ." His voice grew weaker. "Two miles outside of Rocky Creek. They sent me to Missouri to fetch the prisoner and bring her back." After a beat, he murmured, "My . . . my family . . . ?"

Justin leaned close. "You have my promise. I will do whatever I can to help your family." He didn't know how or even if he could help them, but he was determined to try.

Owen stared up at the sky for several long moments before his eyelids drooped shut.

Justin pulled out his Bible and read the Twenty-Third Psalm in a low, mellow voice. "The Lord *is* my shepherd . . ." He had committed the psalm to memory, of course, but he found that by reading it, he always discovered some new meaning, some depth of understanding that had previously escaped him.

The words seemed to have an immediate effect. Owen's breathing slowed, and he seemed less agitated.

One of Justin's early mentors told him to listen carefully whenever he attended a birth or death. Justin followed the older preacher's advice and was amazed to discover that a newborn babe's first breath made a *yah* sound and the last breath of the dying sounded like *weh. Yahweh*. The biblical name for God.

No sooner had Justin finished the psalm than he heard the unmistakable sound of Owen completing God's name—the last task of the living.

The silence that followed was broken by a strangled gasp behind him. He turned to find Sarah standing a few feet away, her eyes round in horror.

～

Sarah stood on the crest of a hill, staring at the mound of fresh dirt at her feet. She thought about her parents' graves nestled in the arms of a little white church in Texas. Though it had been years since she visited their final resting place, it comforted her to know they weren't alone.

She couldn't imagine anything worse than to be buried out here in the wilderness with only the wind and sky for company.

Together she and Justin had taken turns digging the grave with the one spade they had. It had been hard work to break through the claylike soil, but no more so than carrying the marshal's body up the hill, which Justin did without complaint.

She'd picked out the site herself,

choosing a spot at the base of a sturdy cottonwood whose branches spread far and wide to provide ample shade. The hill commanded an impressive view of the meandering stream below. It would have been easier had she chosen a resting place closer to camp where the soil was softer. But it was too close to the water's edge and she worried about possible flood waters.

She helped Justin cover the grave with rocks to discourage animals from digging up the remains. Then she wandered through the brown prairie grass to pick blue buffalo clover, which she scooped up by the roots and replanted near the grave.

The air, heavy as a wet wool blanket, was hard to breathe. Even the shade beneath the tree offered little respite from the heat of the day. Her throat felt like it was lined with burlap and her eyes stung, partly from the oppressive heat but mostly from unshed tears.

Justin's soothing voice washed over her as he read from the Bible. "Ashes to ashes . . ." Despite the heat, he wore his collar and black frock coat, which made him look even more imposing than usual.

After a long while, he closed the Good Book. In all the confusion that had followed Owen's death, he'd forgotten to handcuff her. Not wanting to remind him, she held her hands behind her back.

"I prayed for him to get well," she said. The accusations in her voice crept in unbidden, but she didn't care. God had let her down, yet again, and she didn't care who knew it.

"Your prayers were answered," he said softly. "Owen is well. He's with his heavenly Father."

Eight

Sarah couldn't move, her hands tied behind her back. She struggled to pull free, to no avail. Looking up, she gasped. The hangin' rope descended from a beam overhead. She watched in horror as the circle of hard fiber cord fell over her head. Her throat closed in protest. She opened her mouth, but the rope at her neck prevented her scream . . .

A male voice cut through her sleep-dazed brain. "Don't move."

Her eyes flew open. A mean-looking hombre stood over her. Her mind scrambling, she fought to sit up, but he held her down with a boot to her chest.

A short distance away, Justin lay on

his back and stared at the shotgun pointed straight at him, mere inches from his nose.

A deep baritone voice belonging to a barrel of a man said, "Hold it right there, mister."

Sarah recognized the two gunmen as the Mitchell brothers. The voice belonged to the older of the two, a round-bellied man with a pock-marked face and a broken nose, named Pete. His brother, called Shorty though he stood over six feet tall, was thin as a snake on stilts and had the disposition to match. A scar ran down the length of his cheek to his chin, making his face appear lopsided.

Pete prodded Justin with the barrel of his weapon. "Throw down your gun," he drawled.

Justin didn't move a muscle. "I-I don't have a gun."

The man's face darkened. "A lawman without a gun? What do you take me for? A fool?"

"Leave him alone, you—" Sarah held back the name that sprang to the tip of her tongue. Justin looked distraught

enough without her adding to his dismay with unsavory talk. "He's not a lawman. He's a preacher," she said. She
doubted the good-for-nothin' Mitchells
respected anythin', let alone a man of
the cloth, but it was worth a try.

The man's eyebrows disappeared beneath the brim of his dusty felt hat. "A
preacher?"

"Yeah, and if you bother a preacher,
God will punish you, He will."

The man nodded toward the handcuffs on Sarah's wrists and spoke to
Justin. "Don't tell me you preach so bad
you have to handcuff people before
they'll listen to you."

His brother laughed at the joke and
grabbed Sarah roughly by the shoulder.
She glared up at him. It had been years
since she'd last come face-to-face with
him, so it wasn't too surprising that he
didn't recognize her. "We got no money.
We got nothing. So jus' leave us alone,
you hear?"

Shorty's beadlike eyes raked the
length of her. "I think the little lady un-
derestimates her true worth. What do
you say, Pete?"

Pete grinned. "I say it's worth checkin' out."

Shorty knelt beside Sarah, grinning. "It'll be my pleasure."

Justin tried to sit up, but Pete stayed him with his shotgun. "Hold it right there, Preacher."

"Leave her alone," Justin warned, his lips thin with anger. "If you touch her, I'll—"

Pete laughed in his face. "What do we have here? A preacher making threats?"

"I'm asking you in the name of God to leave her alone." When his plea went unheeded, Justin struggled to sit up again, but his efforts were rewarded by a whack on the side of the head with the barrel of the gun.

Justin fell backward with a groan, and Sarah cried out. There wasn't much she could do with Pete holding a rifle on them and Shorty leaning over her like a bull in heat.

He groped her and she kneed him. He fell back and eyed her in surprise. "Well, now, ain't you a little spitfire? How lucky can I git?"

"You touch me, and my brothers will

be on you faster'n you can crack a whip. The last time you crossed my brothers, you ended up with a scar the size of Texas. This time you ain't gonna be so lucky."

Shorty released her, his hand flying to his cheek. "You're not—"

"My name's Prescott," she said, enjoying the look of horror and disbelief on his face. "Sarah Prescott."

He couldn't have jumped back faster had he stumbled upon a nest of rattlers. "Come on, Pete. Let's get outta here. With that, he ran toward his horse.

Pete responded with a curse and then raced after his brother, his spurs jingling like silver coins in a gambler's hand. The two men mounted their horses and took off running.

Sarah laughed. "Would you look at that! They ain't got enough guts to hang on a—" Upon seeing the preacher's horrified face, she broke off in midsentence. "Don't tell me . . . a lady ain't supposed to mention body parts." Proud to have figured that out for herself, she gave her head a triumphant toss. "Ain't that so?"

"Uh . . . no. I mean yes." He grimaced and rubbed the side of his head.

Alarmed, she scooted to his side, her cuffed hands held in front. "Looks like you got yourself a bruiser," she said. "At the rate you're goin', you ain't gonna make it to Texas with or without me."

He brushed away her concern. "Did I hear you right? Did he say you were a . . . Prescott?"

She bit her lip. "I reckon there ain't nothin' wrong with your ears."

He groaned but whether from pain or something else, she couldn't tell. "This is worse than I thought," he said.

"I guess you heard about us," she said.

He sat up and shook his head as if warding off a dizzy spell. "I heard that they killed a Wells Fargo passenger."

"My brothers ain't killed no one," she stormed, "and don't say they did."

He looked at her long and hard, his thoughts hidden behind his dark expression. Finally, he pulled the key from his pocket and took off her handcuffs and heaved them away.

"Handcuffs make you too vulnerable,"

he explained. "If there's a problem, you can't defend yourself."

She laughed. "I defended myself jus' fine ag'inst the Mitchell brothers."

"You might not be so lucky next time."

She boldly met his eyes. "Ain't you 'fraid I'll get away?"

The question seemed to put him in an even more solemn mood than before, and he continued to watch her with dark, probing eyes that were maddening in their ability to hide his thoughts.

"You and I both know that if you've got a mind to escape, I can't stop you."

"You're gonna let me go, just like that? After you promised Owen?"

The muscle at his jaw tightened. "I had no right making promises I can't keep."

Hands on her waist, she glared at him. "What happened to your big plans to save me?"

"I'm no longer certain that's possible."

"'Cuz I'm a Prescott?" she asked.

"I doubt that even the best lawyers in Boston could save a Prescott. All I ask is that you go during the daylight hours. I don't want to have to haul you out of trouble again."

Annoyed that he could so easily discount her, she clenched her hands tight against her side. "Out there ain't nothin' but prairie. Not much protection ag'inst Indians or outlaws."

"I thought that most of the Indian problems had been resolved, now that they're living on reservations."

"The only ones livin' on reservations are the harmless ones," she said. "The ones willin' to give up their freedom. It's the renegades you best worry about."

"Sarah *Prescott*." He grimaced as if it pained him to acknowledge her full identity. "Are you saying you're afraid?"

She drew back in surprise. "Me?" she sputtered. Fear was for chickens, not the likes of her. "You're the one who sends up smoke signals wherever we go."

"At least I'm not impulsive like you."

"I don't think—"

"That's the problem, Sarah. You don't think. You do the first thing that crosses your mind and never give a thought to the consequences."

She glared at him. "I suppose you want me to be like you and chew o'er every idea until it ain't worth fodder."

He frowned. "Maybe if you'd do a bit more 'chewing' as you call it, you wouldn't be in so much trouble."

"And maybe if you'd do less chewin', you wouldn't be wound tighter than a banjo string!"

He pulled back in surprise. "Banjo string?" He stared at her. "Banjo string?"

He threw up his hands and stalked away, then stopped. He glanced back over his shoulder. "Banjo string?" he mouthed. Shaking his head, he kept walking.

Sarah seethed for the rest of the day. She was annoyed at herself for letting those scalawags sneak up on them. Sleeping by a stream with little protection was plumb asking for trouble, and she blamed the preacher for her carelessness. Crazy as it sounded, he made her feel safe. So safe, in fact, she had almost believed he could save her from the gallows.

It was more than crazy. It was insane. The man didn't even own a gun, and he probably ain't never made a fist in his life. If he ever got in a fight, he'd no doubt turn it into a prayer meetin'. Why, she'd be safer in a den full of grizzlies than in the company of *Reverend* Justin Wells. Trusting him had been a mistake, that's for sure, and it wouldn't happen again.

Nine

It started to rain around midnight, and the downpour continued for the rest of the night and most of the next morning. The gully-washer turned the trail into a muddy mess that slowed down travel and erased any tracks that could signal danger ahead.

Though inconvenient, Sarah considered the rain a blessing. The Midwest had suffered a three-year drought causing even more hardship than usual on travelers and cattlemen. But this year's spring rains had provided plenty of water, and that was one less thing to worry about.

Justin saw the rain as a nuisance and

clearly thought that Sarah had lost her mind when she greeted the rain with outstretched arms and a loud whoop.

As they rode along the muddy trail, she explained, "Last year it was so dry, bushes followed dogs around."

The statement drew an unexpected laugh from him, and she grinned in response.

Rain dripping off his hat, Justin leaned forward in his saddle and patted his horse's wet neck. "What do you say, Noah? Do you believe in dog-chasing bushes?"

Noah nickered and shook his head. Behind him, Moses hee-hawed.

"You can laugh if you want, but my brothers and me traveled three days without a drop of water. Didn't think we were gonna make it."

Justin had one oiled canvas slicker, which he insisted Sarah wear, but it kept her only partially dry.

Water puddled beneath Blizzard's hooves, splashing mud on her boots and making a sucking sound each time the horse lifted a leg.

But it wasn't the rain or even her lack

of sleep that kept her on edge. The tension between the two of them was thick as syrup. Now that he knew her true identity, things between them had definitely changed.

Well, fiddle on him. So what if he didn't want to help her? See if she cared! What did she need with an uptight preacher? Especially one who accused her of being impulsive.

Sounded just like her brother, he did. George continually harped on her for being impulsive. It was the one thing they fought about. She couldn't help it. She was tired of having to watch every action, every word, every thought.

In her heart she was a rebel, and it was growing increasingly difficult to curtail her true nature. She longed to run through the grass barefoot. To ride with the wind in her hair, to hold a puppy in her arms.

To kiss a man without having to worry about all those silly society rules.

The last thought brought an unexpected warmth to her cheeks. She glanced at Justin's profile. As if sensing her eyes on him, he turned to look at her. In that moment, reality was an arrow straight on target. Reminded of all that she could never have—could never be—she dug her heels into her horse and quickly took the lead.

The mud almost buried a sign that read *Stonewell*. It was all that was left of the town except for a few stone chimneys.

Justin rode to her side to see why she had stopped. "Looks like a prairie fire swept through here," he said.

Sarah bit back her disappointment. She had her heart set on a hot bath and a decent meal. "Once a fire starts out here, there ain't nothin' to stop it."

"It wouldn't have done Owen any good had he held on this far."

The thought had a sobering effect on them both, and they rode side by side in silence.

Fortunately, by midday the clouds began to part, and patches of blue sky appeared overhead. She sat straight in the saddle and scanned the horizon ahead. Prairie dogs popped in and out of burrows. Deer grazed on the grass, and one of the few remaining herds of buffalo roamed on a distant hill. A turkey hawk with rigid wings flew overhead in ever widening circles. Animals would be the first to sense trouble ahead, but for now, at least, the countryside appeared calm.

"Look," Justin called from behind, pointing to the northern sky. "A rainbow."

She pulled back the hood of the slicker and shook out her hair. "I've seen rainbows before," she said irritably. Last night, she'd spent most of the night trying to stay dry and had gotten little sleep. Nevertheless, she had forced herself to stay alert on the trail, though her muscles ached with fatigue.

"You can never see enough," he said, clearly trying to humor her out of her bad mood. "A rainbow is a promise from God."

She rolled her eyes, and guided her horse around the skull of a dead buffalo. "Next you'll be tellin' me that there's a pot of gold at the rainbow's end."

"Maybe there is," he said. "Maybe there is."

Sensing some hidden meaning to his

words, she studied his handsome face and recalled how he looked without his shirt. Every detail of his broad shoulders and surprisingly muscular chest came to mind. The memory was followed by a jolt of awareness that made her stiffen her back and chew on her lower lip.

Both embarrassed and annoyed by her thoughts, she blurted out, "There ain't no gold, and there's not a promise in the world that's worth a wooden nickel." With that she galloped ahead of him so she could study the trail without distraction.

The grasslands fell behind them and they followed a deep-rutted buffalo trail through rugged hills, around buffalo wallows, and across fast-running streams. For the most part they rode in silence.

Suddenly, she saw something that alarmed her. Reining in her horse, she pointed to the ground.

"Indian tracks," she called. "Looks like they're recent. A day or two maybe."

He looked up sharply. "How can you be sure?"

"Only man can make a horse walk in

a straight line. Wild horses wander," she explained, "and they travel with colts. These horses are mature." She pointed to a U-shaped print at the water's edge. "Two horses are shod. Probably stolen." Stolen horses meant the tracks likely belonged to renegade Indians.

"I guess we're lucky they're ahead of us rather than behind us." He probed her face. "We are lucky, Sarah, right?"

"It depends," she said.

"On what?"

"On whether you druther be attacked from behind or ambushed in front."

A couple of miles later, the tracks vanished from the trail. The horsemen must have cut through the grass and taken off in another direction. Sarah sighed in relief, but she remained alert, her eyes in constant motion as she scrutinized the countryside. For the most part, the land was flat with only a few worrisome hills.

Her horse started to favor one leg. Sarah slid off the saddle and led Blizzard to a grassy area to take a look.

Justin galloped to her side. "Is there a problem?"

"I think Blizzard picked up a stone."

Justin regarded the hill that rose ahead of them, his saddle squeaking beneath his shifting weight.

"I'll take a look," he said. He slid off his horse and tethered Moses to a bush. Mounting his horse, he tugged on the reins. "Stay here."

"Wait!" she called after him. "You be careful, you hear. And . . ."

He lifted a brow and waited.

"I'm sorry 'bout callin' you a banjo string."

He considered this a moment. "I'm sorry I said you were impulsive."

Hands on her hips, she pursed her lips, wondering if he was sincere. "Are you sayin' it's not true?"

"Oh, it's true, all right. I'm just sorry I said it."

She made a face, sticking out her tongue as she often did to her teasing brothers.

He winked back, a glint of humor in his eyes. He then pressed his heels into Noah's sides and urged his horse into a full gallop up the grassy incline.

Feeling a sense of unease, she watched him ride away.

Upon reaching the crest, he reined in his horse and adjusted his hat against the sun. He then rose in his stirrups to peer at the valley below.

Telling herself she was being overcautious, she tethered her horse to a small tree. Keeping one eye on Justin, she searched the ground until she found a sharp, pointed stick. She stroked the horse on the neck, talking in a soft voice. "Atta boy."

Leaning against his shoulder, she pushed until the horse rebalanced its weight to the other side. She ran her hand down the horse's foreleg, squeezing the hard callus on the inner surface of his leg until he raised his foot.

Working from heel to toe, she scraped away the mud, grass, and pebbles embedded in the hoof. Then she walked the horse in a circle until she was satisfied that the limp was gone.

Justin returned just as she finished the job, his face grim.

"Let me guess," she said. "There ain't no gold at the end of the rainbow."

Seldom did Sarah regret anything she said, but moments later, standing at the top of the hill by Justin's side, she would have given anything to take back her carelessly spoken words.

The burned-out remains of a wagon train lay scattered along the trail below. It was a short train with only a couple of wagons and a buckboard. There were no signs of oxen or horses.

Sarah turned her head and spotted a dead Indian half hidden in the tall grass. Retching, she covered her mouth but nothing could block out the stench of decaying human flesh. Nearby, a discarded boot lay in the dirt, the shaft missing. Sarah had heard that Indians used the soft leather tops of boots for moccasin soles.

Justin walked over to the body, then squinted against the sun to better view the overturned wagon a short distance away. "Stay here and keep watch while I see if anyone is still alive."

Though she was tempted to run, she nodded. The stench was making her sick to her stomach. The thought of what Justin was bound to find in the ill-fated wagons filled her with horror.

He took one last look at her before mounting his horse and riding away.

From the distance, she watched Justin check an overturned wagon before moving on to the next one on foot. He moved quickly and with far less caution than circumstances required.

"Justin Wells, you're gonna get your fool head blown off one of these days," she muttered to herself.

She shaded her eyes against the sun and scanned the surrounding hills. Every shadow, every bush, every rock suggested possible danger and demanded close scrutiny.

Time seemed to stand still. She could have sworn she'd stood in that same spot for hours, waiting for an arrow, a war cry, or some equally horrible occurrence. But the sun remained stubbornly in place, telling her that only a few moments had passed.

Adding to her unease was the eerie silence. Not even the song of a bird could be heard in the valley. What did nature know that she didn't?

Justin vanished behind an overturned wagon. When he didn't reappear, she grew anxious.

"Where is he?" she muttered under her breath, her imagination taking flight. What if he had been ambushed by an Indian? Her heart nearly stood still. What if he had been stabbed or other-wise wounded? What if she lost him?

Sweat broke out on her forehead. What was wrong with her? The man with all his virtuous qualities couldn't protect himself against a tin soldier. He needed her, and here she was, useless as a bucket under a bull.

Unable to stand still for another sec-ond, she tethered her horse next to Moses. With lowered head, she ran down the hill and toward the nearest wagon, taking cover next to an over-turned wagon. Pots, pans, and other belongings were strewn everywhere.

A copy of Henry James's *The American* lay spine-up in the dirt. The portent smell of whiskey rose from a broken glass bottle.

Checking first to see that the way was clear, she made a beeline for the covered wagon a short distance ahead.

Without warning, the sharp retort of a gun broke the silence, and she dived for cover.

Ten

The bullet missed Justin, and that in itself was a miracle. Warned in advance by an almost imperceptible clicking sound, he'd hit the ground mere seconds before the rifle fired. The bullet missed him, but it had been a close call.

Shaken, he lay facedown for a moment, then he slowly rose on hands and knees. "Don't shoot!" he cried. "I'm not going to hurt you. I'm a preacher. I'm here to help."

His plea was met with a soft groan. He bent his head and peered cautiously beneath the overturned wagon.

A young woman no more than eighteen lay huddled beneath a blanket, her eyes glazed. She spoke through blistered lips, her voice hoarse, but he couldn't understand a word she said.

Crawling beneath the wagon, he lifted the rifle from her shaking hands. She was burning with fever.

"Where are you hurt?" he asked, inching to her side. He smoothed her damp blonde hair away from her face. A broken arrow shaft lay nearby, and she lifted her arm to show him where the stone head remained embedded in her side.

He pulled the knife out of his boot and carefully cut away the blood-soaked fabric, then he examined the dark, swollen wound.

"My name is Reverend Justin Wells," he said, trying to distract her from his probing fingers.

The arrowhead held tight. She cried out and he pulled his hand away, looking around for something to stop the fresh flow of blood.

"You . . . you're a . . . a preacher?" she whispered.

He nodded. At that moment he wished he was a doctor, but judging by the look of her wound and feverish eyes, he doubted that even a surgeon could help her now. Still, he wasn't ready to give up so easily. Perhaps there were medical supplies in one of the other wagons.

He leaned close to her. "I'll be back."

Her eyes widened in alarm. "No," she whispered. "Don't . . . don't go."

"I'll only be gone for a short time. I'll get you some water to drink and something for your wound. I'll also bring my friend. She knows a lot about medicine."

"Promise me . . ." Her voiced was weak and fading fast, but he nonetheless sensed the urgency behind her plea.

His stomach clenched into a knot. He seemed doomed lately to making promises to the dying. Despite his reservations, he leaned closer to catch her every word.

"What do you want me to promise?"

"That you'll b-baptize her."

Startled, he drew back. "Baptize who?" he asked, glancing around.

"Elizabeth," she said faintly. Her eyes

closed. With a soft gasp that he instantly recognized as the completion of God's name begun at birth, she fell limp against his arm.

He shook her gently. "Who is Elizabeth?" he asked, to no avail. The poor woman was dead.

Justin said a prayer. Lifting the blanket to cover her face, he stopped and stared.

A tiny infant lay by her side. At first he thought the child was dead, but then the baby made little sucking motions as if to nurse.

Based on his limited experience, he guessed that the baby was probably two or three months old.

He carefully wrapped the child in a blanket. He then pushed himself from under the wagon and reached for the bundle. Pulling the baby out gently, he lifted her into his arms and stood.

"Well now," he said, gazing at the tiny round face and big blue eyes. "You must be Elizabeth."

Where is he?

Sarah frantically checked under each overturned wagon. "Justin! Answer me this minute! You hear?"

She stopped to pick up the Colt Peacemaker that lay by a dead man's side. She spun the chamber to check for bullets, then held the gun to the ready.

Justin stepped from behind a wagon, and she almost fainted with relief. She'd been so certain he was dead.

"It's about time," she scolded, hiding the pistol in the waist of her pants, hiding even her relief at seeing him alive. "You like to scare the life out of me."

Spotting the infant in his arms, her jaw dropped. The baby seemed unbelievably tiny next to Justin's broad chest.

He moved the blanket so she could get a better look, and her breath caught in her throat. Except for patches of dried blood, the baby was perfect in every way, like a little porcelain doll Sarah once saw in the window of an emporium. Her mouth looked like a rose about to bloom, her wispy hair golden in color.

Cradling the baby in one arm, Justin walked with quick strides up the hill to where the horses were tethered. Sarah followed close behind.

A baby? She couldn't believe it. What in tarnation were they gonna do with a baby?

"Her name's Elizabeth," he explained when they'd reached the horses. "Her mother . . ." He didn't finish, and Sarah felt a sinking feeling inside.

In a brighter tone, he added, "Her name's in the Bible too."

Snatching her gaze away from the tiny infant, Sarah met his piercing blue eyes. "That don't mean a hill o' beans," she said, frowning. "She's still an orphan, and that gives her a tough row to hoe."

"She hasn't got a chance of making it without her mother's milk," Justin said, his voice solemn as the expression on his face.

Sarah swallowed hard and turned her head away. Never had she felt at such a loss for words. "What . . . what do we do now?"

"I need you to watch the baby while I check the other wagons. There could be more survivors," he said, though judging by the tone of his voice, he didn't hold much hope of finding anyone else alive. "I'll see if I can find some baby clothes."

She tossed her head back and boldly met his eyes. "I ain't watchin' no baby." A body who didn't know what she was doing could drop a thing that tiny . . . that unbelievably perfect.

"Sarah, I don't have time to argue with you."

"I told you, I ain't takin' care of no baby, and that's—"

Justin surprised her by thrusting the child in her arms. Without another word, he turned and walked away, a man clearly on a mission.

"Come back. You hear? Come back here!" she cried, but he kept walking and didn't so much as glance back at her.

"Oooh!"

She stared at the bundle in her arms.

Fearing she would drop the infant, she sat ever so carefully on the nearest rock. Afraid to as much as breathe, she held on with both hands, as she would a piece of fine bone china that might break with the least bit of pressure.

The baby peered up at her with big blue eyes, and something tugged at Sarah's heart. Never had she felt more protective or more helpless than she did at that moment.

"Poor little thing," she cooed. "You deserve better than to spend your last hours on earth with the likes of me."

She carefully laid the baby on a soft patch of grass. Beneath the blanket, the baby was dressed in a full-length gown with layers of petticoats beneath.

"Would you look at that?" Sarah exclaimed. "You have more fofarraw on you than a Southern belle." She obviously needed to be changed, and Sarah waved the unpleasant odor away with her hand.

Carefully, she undressed the baby, her heart pounding nervously. She then emptied the water in her canteen onto her kerchief and, ever so gently, washed the infant's soft pink skin.

When she was done and with no clean clothes available, she wrapped the baby in the blanket and rocked her. She wanted to sing to her and wished she could remember the lullaby her mama had sung so many years ago. All she knew were the bawdy bar songs her brothers taught her. She couldn't bring herself to sing such lyrics to this precious, sweet child. Instead, she hummed.

The baby started to cry, and Sarah hummed louder. Then the baby's face turned an alarming shade of red, and it was all Sarah could do to keep from crying herself.

By the time Justin returned carrying bundles filled with baby clothes and a generous supply of dried meat and hardtack bread, Sarah was nearly frantic.

"It's 'bout time." The instant he dumped his bundles, she handed the child over to him and brushed her hands together.

"She's probably hungry," Justin said, jiggling the baby up and down.

"We can't do nothin' 'bout that."

Justin winced as if in pain but said nothing. Instead he carefully placed the baby on a blanket he'd spread on the ground. After much fumbling with the nappy, he finally got her partially dressed.

Sarah sighed in relief. She'd held her breath the entire time he'd tried to pin the baby's britches on. Not that she could have done any better. But by cracky, she couldn't have done much worse.

Taking Sarah's hand, Justin pulled her away from the still crying child, eager to show her all that he found in the wagon train.

"Look, Sarah, a dress." He held the garment up for her to see. It was a simple blue gingham day dress with a flared skirt and fitted waist. The narrow collar, long sleeves, and hem were finished with a white band of fluted ruff. A row of porcelain buttons held the darted bodice closed.

"Matches your eyes perfectly." He shoved the dress into Sarah's hands.

The fabric felt smooth and velvety to her touch. Sarah didn't know a hog's hair about fashion, but she knew a pretty dress when she saw it, and this one qualified on all accounts. How would it feel to wear something this soft? This beautiful? This feminine?

Feeling guilty for her petty thoughts, she tossed the garment back and it fell to the ground. "That ain't gonna feed no hungry baby!" she cried.

A muscle tightened at his jaw. "I'm afraid there's not much we can do for Elizabeth," he said, his voice husky. "But that doesn't mean we can't save you. Like I said, they'll think twice about hanging a lady."

Covering her ears with trembling hands, she turned away. "A body who lets an innocent baby die deserves to be hanged!"

He grabbed her from behind and spun her around. "Don't say that. Don't ever say that."

She fell to her knees, sobbing, and he followed her downward.

With a choking sound he hugged her tight, burying his face in her hair. For several long moments they clung to each other, but it was no use. His arms—his strong, warm, comforting arms—could block out the past and make her forget the future, but they could do nothing to stop a poor baby's fate.

Pulling away from him, she stood. "Why, why?" she cried, tears streaming down her face. Raising a fist to the sky, she lashed out at God, at the world, at the unfairness of it all. Seeing his stricken face, she wanted to die. She laid her hand on his arm and added in a softer voice, "My being a lady won't change a thing." She glanced at Elizabeth. "Don't you see? Not a thing."

His face a mask of frustration, he plucked the garment off the ground and stuffed it into Moses' pack. "The fabric might come in handy," he said.

He then picked up the crying infant. "Come on, little one." Walking with quick, even strides, he carried the baby to a spring-fed stream.

"What are you doin'?" Brushing her

tears aside, Sarah ran after him. She didn't want to be saddled with no baby, but that didn't mean she didn't care what happened to the poor thing.

"I'm going to baptize her, just like her mother requested." Bending over, he cupped his hand and reached into the water. Sarah gasped and snatched the child out of his arm with an indignant swoop.

"Have you gone loco? That water's cold enough to freeze the fur off a bear."

"It's only a few drops," he protested. "And it's not that cold. It just feels cold because the air is so warm."

"Hasn't this poor child been through 'nuff already? The least you can do is heat the water."

He stared at her. "I've baptized a number of people in the dead of winter, and no one ever complained about the temperature of the water."

"That's 'cuz they were too cold to complain," she retorted.

Justin shook his head as if he didn't believe his ears. "It's not that cold," he protested. Nonetheless, he started gathering up twigs and set to work building a fire.

Meanwhile, Sarah cradled the bawling baby in her arms.

Once the water had been heated to Sarah's satisfaction, Justin took the child in his arms and performed the simple ceremony. Elizabeth's cries subsided, and she latched onto Justin's finger and sucked hungrily.

He glanced up at Sarah. "As the child's godmother, do you promise to do right by her? To bring her up in accordance with God's Word?"

She gaped at Justin and shook her head. "I ain't no godmother, and don't go sayin' I am, you hear?"

"It's just you and me, Sarah. If we're not her godparents, who else is there?"

Sarah's lips parted, but she couldn't for the life of her think of anything to say.

Justin gave a grim nod. "I'm going to take that as a yes," he said. Elizabeth began to cry, and he shifted her onto his shoulder.

Sarah felt trapped. More than that, she was scared. She had escaped her own lynching, outrun more outlaws and lawmen than she cared to count, had even plunged a knife in an attacking bear, but never had she faced such a challenge as this.

"It'll only be for a short while," Justin said, as if that could make her feel any better. "Without her mother's milk . . ."

Giving up on Justin's finger, Elizabeth began crying so hard that her whole little body shook. Her face turned red as a ripe summer tomato. It was all Sarah could do to keep from crying herself. Shouldn't a godmother know what to do?

Finally she could stand it no longer. She didn't have it in her to wait around while a helpless infant starved to death in front of her very eyes. She grabbed hold of the leather horn of her saddle, shoved her foot into the stirrup, and swung herself hard onto the horse.

Justin, rocking Elizabeth, looked up. "Sarah!"

He tried to grab the reins with his one free arm, but she pulled out the pistol she'd found earlier.

He fell back, mouth open, eyes round with astonishment.

"I'm sorry," she whispered, her words drowned out by the infant's frantic cries.

His face dark, he pleaded with her. "Please, Sarah." He lifted his voice to be heard. "Don't go. We can get through this together, I know we can."

Something like a knife twisted inside her. She had been prepared to stand by his side until it was time to go their separate ways, to face any adversity. She would have gladly fought Indians, outlaws, and whatever nature had to offer, but not this.

She met his beseeching eyes, then glanced down at the red-faced infant in his arms and wanted to die. Swallowing the lump in her throat, she pressed her heels into the side of her horse and rode away.

⌇

For the longest while, all Justin could do was watch until Sarah was no more than a tiny spot in the distance, his head filled with Elizabeth's frantic cries.

He didn't blame Sarah for leaving. Didn't blame her one bit. He was tempted himself to run away and leave the horrors of the ill-fated wagon train behind. But he couldn't bring himself to leave until he'd given Elizabeth's mother a proper burial. His heart squeezed tight at the thought of having to bury the beautiful child he held in his arms. If only there was a way to save her.

Never had he felt so utterly, utterly alone.

Sarah was no longer in sight, and any hope he had that she would return began to fade.

Holding the baby close to his heart, one hand cupping her tiny head, he rocked her gently. Elizabeth was clearly exhausted, and her eyes began to droop.

"You've got some mighty fine tonsils," he said, soothingly. "Reminds me of old Mrs. Spindlemeyer. She sang at our church last Christmas and her voice nearly raised the roof." Just thinking about his church in Boston made him feel even more depressed, but since his voice seemed to have a soothing effect on Elizabeth, he continued to talk. Not about his church. Instead, he found himself talking about Sarah.

Calmed by his low, soothing voice, Elizabeth's cries stopped altogether, and her little body grew still.

". . . and there she was, up to her chin in mire. You never saw such a sight." He chuckled softly to himself. He glanced down at the infant in his arms, noting with satisfaction that she was sound asleep.

Moving ever so slowly, he spread a blanket beneath the shade of a tree. Taking care not to wake her, he laid her down. Elizabeth cried out once before closing her eyes and drifting off to sleep again.

Justin stood watching her. Never did he feel so helpless.

"Now what, God? Now what?"

He knew he was close to the Kansas border, but according to his map, he was still miles away from any town or forts. He doubted there were any farms or homesteads. But first things first. If by some miracle Elizabeth survived this ordeal, he wanted to be able to tell her that he gave her mother a decent burial.

He pulled his spade from the mule's saddle, picked a spot a short distance from the sleeping child, and began to dig. The sound of approaching horses made him freeze, a shovelful of dirt in his hand. His mouth went dry. He spun around. Three horsemen headed his way, riding fast.

Dear God . . . no! Please don't let it be Indians.

Eleven

Sarah rode away without looking back, her heart so heavy she could hardly breathe. Blizzard's hooves flew over the buffalo grass, pounding the ground and kicking up dust. Prairie dogs scattered from the path and popped into the nearest holes.

Never one to stand around, she had to do something. Anything. There had to be a way to save that poor babe. But how?

Hot tears streamed down her face.

She hated to leave Justin alone, but standing around and watching some poor baby die was more than she could bear. She'd seen enough people die to last a lifetime, but never before had she witnessed the death of someone so young.

Digging her heels into the side of the horse, she rode hard through the valley, blinded by tears. Normally, she would never think of riding through such an area without scrutinizing every rock, every shadow, every indentation in the ground as George had so patiently taught her. Today she didn't care a pig's tail about her own safety.

There had to be something. A farm, a town.

Never had she felt so utterly helpless, so completely unworthy. The youngest in her family, she'd never had to take care of anyone, never knew what it was like to be needed. And the moment someone needed her, what did she do? She panicked!

Think, Sarah, think!

She rode until she came to a grove of trees clustered along a sparkling stream. She dismounted and let her horse drink from the cool waters. Falling to her knees, she cupped her shaking hands and splashed water on her tear-stained face.

She closed her eyes, but all she could see was Justin's face as she rode away, the baby's desperate cries ringing in her ears.

If only she were a praying woman—

She glanced upward, then lowered her head. Justin believed in miracles, and if ever she needed one, it was now. Bracing herself with a deep breath, she began to pray as she had heard Justin pray so many times before.

"Dear heavenly Father, Almighty God, Creator of heaven and earth . . ." She stopped. What came next? She couldn't remember.

She threw up her hands. This was a waste of time. The words sounded foreign—meaningless even—to her ears. She jumped to her feet and paced back and forth. She gazed at the sky and wondered if heaven really existed, if there really was a God.

"Are You up there?" she called. "God, are You there?" She listened, but all she could hear was the distant song of a bobwhite and the sound of rushing waters.

She fell to her knees again and lifted her hands upright. "God, I've only asked You for a couple of things in my life. I asked You to save my papa, but he died anyway. I asked You to save my ma, but You didn't see fit to help her. After that, I never bothered You again. I figured You were too busy for the likes of me.

"Maybe You still are, but I'm not askin' for me. I'm askin' for that little babe who doesn't deserve to die. She needs Your help. God. If You answer this one prayer, I promise I ain't never botherin' You again. I'll . . . I'll act like a lady, I will. I'll use proper words, and I ain't never gonna to throw myself at . . . anyone.

"And that rule—you know, the one about doin' unto others . . . I promise, God, I'll be the best person I can be. If You would only grant me this one thing, it'll be the last You ever hear from me."

She dropped her hands to her side and stood. Then she remembered something and quickly fell to her knees again. "Amen."

She waited, for what she didn't know. A bolt of lightning? The parting of the waters? Something. But nothing changed. The sky, the sun, everything was the same.

And a short distance away, an innocent babe was dying.

"Sarah Prescott," she muttered, "you're nothin' but a fool."

She jumped to her feet and, not knowing what else to do, started for her horse.

A rustle in the nearby bushes startled her. She drew out her pistol and spun around. Heart pounding, she crouched low and called out, "Who—who's there?"

The rustling continued. Moistening her dry lips, she made a wide circle around the bushes and closed in from the rear. Seeing a movement ahead, she froze.

Suddenly, a bleating sound broke the silence, and she burst out laughing. She fought her way through the heavy undergrowth until she spotted a white goat. The rope tied to the goat's neck was caught on a bush. The poor animal shook its head from side to side in an effort to free itself, bleating as if blaming her for its predicament.

Slipping her gun in the waist of her pants, she petted the animal's rump. "If that don't beat all." Talking gently to the animal, she dropped to one knee and untangled the rope. That's when she discovered the most amazing thing; it was a nanny goat with teats full as a peddler's bags.

"Well, if you ain't a sight for sore eyes." The female goat must have run away from the wagon train during the Indian raid.

She couldn't believe her good fortune. It was the answer to her prayers. It was a miracle, that's what it was. A miracle. Fresh tears streaming down her face, she glanced at the sky.

"Thank You, God. Thank You."

Tugging on the rope, Sarah pulled the goat away from the bushes and led it to her horse. "Let's hope we make it back in time."

Twelve

It was dusk by the time she spotted what could only be Justin's campfire ahead. Who else but a greenhorn preacher would make a campfire out in the open?

Great snakes! The fool man was going to get himself killed.

He couldn't have made his presence more obvious had he fired cannons. Shaking her head in alarm, she tried to coax the goat into walking faster, but the animal was clearly exhausted.

It was dark by the time she reached the campsite, which only made the fire stand out that much more. She slid off her horse, calling Justin's name.

"You won't believe this," she yelled, "but I done found myself a miracle!"

No one was by the fire, and she stopped, her heart frozen in fear. The eerie quiet filled her with dread. It was too late, she was certain of it. The baby was dead, and Justin was off somewhere digging her grave.

Torn between running away and comforting Justin, she hesitated. She couldn't do anything for the baby, and she wasn't even sure she could do anything for Justin, but she had to try.

A tall form stepped out of the darkness. Her mouth dropped open in surprise. "I never thought you'd find me."

Her brother gave her a crooked grin. "I reckon we'd have to be blind as a fiddle not to see the signs you left."

Robert had Sarah's same red hair and big blue eyes. A man of few spoken words, he nonetheless scribbled up a storm every chance he got, filling notebook after notebook with poetry and prose that he refused to let anyone but Sarah read.

"Where's Jed and George?" she asked.

"Right here," George said, walking out from a clump of trees. George was the oldest and had inherited his father's dark, brooding looks.

Jed walked in George's shadow, as usual. A poor imitation of the older brother who headed the family, Jed was shorter, thinner, and less inclined to give George grief than she was.

Sarah tied the goat to a bush and ran into the waiting arms of her brothers. They all talked at once, except for Robert, of course, ever the watchful one.

"Been trailing you for days," Jed explained. "Ever since that U.S. Marshal got hold of you. Then we bumped into the Mitchell brothers, and they swore up and down that you were travelin' with some preacher. Didn't sound like somethin' you'd do."

"You're lucky you're still alive," George said, his face dark. "I swear, Sarah, If you ever disobey me ag'in, I'll—"

Sarah paid George no heed. She was too busy looking around for Justin.

Spotting him tied to a tree, she cried out in dismay.

"What ya have to go do that for?" She reached for the leather sheath at Jed's waist and pulled out his dagger. Before anyone could stop her, she hurried to Justin's side and began working on the rope at his hands and feet.

Justin searched her face as she freed his wrists. "You came back," he said softly.

"Of course I came back. What do you think I am, some chicken-bellied—?"

"I . . . didn't know what to think."

His uncertainty filled her with despair. Did he really think she'd run off when he most needed her? "The . . . the baby?"

Rubbing his wrists, he pointed to the little bundle a short distance away. "Poor thing cried herself to sleep."

Her heart jumped with joy. "Then she's still—"

He nodded. "But I don't know how much longer she can go without milk."

"That's what I was tryin' to tell you." She kept her voice low so as not to wake Elizabeth. "I found a goat. We have milk!"

Quickly, she cut the last piece of rope away from his ankles and, jumping to her feet, whirled about to face her brothers.

"Don't just stand there!" she ordered. "We have a baby to feed."

She met George's cold-eyed stare without flinching. He wasn't used to his younger sister giving orders, nor, judging by the dark scowl he gave her, had he forgiven her for the latest trouble she'd gotten herself into. But there was no time to worry about that now.

Justin scooped the sleeping baby in his arms, and she immediately began to wail. Sarah never thought she'd hear a more beautiful sound.

Fighting tears of relief, she grabbed a tin cup. "Hold on to the goat."

Kneeling beside the squirming animal, she massaged the animal's udder. "I'm gonna call the goat Mira," she announced. "Short for 'miracle.'"

She squeezed hard, letting the first few squirts of milk dribble onto the ground. Satisfied that any dirt had been washed away, she held the tin cup beneath the goat. In no time at all, the cup was filled to the brim with pure white milk.

It took four of them to feed the baby. After a few false starts, Robert finally tried soaking a piece of clean fabric with milk and letting the baby suck on it. The baby cried in frustration at first, but once Robert learned how to keep the flow of milk constant, she soon settled down and frantically began to suck.

It took nearly an hour, but little Elizabeth finally had her fill and drifted off to sleep, looking contented as a bear ready to hibernate. Her brothers had gone to unsaddle their horses, leaving her and Justin alone.

Justin gave her a look of admiration and her heart skipped a beat. He wrapped the baby in a warm blanket and placed her a safe distance away from the fire. "You saved her life."

Not usually one for false modesty, Sarah was uncharacteristically hesitant to agree. Something was at work in her life that she couldn't fully understand.

"I had a little help," she allowed.

"Help?" Justin stared at her as if he

hadn't heard right. "You aren't suggesting that . . .?" He pointed upward.

She blushed. She hated showing any sign of vulnerability or weakness in front of her brothers, and such talk would clearly qualify as both where they were concerned.

"Now don't go thinkin' I'm a saint or anythin' just 'cuz I had a divine interruption."

"Intervention," Justin said gently. "And somehow the word *saint* never came to mind." Thinking she heard a touch of humor in his voice, she eyed him warily. His face told her he was perfectly serious.

George and the others walked back to camp. "Miracles? Divine interventions?" George mimicked. "You sure ain't soundin' like yourself. I think this here preacher has done gone and messed with your brain."

"No one's messed with my brain," Sarah snapped. "I know what I know, and I'm tellin' you, findin' that goat was a miracle."

George exchanged glances with Jed but said nothing. Instead, he reached into his vest pocket and drew out a square of brown paper and a rawhide pouch. After rolling a cigarette, he poked a stick into the hot embers and used the glowing red tip to light it.

The five of them stood around the baby, staring down at her.

Nothing ever happened, it seemed, that Justin didn't have a corresponding Bible story to match. So it came as no surprise to Sarah when he likened their finding Elizabeth to the Pharaoh's daughter finding a baby in the river Nile. "She took that babe home and raised him as her own son."

"Don't tell me," Sarah said, guessing. "The baby's name was Moses."

As if to acknowledge his namesake, Moses the mule gave a loud hee-haw, and Sarah and Justin roared with laughter. After the harrowing day, their laughter offered a welcome release. It also chased away any lingering tension between them.

Her brothers, not knowing the mule's name, stared at them as if they'd been nipping at a loco plant.

Wiping the tears from her eyes, Sarah

explained, "Robert, Jed, George. Meet Moses, the mule."

Though Robert and Jed chuckled upon learning the mule's name, George continued to stare at her with an odd expression.

Later, George shot a rabbit, and while it roasted over the fire, Robert took Sarah by the elbow and led his sister a short distance away from the others. "Are you gonna keep that baby?" he whispered in her ear.

Surprised by the question, she quickly turned to face him. "Are you joshin' me? What am I gonna do with a baby?"

"I thought maybe you planned on marrying yourself a preacher. Be one of those respectable ladies that serves tea and makes quilts."

"That'll be the day," she said dully, feeling a sudden longing inside that she couldn't name.

Robert studied her thoughtfully. "You aren't sweet on the preacher, are you?"

Feeling her cheeks grow warm, she scowled furiously. "I ain't gone sweet on nobody," she said. It had been a long, hard day, and she was in no mood for such ridiculous nonsense. She walked away to rejoin the others.

A lone wolf howled, and George stared into the darkness. "We're as good as sitting ducks out here. Jed, you better keep watch. We'll leave first thing in the morning."

Justin looked straight at George. "I could use some help burying the victims. It doesn't feel right not to give them a proper burial."

George hesitated. He clearly didn't want to play the part of undertaker, but whether out of gratitude to Justin for saving Sarah's life or simply out of respect for a man of God, he reluctantly agreed. "How long will it take?"

"With four of us working, it shouldn't take more than an hour or two. If we start at the first light, we should be done in no time."

"I wanna be out of here as close to sunup as possible."

Justin nodded. "Understood." He glanced at Sarah as if asking permission for something. "Sarah told me about her trouble in Rocky Creek," he began.

George gave Sarah the look of a disapproving parent. "Did she, now?"

"I offered to help in any way I could."

A cloud of annoyance darkened George's face. "That's mighty nice of you, Reverend, but as long as my little sister stays with us and does what I tell her, we won't be needin' your assistance."

Feathery lines deepened at the corners of Justin's eyes. "Have you considered asking Washington for help? President Hayes has pardoned more people than any other president. I'm sure if you make the case that she wasn't given a proper trial, he'll relent."

George discounted the idea with a wave of his hand. "I doubt that Hayes would do somethin' so unpopular as to pardon a Prescott." He turned his attention to Sarah. "We've wasted a lot of time trackin' you down," he said, his voice low so as to be heard by her ears only. "We missed a big Wells Fargo shipment, and I ain't aimin' to miss another."

Sarah glanced at Justin, who watched

from a distance. As if to guess what George said to her, he turned and walked away.

The following morning, Sarah woke to angry voices.

"I ain't doing it," Jed shouted. "I'm done!"

In the silver light of dawn, Sarah scrambled out of her bedroll and hurried to join the men. "Shh, you'll wake the baby." She turned to Jed. "What are you so riled up about?"

"Your preacher friend insists that we bury that dead Indian, and I ain't doin' it."

Justin leaned on his shovel, his stance every bit as stubborn as Jed's. "Everyone deserves a proper burial."

Jed shook his head in disgust and shuddered. "After what those savages did to that poor family—"

"Maybe if we stopped pushing Indians off their land, they wouldn't feel the need for revenge," Justin said quietly.

"That's not revenge," Jed spit out. "That's cold-blooded murder."

"Jed should know," Sarah said.

"When it comes to revenge, us Prescotts are experts."

Jed whirled around to face her. "We rob stages. We don't kill people." He kicked a mound of dirt and started back to camp.

George gestured impatiently. "I say we stop jawing and finish the job. I want to hit the trail."

Without another word, Justin resumed digging.

Sarah glanced at the body of the Indian and quickly turned away. It was the Comanche custom to lay their dead to rest in caves, but they were miles away from the nearest mountain. They had no choice but to bury him in the ground.

Knowing that Justin would want to do everything right, she said, "Break his weapon and bury it with him."

Justin stopped digging and looked up.

Robert explained, "Everything a Comanche owns is buried with him so he'll have it with him in the afterlife."

George pushed back his hat. "I don't

think he's gonna need it where he's goin'."

Justin scooped a shovel full of dirt and tossed it behind him. "That's for God to decide, not us."

Sarah walked back to camp and checked on Elizabeth, who was still asleep. Knowing that she would soon be riding off with her brothers, she found herself close to tears. A searing pain shot through her, lodging in her chest.

In a very short time, this tiny babe had managed to work her way into Sarah's heart. How was such a thing possible?

Staring down at the child, Sarah pondered the future. How would Elizabeth react upon learning how her mama was killed? Would she seek revenge as Sarah's brothers had done? Or would she, instead, choose Justin's way and leave things in God's hands?

Sarah closed her eyes and imagined Elizabeth all grown up. But the life she envisioned for Elizabeth, hoped for her, wanted for her, was nothing like the reality of her own life.

"Dear little one," she whispered, "choose Justin's way. You hear?"

She left Elizabeth's side and made a fresh pot of coffee, but she couldn't shake off the depression that settled over her like a dark cloud.

The sun rose, its golden rays spilling across the flower-decked prairie like warm honey, but even the cheery brightness failed to lift her spirits.

The air was eerily still, without so much as the trill of a bird to break the silence. The quiet pastoral scene seemed all wrong for the grisly task of burying the dead.

In the distance, Justin and her brothers stood in a circle, George and Robert with their hats on their chests. Justin lifted the Indian's arrow above his head, holding it with both hands. He snapped it in two and tossed it into the grave.

Across the way, a flock of curlews suddenly took to the air with piercing cries that ended in a long, drawn-out whistling sound.

Watching them, an inexplicable chill shot through her. Her neck prickled.

She dropped down and grabbed her weapon from her bedroll.

Jed crouched next to her, hands on his own shooting iron. "What's wrong?"

"I think I saw somethin' move in those there trees."

Jed shaded his eyes against the sun. "I don't see nothin'. Maybe it was a deer."

Would a deer frighten away birds, she wondered? Maybe. "You don't think they'll come back, do you?" she whispered.

"The Comanches? Nah. They got what they want. They won't be back."

"They don't usually leave their dead behind," she said.

"It was a small band. Probably had their hands full stealin' the animals."

Elizabeth cried out, and Sarah rushed to her side.

Jed's assurances did little to ease her nerves. While she changed and fed Elizabeth, she kept her weapon handy at her side and her eyes and ears alert.

The others returned, their faces grim. Justin tucked his Bible into Moses' saddle while George and Robert helped themselves to the freshly brewed coffee.

After washing and changing his shirt, Justin took over the care of Elizabeth.

"How's my girl?" he said, jostling the baby up and down.

"Careful, she just ate," Sarah cautioned, but her warning came too late. Elizabeth spit up all over him.

This meant having to change the baby again, which Justin attempted to do with great difficulty. Sarah watched in dismay as he struggled to get the baby in and out of her clothes. Finally, unable to watch a moment longer, she took over the task herself.

She kept her back toward Justin so he couldn't see her own awkward efforts in fitting the garment over the baby's head and working her little arms into the sleeves.

A short while later, she sidled up next to George. "I'm worried about leavin' Justin by himself," she said. Now that he had a baby to care for, his journey was all that more difficult.

"He's not your problem," George replied gruffly.

"It's not just him," she said. "I'm worried about Elizabeth."

"What do you want me to do about it?"

"I want us to stay with them," she beseeched. "Just to the Texas border."

George tossed the dregs of his coffee into the dying fire. "We've wasted enough time trackin' you down, girl. There's a big shipment of gold headin' toward Abilene, and if we don't hurry, it will be loaded on the train and sent East before we get there. We ain't got no more time to waste."

George motioned to Jed with a toss of his head, and the two of them picked up their saddles and headed for the horses. Robert stayed behind and waited until he was alone with Sarah.

"It's not too late, sis," he said earnestly. "You can change your name. Move to the city. Find yourself a good man."

She squeezed Robert's arm. She always felt closest to Robert, who was only two years older. George showed her how to fish and shoot, but it was

Robert who taught her to read and write.

"What would a good man want with the likes of me?"

"I'm serious, Sarah. Do you ever think about what life would be like if we didn't belong to the Prescott family?"

"I think about it," she said truthfully. "I think about it as often as a goose goes barefoot. But thinkin' don't make it so. We are who we are, and ain't nothin' goin' to change that."

Jed called to her. "Ready, Sarah?"

"Be there in a minute," Sarah called back.

She was painfully aware that Justin stood a short distance away, staring at her, a world of emotions in his eyes.

It hurt to think she might never see him again, hurt more than she ever thought possible. A lump rose in her throat, and she closed her eyes so as not to look at him. If she did, she feared that propriety wouldn't have a chance against the overwhelming need to feel his lips on hers once again before she left, this time for good.

"I guess this is . . . good-bye," she said.

He took a step toward her. "Sarah—"

She wheeled around and started toward the horses, but some invisible force prevented her from moving more than a few feet away. Feeling her defenses desert her, she turned. "I can't go," she said, her voice low. "I can't leave you alone with Elizabeth."

He gave her a worried frown. "Are you ready to return to Rocky Creek?" he asked. "To put your fate in God's hands?"

"I ain't meanin' to do that," she said. "I'll just stay with you till the Red River. After that, you're on your own."

He shook his head, but before he could protest, she hastened to add, "I know the territory. I can get you through the Nation safely. If you wander too far away from the reservations, you'll be in more trouble than a Texas twister."

His eyes dark with appeal, he moved toward her and laid his hand on her cheek. "If you stay with me, you risk getting caught."

His touch sent tingles down her spine, but it was the concern on his face that made her heart swell. She reached up to place a hand on top of his.

"We have to think 'bout what's best for Elizabeth."

She saw the pain in his eyes, the indecision. He drew his hand away and turned to gaze at Elizabeth, who lay on her back, her little legs and arms in constant motion.

"It won't be easy," he conceded. "I never milked anything, much less a goat, in my life, but I'll learn. I won't let anything happen to her. You have my solemn word."

"It ain't easy feedin' her," she persisted. "You ain't got a rat's chance in a hawk's nest of managin' on your own."

"I . . ." The eyes that had moments earlier showered her with tenderness now implored her. "I would never forgive myself if something happened to you."

"It won't," she said.

"You don't know that."

"Maybe not," she admitted. "But I druther take my chances with you than

watch my brothers rob another stage."
There, she said it. She loved her brothers, would always love them, but she no longer wanted to stay with them.

Some, if not all, of his objections seemed to melt from his face. "I don't want you with them either. I only wish there was something I could say or do to make them give up their ways."

"I don't think there's anythin' anyone can say to make them change their ways," she said. "Let me stay with you, Justin. Just for a while."

"If you're sure . . ."

She lifted her chin. "Seems like I'm more sure than you."

A shadow of indecision crossed his forehead. "I want you with me, you have to know that. Not just for Elizabeth's sake, but . . . for my sake as well. It's just—"

She searched his face, certain he was about to break her heart by making her go with her brothers. "What?"

"I'm a preacher."

She tilted her head to the side. "I ain't likely to forget that."

"The problem is . . . I'm afraid *I* might forget."

Startled, she blinked, afraid to believe what she heard in his voice, saw in his eyes, felt in her heart. Was he really saying what she thought he was saying? A man of God? A man whom she suddenly realized she trusted with her life? Was such a thing even possible?

When at last she found her voice, she asked, "You talkin' about that man and woman stuff?"

He didn't answer her. Didn't need to. His tormented face told her all she needed to know. Instead, he stared at the fire as if waiting for the dying embers to consume any improper feelings that might have passed between them.

She took a step toward him, but he stiffened and the all-too-familiar mask of denial fell firmly in place. "You ain't never gonna forget," she said. She didn't know how she knew this, she just did. Just to be on the safe side, she added, "I ain't never gonna let you forget."

God had saved Elizabeth, He did, and

she wasn't about to do anything to displease Him. She would keep a clamp on any untoward musings. No more thinking about manly things or womanly things, and especially not man and woman together things. From now on, she would be as virtuous as an old school marm. Even if it killed her.

His gaze held hers for a moment as if to determine the sincerity of her promise. After a moment, they both looked away.

Sarah stared at the ground. "Well, have we got a deal or ain't we?"

"And what kind of deal is that?" George asked, from behind her.

Bracing herself with a deep breath, she turned to face her older brother. She'd done her share of rebelling over the years, but she'd never really stood up to him. Not even Robert and Jed had managed that.

Her brother was quick to pick up a weakness. If she showed the least bit of hesitation, she wouldn't have a hare's chance against a fox of getting her own way.

She straightened her shoulders in an effort to gain confidence. Refusing to look at Justin, she said, "I ain't goin' with you."

Thirteen

For the longest while, no one moved. Even Elizabeth seemed to sense the tension in the air and stared at them with unflinching eyes.

George impaled Sarah with a steely look and, though her knees felt weak, she matched his demeanor. When she didn't back down, he wagged his finger in her face.

George spit out a stream of tobacco. "I've had enough of you and your wild ways, Sarah. Every time you strike out on your own you get yourself in trouble. From here on in, you're stayin' with the family—and there ain't gonna be no argument."

Jed nodded. "Family sticks together no matter what."

Sarah stood her ground. "I told you, I ain't goin' with you. I promised Justin."

George's eyes blazed with anger. "You'll do what I say or—"

"Back off," Robert said, quietly, his thumbs looped around his suspenders.

George spun around and thrust a finger in Robert's face. "No, you back off. Sarah's life is in danger, and we're the only ones who can protect her."

Sarah's temper flared. She was tired of her brothers acting like she didn't have a brain in her head. "You know full well I can take care of myself."

"You ain't done a very good job of it," George bellowed back. "Otherwise there wouldn't be a noose in Texas with your name on it."

"It wouldn't have my name on it if you weren't so determined on rightin' a wrong done sixteen years ago."

George's jaw dropped. "Are you sayin' we're supposed to forget what they did to our parents? Is that how you want to honor their memory?"

"This ain't about our parents," she

said with sudden insight. All these years, she'd believed that whatever George said was true. Now she questioned his motives, questioned even their right to lash out at society for the wrongs committed by a misguided few. Where was the honor in that?

"This is about what we've done to ourselves," she said. "We're outlaws, George. And that's how we're gonna die if we don't—"

"You don't know what you're talkin' about." He stabbed his chest with his thumb. "I'm the one who makes the decisions around here. Not you. Not Robert. Not anyone else. Me! Now get your backside on your horse, and—"

Arms crossed in front, she lifted her chin and boldly met his eyes. "I told you, George. I ain't goin'."

Grabbing her by the shoulder, George's nostrils flared with fury. "I said, get on that horse!"

"Leave her alone!"

At the sound of Justin's voice, George released her, the veins in his neck bulging. "This ain't your business, preacher. This is a family matter."

"And I believe the matter has been settled. The lady said she's not going."

Making a fist, George swung around to face the preacher. Sarah gasped, but George caught himself just in time. He slammed his fist into his palm before dropping his clenched hands to his side. He offered no apology. Instead, he glared at Justin, his face red with rage.

"So help me God, if you weren't a preacher—"

Justin nodded. "I understand your frustration." He pressed his own fist into his hand. "If you weren't Sarah's brother—"

Jed laughed out loud, and George glowered at him before turning back to Sarah.

"Please, George," she pleaded. "Soon as I know the baby's safe, I'll . . . I'll catch up to you." It pained her to make such a promise, but the truth was she didn't know what else to do. The few times she'd struck out on her own, she'd failed. A single woman with no formal education and a rope hanging over her head had no future except with her brothers. "It will just be for a short time. I promise."

"No!"

Toe to toe and practically nose to nose, she and George continued to argue, each trying to outshout the other. Robert and Jed watched with slackened jaws. Justin picked up Elizabeth and moved her out of earshot.

Not knowing where she got the strength or courage to stand up to her brother's obstinate ways, she wore him down with sheer determination.

"Drats, Sarah, when did you get to be so stubborn!"

"I reckon I take after you," she shouted back.

George appeared conflicted, but at least the obstinate scowl had left his face. He rubbed his chin and fumbled with his tobacco pouch. A man used to giving orders and having them obeyed was clearly out of his element.

"I don't like leaving you. It's dangerous. A woman alone . . ." He waved his hand toward the overturned wagons in the distance. "You saw what can happen."

"I'll be careful."

"Careful?" He mouth twisted in mock laughter. "When have you ever been careful? You wouldn't be in this mess if you'd been careful and done what I told you. Have you even got a weapon?"

She nodded and reached into the waist of her pants, fumbling as she drew out the six-shooter.

George's scowl grew more menacing. "You better be a lot quicker on the draw than that." He called over to Jed. "Give her your gun belt."

Jed protested with a shake of his head. "Ah, come on, George. What am I gonna use?"

"I'll get you another." To Sarah, he said, "Meet us in Fort Smith." He pointed a finger. "If you know what's good for you, you'll be there."

She gaped at him. Fort Smith, Arkansas? Home of the famous hanging judge? She wouldn't have been more surprised had George told her to meet him at the Rocky Creek gallows. Judge Parker's relentless determination to hang every outlaw in his jurisdiction was enough to make her want to run in the opposite direction.

"Are you serious?" she gasped.

George stiffened at the question. "The last place the law will look is under its very own nose," he said curtly.

"I told you, I ain't leavin' that baby till I know she's safe."

Justin moved to her side. "Sarah, I can take the train from Fort Smith to Texarkana. From there, I'll catch the stage to Rocky Creek."

"Is that what you want to do?"

"I don't have much choice, do I? I've got to do what's best for the baby, and right now, the faster I can get to Rocky Creek, the sooner I can find a proper home for her."

She nodded, but her heart wasn't in it. As much as she detested the idea of traveling to Judge Parker's territory, the thought of saying good-bye to Justin left her feeling bereft and desolate.

A satisfied look crossed George's face. "You'll be okay till we get there, providing you lay low. Stay at the Ferris Hotel. You know how to check in. Don't show your face." His voice hardened. "I mean it, Sarah!"

"I ain't doin' nothin' but what you say," she said.

George's eyebrows quirked upward. "I guess there's a first for everythin'." His voice softened. "You should be able to reach Fort Smith in two, maybe three days."

"It'll take us longer 'cuz of the baby."

George scowled and she braced for another argument, but instead he issued a list of instructions about which trails to avoid. "It'll probably be closer to a week before we get there. You just lay low and wait for us, you hear?"

"I said I would."

"You take care, Sarah. If anythin' happens to you—"

"It won't." She threw her arms around his neck, knocking him off balance.

He hugged her back, then mounted his horse. Astride, he stared at her, his mouth tight with disapproval. "Stay out of trouble."

"I will," she promised.

"I mean it, Sarah." George leveled a

warning glance at Justin. "I better not live to regret this. I hope none of us do."

With one last lingering look at her, George galloped away.

Robert shoved a wad of money into her hand.

"I can't take that," she said, handing it back. "It's not our money. It's stolen."

He studied her, a look of sadness in his eyes. He nodded but, nonetheless, pressed the money into her palm. "Take it for the baby's sake," he said, nodding toward Elizabeth asleep on a bedroll. He winked at her. "A well-placed bribe can get you—and your little orphan—out of a heap of trouble."

Forcing a smile, she tucked the money into her pocket. He was right; it might come in handy at that.

Robert pecked her on the cheek and mounted his own horse, touching a finger to the brim of his hat. "Good luck, Sarah."

Jed handed her his holster and gave her a big hug. "Take care, you hear?"

She nodded. "See you soon." Her spirits sank as she watched the three men gallop away. "I love you all," she called after them, waving until they were mere specks in the distance.

Justin put a hand on her shoulder. "Thank you for staying," he said, his voice low.

She turned to face him, soaking up the warmth of his eyes like flowers in the sun. "They raised me. Taught me everything I know," she said, her voice hoarse. "I love my brothers. I know what they do ain't right."

"Forcing you to be part of that is also not right."

"I never actually robbed a stage," she said. "George said I was a girl and girls have no business on the front lines. He told us we were only takin' what was ours." Her voice broke. "We believed him. *I* believed him."

"You were a child when your parents died," he said simply. "You had no choice but to believe what he told you."

She bit her lip, determined to hold back her tears. She loved her brothers with all her heart, but it was becoming increasingly difficult to defend them, even to herself. Still, old habits die hard, and though she hated what her family had become, she couldn't bring herself to turn her back on them. Not completely.

"My brothers, they would do anything . . . anything in the world for me." Feeling at once embarrassed and ashamed, she lowered her lashes. "All these years they've cared for me and protected me."

He lifted her chin, forcing her to look at him. "Sarah." The touch of his fingers sent warm shivers coursing through her. "You have no idea what it means to be cared for," he said, his eyes soft. "Or protected."

Something in his voice, in the way he made her tingle when he said her name, in the way he gazed at her, found a need so deeply buried that she hardly knew it existed.

She rested her head on his chest, dizzy with the scent of him. Suddenly— inexplicably—she found herself sobbing. Hot tears spread across the bib of his shirt in a widening circle.

She cried for the little girl who had lost her parents and who, at the time, had not been able to shed a tear. She cried for her brothers whom she feared she would never see again. She cried for the past she despised and the future she dreaded.

But most of all, she cried because she was twenty-two years of age—an old maid by some accounts—and she had never before been held like Justin was now holding her.

Fourteen

They traveled across the southeast corner of Kansas and into Indian territory, the boundaries dotted with government signs. It was now June, and the farther south they traveled, the hotter it got. Sarah's clothes clung to her body, and rivers of sweat trickled down her face. Despite the difficulties of travel, she was greatly relieved to leave the horrors of the wagon train behind.

Justin carried Elizabeth in a sling made from one of his shirts. Tied around his neck, the carrier cradled the baby next to his chest. This left his hands free to hold the reins. From time to time, he waved a kerchief up and down to fan the child.

He preferred carrying the baby to dealing with the goat, and Sarah let him. At times, it was a battle to get Mira to do what she wanted the goat to do, but she was better at it than Justin.

Elizabeth grew fussy, and Sarah was convinced it was because Mira's milk supply had dropped. She stroked the goat's side, trying to get it to relax. "I think Mira's plumb worn out from all the walkin'."

"Let's try strapping the goat onto your horse," Justin suggested.

"She ain't gonna like that much."

Justin lifted Mira by her front legs and Sarah grabbed the back, but it was all they could do to hold on to the struggling animal. They finally managed to force the goat on top of Blizzard, belly-down in front of the saddle. Forelegs dangling on one side, back legs down the other, Mira's bleats turned into high-pitched screams.

Blizzard whinnied and pawed the ground. Not to be left out, Noah snorted and let out a loud squeal followed by the mule's harsh cry. All the commotion woke Elizabeth, who immediately began to wail.

Battling with Mira, Justin was clearly out of his element. Sarah couldn't help but burst into laughter.

Amusement flickered in his eyes, and his mouth quirked upward. "The things they don't teach you in seminary." He shouted to be heard above the racket.

It took close to a half hour before the animals settled down enough to continue the journey.

Sarah mounted her horse. With one hand on the reins and the other on the goat, she followed Noah along a rutted trail, Mira grunting all the way.

Elizabeth slept fitfully during the next two hours, then she began to wail. Justin found a shady spot and dismounted. Laying Elizabeth beneath a tree, he then lifted Mira off Sarah's horse.

The goat wobbled around before finding its footing and began to graze.

"We have milk," Sarah cried after a while, clapping her hands together. She milked the goat and Elizabeth hungrily sucked on the nourishing cloth.

Justin sat on the grass next to Elizabeth and gently dabbed the milk from her mouth, cooing to her. When Elizabeth cooed back, Sarah laughed. "You two sound like a couple of doves," she said.

He grinned up at her, but his smile suddenly died. "What's that noise?"

Sarah stilled. "Sounds like someone cryin'," she said.

Justin jumped up and hurried through the brush. Elizabeth in her arms, Sarah quickly followed. The sobs grew louder.

"Over there," she called. She pointed to a man sitting beneath a tree, his hands covering his face.

Justin walked up to the distraught man. "Is there a problem, sir?"

The man lifted his head and was clearly surprised to see them. A young man, no more than twenty or so, his red puffy eyes were filled with despair. Unruly sandy hair offered an odd contrast to his neatly clipped mustache.

The man showed no embarrassment at his emotional display, nor did he offer an apology. He simply glanced at Sarah and the baby in her arms and, hiding his face in his hands, started bawling again.

Justin dropped down on his haunches, his hand on the man's shoulder. "I'm Reverend Justin Wells and this is Miss . . . Sarah."

The man moved his hands away from his face. "Logan Hobbs," he said, his voice thick with anguish. Hobbs looked Justin square in the face. "Maybe you can tell me why God took my wife and baby."

"Your wife and baby . . . Are they—"

Hobbs nodded. "Measles."

Justin sat back on his heels. "When did this happen?"

"A few days ago," Hobbs said, his voice choked.

"Where?"

"Fort Smith. There's an epidemic."

Justin glanced at Sarah, his face suddenly drained of color.

"So what's your answer, Preacher? Why did God have to go and take my family?"

"God didn't take your loved ones,"

Justin said gently. "He received them with open arms."

The man broke into fresh sobs.

Never had Sarah seen anyone so distraught, and her heart went out to the man. She didn't know how to comfort Hobbs, how to comfort anyone who had suffered such a terrible loss. Justin knew exactly how little or how much to say, his voice soft, his touch gentle, his words comforting.

Standing there watching him was like watching her whole world crumble. It was as if someone had removed a blindfold allowing her to see what had previously been hidden. Preaching wasn't just a profession with Justin. Not like being a farmer or blacksmith. It was a vital part of who he was. Maybe she always knew that about him. What she hadn't known—what she didn't want to know—was that if anything kept him from his calling, it could destroy him. *She* could destroy him.

Sensing that Elizabeth's presence only added to Hobbs's distress, she moved away and made camp. She couldn't stop thinking about Justin and the impossible situation she had put him in.

If only she wasn't a Prescott. Why hadn't someone helped her and her brothers through their grief following the loss of their parents? Someone like Justin? Would that have made the difference?

The town had pretty much turned their backs on her family following her papa's hanging. By the time the truth of his innocence came out, it was too late. George wanted nothing to do with the townsfolk. She pushed her thoughts away with a sigh, but there was nothing to be done about the heaviness in her heart.

It was almost dark when she heard Hobbs ride away on his horse.

Justin joined her by the fire where she sat feeding Elizabeth and yawned. His face was drawn, the fine lines at the corner of his eyes a notch deeper.

"He okay?" she asked.

"I think so. I invited him to join us for supper, but he declined. He said he wanted to be alone."

She sighed. "Poor man. He's lucky we found him."

"God always sends the right people in time of need."

Anger spurted up like steam from a kettle. "He didn't send no right people to me and my brothers when we needed them," she retorted.

"He always sends the right people, Sarah. It's up to us to accept their help."

She wanted to believe what he said was true, but she couldn't remember much beyond the grief that consumed her following her parents' death. She bit her lip. "You told Hobbs that God didn't take his family."

Justin sat on a fallen log opposite her. "He didn't take yours either," he said. "But He did receive them."

A weight fell from her shoulders, and for the longest while all she could do was bathe in the comfort of her new knowledge. God didn't take her parents away from her, he didn't, and knowing that made all the difference in the world.

"Sarah . . ." His voice was earnest, almost apologetic in tone. "I can't go to Fort Smith."

She stared at him. "You can't travel to Texas alone."

"I'd rather take my chances on the trail than chance Elizabeth getting measles."

"That's crazy talk."

He shrugged. "Maybe. But I lost two sisters to measles, and I'm not taking any chances."

She gasped in dismay. "Oh, Justin, I'm so sorry. I rattled on about my own losses and here you—"

"There was no way you could have known."

She leaned forward. "Measles is a terrible thing, but travelin' through the Nation ain't no picnic. So far we've been lucky, but luck is unpredict'ble as an unbroken horse."

"I think running into Hobbs might be a warning from God."

She swallowed hard, not knowing what to say.

He rested his elbows on his thighs, his hands clasped beneath his chin. He spoke in a low voice. "Their names were Louise and Claudia. They died in their early teens, within two days of each other. It was a terrible thing to live through. I was only eighteen when it happened, and I went crazy. I started drinking."

Her eyes widened. "That don't sound like you."

"I'm far from perfect, Sarah. Fortunately, God doesn't require perfection."

"Loss can sure ruin folks," she said. Look what it did to her brothers. To her.

"Instead of turning to God, we try to comfort ourselves with worldly things," he said. "That's where the danger lies."

"What made you change?" she asked.

"The right person at the right time," he said. "One night, after getting drunk, I got beat up and was left in the gutter. I was in bad shape. To make matters worse, it was the middle of winter and I was freezing. I stumbled into a church for warmth. A woman stood on the altar and talked about coming to this country in chains as a young girl and how she was now free. She then sang 'Amazing Grace.' That's when I decided I wanted to be free too."

She studied him. "So who did God

send? The one who beat you up or the singer?"

He laughed. "I guess you could say both of them." His face grew serious. "God works through everything. The good and the bad."

Sarah closed her eyes. How would it feel to be free? Free from the past? Free from the future? Free to love . . .? With a heavy sigh, she pushed the thought away, but the longing remained and her heart ached. "I don't blame you none for worryin'. If anythin' happened to Elizabeth . . ." She shuddered. "If you ain't goin' to Fort Smith, then I ain't goin' neither."

"But I promised your brothers—"

"I don't care! I ain't lettin' you travel alone with no baby."

He sighed as if he knew he was in for a fight even as he beseeched her. "Sarah, don't make this any harder than it has to be."

"You're the one makin' it hard."

"I can't take Elizabeth to Fort Smith, and you can't travel to Texas."

Sarah lay the sleeping baby on a blanket, then stood and faced Justin, hands on her hips. "And how do you plan to take care of her? A woodchuck could milk a goat better'n you can."

"I'll learn."

"What 'bout outlaws? And Indians? You saw what they can do."

Justin stared into the fire, his face dark. "I'm not going to Fort Smith." There was a finality to his voice that told her arguing would do no good. He believed God had sent Hobbs for a purpose, and deep in her heart, she wanted to believe it was true.

She stood. "I'm sorry 'bout your sisters," she said. Without another word, she gently picked up Elizabeth and headed for her bedroll.

For the next couple of days, Sarah avoided the subject, but it was evident from Justin's determination to learn to milk the goat that he hadn't changed his mind.

But then, neither had Sarah.

One afternoon they reached the edge of a dense forest. Noah halted in his tracks. Shaking his head from side to side, the gelding swished his tail and pawed the ground. Justin pressed his legs into the horse's side, but the animal refused to budge.

"Maybe he's thrown a shoe," Sarah said. She slid out of her saddle to take a look. Too late, she realized her mistake.

A small band of Indians riding paint horses emerged on the trail a few feet in front of them. Comanches!

Fifteen

Sarah froze, her hand on her weapon. Fear gripped her, and her throat went dry.

There were four of them altogether, all dressed in buckskin breechcloths and loose buckskin fringed shirts. Their black-striped foreheads all but hid the absence of eyebrows. All four wore their greased hair parted in the middle, thick shiny braids hanging in front. But it was their feet that sent chills down her spine. The leader of the pack wore the shaft of a cutoff boot around his ankle. A white man's boot.

The leader pointed to Noah and yelled, "Puuku!" Sarah's heart sank.

"What do they want?" Justin asked.

"Our horses," she said, her voice shaking.

One brave dismounted and walked over to Blizzard, grabbing the horse's reins. Six feet tall with a strong, muscular body, he looked no less forbidding on foot. As if sensing danger, Mira bleated and kicked her legs and a second brave hurried to help.

"No!" Sarah yelled. She dived forward, but the brave pushed her to the ground with a single thrust of his powerful arm.

"Leave her alone," Justin thundered. He nudged his horse closer to Sarah, but already she was on her feet.

"No!" she cried again. She pulled out the wad of money that Robert had given her and waved it. When that failed to make an impression, she pointed to the goat and then to Elizabeth.

The leader grunted and made the sign for *no.* Then he brusquely motioned for Justin to dismount.

One of the other braves spoke and a lively conversation followed. All four Indians stared at Justin.

"Why are they looking at me like that?" Justin asked, his face white. He turned his body sideways to shield Elizabeth.

"I don't know," she said. She tightened her hold on her gun. Her teeth bit down on the metallic taste of fear that filled her mouth. She'd never shot a man, but if one of them made a move toward harming Justin or Elizabeth, she wouldn't hesitate a moment.

The leader grunted and motioned with his hand in the sign language that plains Indians used to communicate between tribes. She only knew a couple of signs, but it was enough to know they were in a whole peck o' trouble.

"You better do your thing," she whispered, her stomach clenched into a knot.

A muscle tightened at Justin's jaw. "You're asking me to pray? Now I know we're in trouble."

"He's talking about a burial," she said, her voice strained. She recognized the sign for grave.

His eyes wide with horror, Justin's

gaze swung back to the leader. "Talk to them. Say something."

Sarah made a series of motions with her hands. Then dropped her arms to her side and waited. All four braves stared at her.

"What did you say?" Justin asked.

"Hello, good-bye, grave, and spring of year," she said, adding defensively, "That's 'bout the only sign language I know."

His forehead lined with worry, Justin handed her the baby. "Hold Elizabeth and let me try."

He turned to the leader. "Thou . . . shalt . . . not . . . kill." He punctuated each word with dramatic gestures. He then pointed toward the sky and the eyes of all four Comanches followed his finger upward.

"That's a big help," Sarah muttered.

The leader again leveled his gaze at Justin, then lifted his hand and said something to the others. Without a word, the brave released Blizzard and the two Comanches mounted their paints.

The leader pulled out an arrow and

Sarah gasped. Ignoring her, he held it in both hands toward the sky. He nodded at Justin, made a sign with his hand, and the four of them rode away.

For several moments, Justin and Sarah didn't move. They stared after the four Indians as if they had seen an apparition. Suddenly, it dawned on Sarah what had happened, and she threw her head back and laughed.

The puzzled expression on Justin's face made her laugh harder.

"What happened?" he asked, dismounting. "What made them take off? Was it God's commandment?"

"Hardly," Sarah said between guffaws. "That Indian you buried . . . They must have seen you." She remembered telling Jed about a movement in the trees, and obviously she had been right.

She jiggled Elizabeth up and down as she danced around. "They spared our lives because you done showed honor to their dead."

Disbelief flitted across his face then melted into a broad smile. He raised his face to the heavens and shouted, "Thank You, God!"

She stopped dancing and stared at him. "That's it? No long-winded prayer?"

He laughed. "There'll be time for that later."

Sarah grew serious. "Oh, Justin, I thought we were goners."

He placed his hand on Elizabeth's back. "Me too," he said. "Me too."

She looked away from him, feeling uncommonly shy. "I-I promised God I wouldn't bother Him again . . ."

"God wouldn't want you to keep a promise like that," he said.

She met his eyes. "Are you saying it would be okay if I thank Him?"

"You can say whatever you need to say to God."

Sighing in relief, she bowed her head. "God . . ." She opened one eye to make sure she was doing it right. She had never prayed in front of anyone before. Justin gave her a nod of encouragement.

Gathering her courage, she closed her eyes again and finished her prayer in a rush of words. "You sure did get us out of a whole peck o' trouble, and I'm mighty obliged. Amen." She opened her eyes and felt her heart sink. If the frown on his face was any indication, she sure had a lot to learn about prayin'.

It was later that she learned what was really on his mind, and it had nothing to do with her praying. "I have no business traveling alone," he said. "I'll go to Fort Smith and take the train to Texarkana. Somehow, I'll find a way to keep her safe."

When she made no reply, his face darkened with suspicion. "Sarah?"

"Now don't you go gettin' yourself in a lather, you hear?"

"Sarah!"

She backed away. "We passed the Fort Smith cutoff two days ago."

He stared at her in disbelief. "What? When were you going to tell me that?"

"Sooner or later you'd have figured it out for yourself."

He threw his head back and roared with laughter.

Surprised, she stared at him. Then recognizing his laughter as a release from the tension of all that had happened these last several days, she found herself laughing too.

The light mood didn't last long. That night, she woke in a sweat, her heart pounding so hard it was a wonder it didn't wake Justin and Elizabeth. In her dream, she stood on a wooden platform, a rope around her neck. The dream had seemed so real, she quickly ran her hands along her throat thinking she'd find the rope still there.

Shaken, she stared at the nighttime sky. "God," she whispered. "What's gonna happen to me?"

Sixteen

The following afternoon Sarah reined her horse on the crest of a hill and stared at the valley below. In the distance, a sparkling stream curved through the trees like a carelessly tossed diamond necklace. "That's the Grand River ahead," she called.

The dock was empty when they arrived, and the ferry was nowhere in sight. Sarah knew from past experience that ferry operators in the Indian Nation could be temperamental. Ferries didn't run in the wind or rain, and Sarah and her brothers once waited for two full days to cross a river because the superstitious ferry operator refused to work during a full moon.

"Looks like we're gonna have to wait till tomorrow," she said.

"We'll make camp here," he said.

Sarah sat on a fallen log feeding Elizabeth, while Justin collected pieces of firewood. A cloud of dust on the trail ahead caught Sarah's attention. Worried, she stood and watched until two horsemen came into view.

"They don't look like Indians," Justin said. "Maybe they're just travelers."

She shook her head. Even from that distance, she could see that the men rode fine stallions. Nothing screamed *lawman* louder than a well-bred horse. "They're U.S. Marshals," she said, heart pounding.

She glanced around for a place to hide.

"Act natural," Justin said. "I'll handle them."

Elizabeth, seeming to sense Sarah's distress, stopped sucking. Sarah took a deep breath, forcing herself to relax, and gently coaxed the milk-soaked cloth into the baby's mouth again.

Justin walked to the middle of the trail to greet the approaching strangers. "Hello there," he called, waving his arms.

The horsemen halted in front of him and the leader touched the brim of his hat in greeting. "I'm U.S. Marshal Shaw and this is Deputy Marshal Cabot." Shaw's copper beard ended in a point just below his chin. His partner's face was pitted with smallpox scars.

"Pleasure to meet you both," Justin said.

Shaw nodded toward the mule. "It's against the U.S. government to carry alcohol in these parts. You wouldn't happen to be carrying any, would you?"

"I'm not carrying any alcohol," Justin said. "I'm a preacher."

Shaw leaned on his saddle horn. "A preacher, huh? If you're here to convert the Indians, good luck to you." He glanced at Sarah and she quickly lowered her head and busied herself wiping the milk off Elizabeth's chin.

"We're just passing through," Justin explained. "Heading for Rocky Creek, Texas."

"Rocky Creek?" Shaw chuckled. "On second thought, you'd probably have better luck converting the Indians." Without another word, he touched his hand to his hat, and the two men galloped away.

Sarah felt almost faint with relief. She kept a wary eye on the trail, but no other travelers passed by.

It was almost noon the following day before the ferry arrived carrying three passengers. The men walked their horses off the flatboat, nodded curtly to Justin and Sarah in greeting, and quickly rode away.

The ferry operator was a craggy-faced Creek Indian with black-and-gray braids and bone ornaments hanging from his ears. He wore moccasins but was otherwise dressed like a white man in denim pants and bibbed shirt.

"No firewater," he grunted. He opened Noah's saddlebags and pawed through them.

"We don't have any," Justin said. "I'm a preacher." This made no impression on the Indian, who continued to rifle through their belongings.

The U.S. government paid ferry operators to report anyone carrying alcohol, but Sarah suspected this Indian kept any bottle he confiscated for himself.

"What's the Indian word for preacher?" Justin asked Sarah.

Sarah shrugged. "How would I know?"

Justin thought for a moment, then turned back to the Creek, who was now rummaging through the mule's pack. "A preacher is kind of like a missionary. Do you understand? Missionary?" He pointed up to the sky and then pressed his hands together and bowed his head, as if praying, trying to get the man to understand him.

The man nodded and looked even more suspicious than before. Keeping a wary eye on Justin, he rummaged through their belongings a second and even third time.

Obviously disappointed at not finding any contraband, the Indian checked for hot ashes in the fire pit and charged them an outrageous eight dollars for burning firewood.

Sarah opened her mouth to protest,

but Justin stopped her. "I'd rather pay the fee than have to swim across the river."

After they boarded the ferry, the Indian guided the boat a half mile down the Grand River to the clay-colored waters of the Arkansas River. He let them off a short distance from the Creek Nation, the boundaries marked with steel poles set a mile apart.

For the next three days, Justin and Sarah traveled across blistering dry plains, rugged hills, and boggy streams. At times, the challenging terrain partnered with the weather to create impassable trails and dangerous detours.

At one point, Elizabeth's newly washed baby clothes blew off the rocks where Sarah had laid them to dry, and Justin chased after them on his horse.

Twisters whipped across the land like giant egg beaters, whisking the air until it was black with dust. Lightning spooked the horses and rain soaked the ground. During one such violent storm, they hunkered beneath a rocky crop and waited for the weather to clear.

It was hard, harder than she could ever imagine to stand so close to Justin and not fall into his arms. As if to guess her thoughts, he looked at her with such longing that it was more than she could bear.

Not strong enough to fight the temptation, she touched his arm. She held Elizabeth, but, even so, he captured her lips with velvety softness.

Reacting as if he'd been burned, he pulled away and dropped his hands to his side. The want and need and, more than anything, frustration on his face matched her own. Still, nothing more could be done. Not with a baby crushed between them. Not with the water and mud at their feet, the hard rocks at their backs. Not with the promises that had been made to God and each other.

Letting out a long, audible breath, he turned and vanished into the pounding rain.

On the fourth day, the wind stopped, but there was little relief from the scorching heat. To make up for lost time, they'd started on the trail hours before dawn. Still, travel was slow out of necessity. Caring for Elizabeth and replenishing the milk supply by providing the goat ample grazing time seemed to consume more and more time.

Just as the sun began to set, they found a place to camp next to a rock-bottom stream.

Sarah cooled Elizabeth down with a wet sponge and then ran along the trail to pick wild berries she spotted a short distance away. Hearing angry voices, she dropped the pan of berries and ran back to camp.

Much to her shock, Justin stood arguing with two Indian women. One woman had her hand on Elizabeth's face, and Justin was struggling with her.

"Let her go," he bellowed.

Sarah ran toward them. "No, no!" She grabbed Justin's arm and pulled him away from the woman, then spun around to confront her. The woman's tattooed face gave her a menacing appearance.

Refusing to be intimidated, Sarah held her right hand at her waist, fingers folded inward, and flipped her first and second finger outward. It was the sign for *no* and immediately, the taller of the two women released her hold on Elizabeth, who let out an indignant wail. Justin swooped the child up and quickly stepped aside, his watchful gaze leveled at the two intruders.

The crying seemed to upset both women, who discussed it among themselves at great length while glaring at Justin with obvious disapproval.

The Indians wore fringed deerskin dresses with a band of green seed beadwork at the hem. Their black hair, slick with bear oil, hung down their backs in long slender braids, as was customary. Only men allowed their braids to hang in front.

The two women eventually left, shaking their heads and talking in their native language.

Justin watched them leave, his face dark with fury. "We better pack up and go. They were trying to smother Elizabeth."

He looked and sounded so worried,

she couldn't help but smile. "They were just tryin' to teach her not to bawl."

"What?"

"Papooses don't cry," she explained. "A cryin' baby gets his mouth and nose pinched so he can't breathe. They were just tryin' to help, is all."

He shifted Elizabeth to his other arm. "What's so wrong with a baby crying?"

"I reckon just about everythin'. A cryin' baby can scare off game and reveal a tribe's location to the enemy. Teachin' a baby not to cry can mean life or death for a tribe."

Her explanation failed to wipe the dark frown from his face. A muscle flicked at his jaw. "It's a good thing you came back when you did."

"Elizabeth was in no real danger," she said.

"Maybe not, but those women were."

Something in his voice told her he was serious. "Maybe you don't need me, after all," she said.

"I need you, Sarah," he said with gravity.

Her breath caught in her chest. The

gentle tone of his voice, the softness in his eyes, the very tautness of his body told her he weren't talkin' about no Indians. She didn't want to keep pushin' him away physically even as he kept stealin' more of her heart, but it was the right thing to do. For once in her life, she wanted to know that she was doing right by God. It wouldn't make up for the past but maybe, just maybe, it would make a difference in the future.

She opened her mouth to protest, to tell him that he didn't need no Prescott, but before she had a chance to speak, he turned and walked away.

Later, after the sun had set and day had turned to dusk, a hushed silence settled over the land. It was as if every living creature held its breath, waiting for the cover of night.

A strange sing-songy voice shattered the early evening quiet. It stopped and started again, an eerie sound that seemed to grow louder following each pause.

Justin jumped to his feet and scooped Elizabeth into his arms. Since the encounter with the two Indian women, he was even more protective of the child than before. "Tell me they aren't on the warpath."

She couldn't help but laugh at the worried frown on his face. "Come," she whispered.

She led the way up a nearby hill.

"Are you sure we should be doing this?" he asked.

"Sure enough to drive a nail in it," she replied.

Justin followed close behind, carrying Elizabeth.

Reaching the crest, Sarah lay face-down on the grass. The valley below was dotted with tepees. Hearth fires blazed behind buckskin walls, turning the conical tents into glowing lanterns.

Justin spread a blanket on the ground for Elizabeth, then lay on the grass next to Sarah, his shoulder touching hers. The very nearness of him caused her heart to flutter.

"So that's what a reservation is like," he said. "I thought it would be more fort-like."

"Like that building over there?" she asked pointing to the government structure in the distance, which also served as a school for Indian youths.

The rigid clapboard building with its square windows and neat chimneys offered a startling contrast to the graceful tepees, which in the darkness looked like hands folded in prayer.

"Yes," he admitted.

"You can put an Indian on a reservation, but I reckon he's gonna wanna keep his ways."

"They seem so . . . peaceful," he said. She detected a note of surprise in his voice.

"They *are* a peaceful people," she said. "Most times."

"You say that even after what happened to Elizabeth's family?"

"It ain't right to judge all tribes for the actions of a few renegade bands."

"I thought the Medicine Lodge Treaty would put an end to the Indian wars," Justin said. The treaty promised government protection for Indians against white intruders. In return, the tribes agreed to relocate to reservations.

"There ain't gonna be no end to the killin's unless the Indians learn to live in the white man's world."

"So you think they should give up their tepees and moccasins?"

She laughed. "Ain't I a fine one to tell someone how to live and dress?"

Justin chuckled with her. "Yet I have to admit, feathers and beads can be intimidating to us city folks. Not to mention war paint."

"And you don't think you look intimidatin' in your black coat and pants?" she teased.

She could feel his eyes on her in the darkness. "So you think beads and feathers would improve my appearance?"

She smiled at the thought. "It's not what's on the outside that divides people. It's the way they think. Indians believe the land belongs to everyone. They ain't got no notion why a white man needs to own property."

"Before . . ." He hesitated as if searching for the right words. "When that Cheyenne put her hand on Elizabeth's face, I wanted to . . . I would have done anything to protect her."

Sensing his distress, she reached out to pat his arm, stopping herself before making contact.

"I never thought to bring harm to another person. It goes against everything I've been taught. Everything I believe in." He spoke in a low voice thick with anguish. "But I can't get the vision of the wagon train massacre out of my head."

She grimaced in an effort to shut out her own memories of that ill-fated scene. "I think about it all the time."

"This land . . . it changes a person," he said slowly. "It's changed me. I'm not the same person I was when I left Boston. I'm not sure if even God recognizes me now."

"This land doesn't change you," she said softly. "It just makes you more of who you are."

"I now know I'm capable of harming another human being, and that's not something I'm proud of."

She longed to touch him but didn't dare. "I ain't got much schoolin' and I don't know nothin' 'bout society ways. But this I do know. You wouldn't hurt no one. You'd have found a way to protect Elizabeth without harmin' that old woman."

She waited for him to respond, but he said nothing.

The eerie voice sounded again, breaking the silence that had suddenly stretched between them. It belonged to a brave who stood at the outer edge of the little village shouting into the hollows of the night. He fell silent, and then an answering voice came from a distance away.

"He's the town crier," Sarah whispered. "He's callin' the news to the next village. The town crier there will pass the news on."

"It sounds like important news," he said. "What do you suppose it is?"

"Probably warnin' the others to watch out for cryin' babies."

Justin's muffled laughter rippled over her like water running over pebbles, lifting her own solemn mood.

The brave fell silent and the sound of drums filled the void.

"Are the drums sending a message too?" Justin asked.

"They use drums to talk to the Great Spirit."

Elbow on the ground, he rested his head on his hand and gazed at her. "Really? That's how they talk to God?"

She smiled at the amazement in his voice and rolled over on her back. Overhead, the first star of the night shone bright. The drums continued until the air vibrated, the thumping beats matching the pulse of the earth.

For several moments, they lay side by side beneath the stars, listening to the beat of drums while Elizabeth slept on the blanket beside them.

After a while, she turned her head to look at him. "You ain't the only one who's long-winded."

His warm, rich laughter brought another smile to her face, and it was all she could do not to follow her heart in a most unladylike way.

As if feeling the sudden tension in the air, the drumbeats grew ever faster. No longer emulating the slow steady rhythm of the earth, they now matched her own galloping pulse.

The scent of him filled her head with pleasant sensations. "I ain't good at this man and woman thing—"

"I thought we agreed to stay away from that."

"We agreed not to . . . go ag'inst God," she said. "It's hard."

He looked at her meaningfully and then sighed. "It's torture."

Not sure how much to say or even if she dare say anything, she bit her lip. "I . . . I was just wond'ring . . . Would it be okay with God if we tell each other how we feel?"

"How we feel?" he asked, his voice muffled.

"I thought it would make it easier, you know, not to—"

"—give into temptation," he finished for her. "Do you think talking will help?"

"Me and Robert used to talk a lot about problems," she said. "About our parents. About . . . different things. It helped."

"We can give it a try," he said, though he sounded dubious.

"Do you want me to go first?" she asked.

"That might be a good idea."

She cleared her throat. She wanted to get this right, but she was surprised to find herself shaking. "I like it when you kiss me. When you hold me. I like it even better when you look at me . . . a certain way." There it was, the honest truth. She held her breath.

For a moment he said nothing and then quietly stood. "Talking doesn't help, Sarah. It only makes things worse."

Unable to see his face in the darkness, she could only stare at his dark form. She'd tossed her heart in the air hoping he would share his feelings with her. Instead, judging by his voice, she had pushed him further away. Swallowing her disappointment, she whispered, "You won't know till you try."

"I know," he said. "I *know*."

He bent to pick Elizabeth off the ground and, slinging the baby's blanket over his shoulder, started down the hill.

No sooner had Justin reached camp when he realized that distancing himself from Sarah hadn't accomplished a thing. The temptation of taking her in his arms was too immense, the lure of capturing her lips far too great to be dampened by space or even time.

I like it when you kiss me . . . when you touch me . . .

The memory of those words blasted a trail of heat through his body.

These last few days, he'd managed somehow to keep his distance from Sarah. It had been difficult and, at times, almost impossible.

Like tonight.

She wanted to talk about it, but he should have known better. Keeping his feelings under control was a matter of self-preservation. The less he had to forget, the easier it would be to say good-bye when the time came for them to part.

Realizing the flaws in his logic, he groaned and covered his face with his hands. He tried to erase the picture of her from his mind, but the vision stubbornly remained. Her words continued to haunt him for the rest of the night. *I like it when you kiss me . . .*

God forgive him.

Seventeen

The next day, they left the Indian reservation behind and followed the hilly trail south. Neither had spoken more than a few words all morning and the tension in the air was like a storm about to break.

Sarah rode ahead, Mira the goat straddled in front of her. She didn't dare look back at Justin, but his soothing voice as he spoke to Elizabeth warmed her heart. For most of the morning, they followed a narrow buffalo trail. The trail widened and Justin galloped to her side.

"Sarah, about last night—"

She kept her eyes focused ahead. "Last night?"

"I'm sorry I hurt you."

"You didn't hurt me," she lied.

"Then why won't you look at me?" Justin pleaded.

Turning her head, she gave him an indifferent stare that hid the turmoil inside. What could she say that would explain the sense of longing and pain she felt every time he drew near?

The tight set of his mouth was at odds with the tenderness in his eyes, and neither belonged with the uncertainty in his voice. "I'm not good with words."

"Well, if that don't beat all," she said. "You're a preacher, ain't you?"

"Preaching's easy. It's talking that's hard." She waited for him to continue, unable to move from his steady gaze. "I don't know what the future will hold." His voice faltered, but the look he gave her was no less intense.

A bugle horn sounded in the distance, its lively tune in blatant contrast to the slow, steady beat of Indian drums. Two distinct worlds clashing with each other.

"Even if they don't hang me, you and I ain't ever gonna be together," she cried. "*That's* what the future holds."

She was furious at him for making her want something she could never have. Furious at herself. "I'm always gonna be a Prescott, and you're always gonna be a preacher. There ain't nothing gonna change that."

She pressed her legs into the side of her horse and rode ahead, but it was a long time before she could breathe normal again beneath the crushing reality she couldn't escape.

At noon, they reached the Canadian River and were lucky enough to find a ferry owned by a former slave waiting to take them across. The man also owned a store where they were able to purchase corn and potatoes. Neither one of them mentioned their earlier conversation, but unspoken words and meaningful glances filled the air with unwanted reminders.

After crossing the river, they traveled for several miles. Moses' pack slid to the side, and Justin stopped to adjust the mule's harness. Sarah lay Elizabeth on the ground and then walked around to stretch her legs and work the kinks out of her back.

Something in the distance caught her attention, an ominous cloud on the far horizon. Hoping she was mistaken, she shaded her eyes against the sun. Much to her dismay, her suspicion was confirmed.

"Quick, grab Elizabeth. Locusts!" She ran for her horse, jammed her foot into the stirrup, and swung into the saddle.

She waited for Justin to scoop Elizabeth off the ground and mount his own horse. His eyes fixed on the advancing swarm, he frowned. "You think we can outrun them?"

"Nothin' to it," she assured him.

Laughing at the dark expression on his face, she took off, keeping one hand on the goat sprawled across the horse in front of her. Despite Sarah's efforts to keep the goat from bouncing around, Mira flopped up and down like an old cellar door, bleating in protest.

Galloping down a grassy knoll, she glanced back to make sure that Justin could keep pace. Moses seemed to have no trouble keeping up with Noah. The pots and pans tied to the mule's saddle clinked and clanked and one pot flew off the pack, but there was no time to retrieve it.

Locusts could travel hundreds of miles in the air without stopping, but this swarm appeared to be descending. She felt encouraged. With a little luck, they could miss most, if not all, of the hoppers.

Several miles down the road, she spotted a cluster of sweet gum trees. She reined in her horse and glanced back. Grasshoppers poured from the sky to the ground in a steady stream. Even from that distance, she could hear the air vibrate with the rasping sound of flapping wings.

Justin pulled up alongside her. Nestled in the sling on his chest, Elizabeth was crying. "She didn't like that fast ride."

Sarah reached over to stroke the baby's forehead. "You're safe now. So don't you go worrying none, you hear?"

A few hoppers began to fall to the ground around them, but they had missed the main swarm.

"Looks like we better stay here awhile

and rest the horses," Justin said, lifting Mira off her horse.

"I think there's a natural well over there," she said, pointing to the green grass ahead. "We better water the animals."

While the horses and mule drank, Sarah rocked Elizabeth in her arms.

Justin had a biblical story for everything and so it didn't surprise her that he would have a tale about locusts. When he finished his story of the ten plagues, she laughed.

"One plague is enough for me. I'd sure hate to live through ten."

The locusts had provided a means by which to break the tension between them.

Elizabeth continued to fuss. "Maybe she needs her britches changed," Justin said.

She handed Elizabeth to him and dug into Moses' pack for a clean nappy. That's when she noticed that the dress he'd rescued from the wagon train was missing. "Oh, no!"

"What's wrong?"

"The dress is gone," she cried, biting back tears.

"It must have fallen off back there aways." His eyebrows rose. "I thought you didn't like it."

"I ain't never said I didn't like it." She handed him the nappy and ran for her horse.

"Where are you going? Sarah? Sar–ah!"

She mounted and kicked her heels into Blizzard's side. The horse took off like a streak of lightning.

A couple of miles down the road, hundreds of hoppers pelted her like wind-tossed hail, all but blotting out the sky's yellow haze. Head held low beneath her hat, she slowed her horse to a walk and frantically brushed the darting insects away from her face.

Barely two inches in length with long wings and brownish bodies, the mass of locusts covered the ground like oozing oil. The air vibrated with flapping wings and the sound of hard-shelled vermin being crushed by Blizzard's hooves. A smell like stale ale rose up from their crushed bodies.

Swallowing her revulsion, she spotted a patch of blue on the trail beneath a dark heap of ravaging hoppers, and she tightened the reins. Unable to reach the dress from her saddle, she had no choice but to dismount.

Grimacing, her hand over her mouth, she reached down and grabbed the fabric with two fingers, shaking it hard. Already, the hoppers had ravaged the gingham, and the skirt and bodice had as many holes as a barbed wire fence. With a cry of dismay, she tossed the dress down.

She flailed her hands and arms to dislodge the insects from her body. Swiping the saddle with both hands, she sent dozens of hoppers airborne before mounting her horse again. She then rode back to Justin and Elizabeth as fast as Blizzard could carry her, her eyes burning with tears.

The loss of the dress saddened her, though she couldn't think why. It wasn't like she planned to wear it or anything. Why, she wouldn't be caught dead in anything so fussy. Still, it was as close to a gift from Justin as she ever expected to get, and she was sorry to let it go.

That evening she sat bouncing Elizabeth on her lap. The baby stared at her with big blue eyes, and Sarah never imagined it possible to love something so small. A lump rose in her throat and she swallowed hard. What in tarnation was the matter with her? Twice in one day, she'd fought back tears, and that wasn't like her. If her brothers knew their sister had grown all weepy over a dress and baby, they would accuse her of growing soft, they would, and that would never do.

Justin leaned against the saddle at his back, watching her. His eyes mirrored the merry flames from the small campfire, effectively keeping his thoughts hidden from view.

Sarah sighed and settled Elizabeth down on a blanket. She stroked the baby's head until she fell asleep. Her mouth curved in a smile; she covered the baby with a light blanket and moved closer to the fire.

"Not much farther to go," she said.

"We'll reach Red River in a couple of days."

Justin gave a curt nod of his head.

As much as she fought against it, it was getting harder not to think about what lay ahead. She gazed down at Elizabeth peacefully asleep. "You find a good home for her, you hear?" she told Justin, her voice breaking.

"Sarah."

"With a mama and a papa who will love her—"

"*We* love her," he said.

His words pierced her already aching heart like arrows. She searched the face she'd come to know so well these last few weeks, a face that would forever be engraved in her memory.

Her gaze met his across the flickering fire. "You're so good with her. You're the kind of papa she should have. Maybe . . . if you found yourself a wife—"

He shook his head and looked away. "Nothing will ever seem right without you." He gave her a beseeching look. "Sarah, I want you to put yourself in God's hands."

"What does that mean?"

"Come to Rocky Creek with me."

"No!"

"Trust that God will help us figure out a way to save you," he persisted.

Her temper flared. He made it sound so simple, and it was anything but that. "You know nothin' 'bout Texas. A drunken judge, a loony sheriff, and power-grabbin' marshal already decided my fate, and they ain't open to reason."

"Nothing is impossible with God," he said gently. Her anger gradually melted. She wanted so much to believe him, to put her faith and trust in God. He had sent that goat for Elizabeth, but helping an innocent babe wasn't the same as helping a Prescott. "I ain't goin' back to Rocky Creek."

He gave her a tortured look. "I wish there was something I could do to help you."

"You can take care of Elizabeth. See that she has a good life. Maybe she'll grow up to be a lady. Wouldn't that be somethin'?"

"I'll find her good home," he said.

She frowned. "You ain't planning to put her in no orphanage, are you?"

He made a face as if the very thought was as distasteful to him as it was to her. "You have my word," he said. "I hope to find a family in Rocky Creek so I can watch her grow up. Tell her about you."

Sarah shook her head. "Don't you dare tell her about me, you hear? She don't need to know that her godmother was an outlaw."

"That's not what I would tell her."

Sarah tilted her head. "What else is there to say? I ain't no lady, and I don't hardly know but a few four-legged words."

"I would say . . . 'Elizabeth, your godmother had long, silky red hair and the prettiest blue eyes you ever did see. She was funny, and her laughter sounded like music.' I would say that she was the bravest woman I ever met. Honest and kind."

Sarah stared at him, speechless. No one had ever said such pretty words to her, not ever.

"Any objections?" he asked.

Not trusting herself to speak, she shook her head.

"Anything you want me to add?"

"Just . . . just tell her that I loved her." With that she rose and settled herself in her bedroll with Elizabeth by her side. It was a long time before she fell asleep.

The next morning, neither of them spoke. Instead, they let their eyes say what couldn't be said with words.

On the trail, Sarah caught him watching her and suddenly felt self-conscious. She tucked the hair he described as long and silky into her hat and was careful not to laugh. For the most part, except for the covert glances she gave him, she kept her eyes firmly focused on the trail ahead.

Sarah learned from her brothers to stay off the main routes, but as they drew nearer to the Texas state line, staying off the beaten path was no longer an option. As the trails began to merge, the way grew more crowded and they met other travelers.

They stopped to speak to a Scottish drummer parked along the side of the trail. He, too, was heading for Texas, his horse-drawn wagon piled high with pots and pans and other household goods. Gilt scrollwork decorated the sides of his wagon along with a wintry scene that seemed as out of place on the flat prairie land as a grizzly on a train.

The man introduced himself as Alastair McKinley.

"Do you happen to have anything for an infant?" Justin asked.

"Aye," came the welcome reply. The man was dressed in gray pants and a gold-trimmed vest. He opened the back of his wagon and produced a green glass bottle with a cork nipple, along with cotton nappies. "I s'pect this is something as ye little one needs."

A baby bottle. Sarah couldn't believe their good fortune.

"You won't find better in Monkey Ward's," the peddler said, an edge of bitterness in his voice. The Montgomery Ward mail-order catalog had cut into the profits of traveling salesmen. For that reason, Justin purchased two bottles, just to show his appreciation.

At first, Elizabeth refused to take the

cork in her mouth. She scrunched up her round face and pushed it away with her little pink tongue. But Sarah persisted until the baby finally caught on, and feeding became less of a chore.

They passed crews of Chinese railroad workers. Justin seemed fascinated with the men and kept stopping to talk to them, but few could speak English.

"I never saw such hard workers," he said, guiding his horse next to hers. Elizabeth, asleep in her sling, was nestled against his chest. "I guess Charles Crocker wasn't crazy after all."

Sarah frowned. "Who's Charles Crocker?"

"He's a railroad contractor who suggested hiring immigrants from China to build railroads. It was the only way he could think to combat the shortage of American workers. Many thought the Chinese were lazy and weak."

"Some say the same about preachers," she said with a wry smile.

He grinned. "Never thought I'd have something in common with the Chinese."

With a click of his tongue, he pulled

ahead of her to make room for the steady flow of wagons filled with buffalo bones coming from the opposite direction. The sun-bleached bones were being hauled to Kansas where they would be turned into fertilizer or bone china.

Most of the bone hunters regarded them with suspicion until they were satisfied that Justin and Sarah had no interest in stealing their haul.

They traveled past another one of the many Indian reservations set up by the government. The tepees were made of woven willows covered with thin sheets of elm bark. A group of scantily dressed children watched them with dark, probing eyes. No matter how hard Justin tried to convince them he was a friend, they continued to regard him with suspicion.

By noon it was so hot they searched for a place to escape the midday sun. Sarah rode her horse up a hill to check out the terrain ahead.

Justin, who had been trailing behind, coaxed his horse to her side.

"We're only two days from the Texas border," she said.

The air seemed to still at the sound of her words. They both knew what that meant. It had seemed they'd been traveling forever, but now with the end in sight, forever hadn't been long enough.

"Sarah, come with me to Texas," Justin pleaded.

"You know I can't."

"I can't bear the thought of not knowing where you are. What you're doing."

"Don't," she pleaded. Silently, she told herself, *Don't think about him. Don't look at him. Don't make saying good-bye any harder than it already is.*

She rode away, taking the lead, her heart so filled with pain it hurt to breathe.

Late that afternoon, a dust cloud on the trail ahead made her bring her horse to a halt. She pointed and yelled, "Cattle. Probably on the way to the shipping pens in Kansas."

"Is that a problem?" he called from behind.

"Depends on whether they're longhorns or shorthorns," she said. "Long-horns are more likely to cause trouble."

A mile up the road, they came to a dugout that had been cut into the rocky hills by Chinese railroad workers.

The dugout was a good ten feet off the ground. Sarah dismounted and climbed up to check it out, leaving Justin on the trail below to watch the animals, Elizabeth asleep in her sling.

The cave used for storage was stocked with supplies. Boxes of can-dles, hard tack, canned food, and dried buffalo meat were stacked in a corner. There was a table and chairs and best of all, a couple of cots.

She stood on the edge of the rocky outcrop overlooking the trail below. "It's as good or better than most of the ho-tels I've stayed at," she called.

The cave offered little if any protec-tion against thieves, as it could easily be seen from the trail, but it was dry and cool and they decided to spend the night there. They made a bed for Eliza-beth out of a wooden crate.

Sarah sat on one of several cots. The tick mattress was thin and the springs felt hard as rock, but it was better than sleeping on the ground.

Just before dusk, they heard hoof-beats on the trail. Justin walked to the entrance with Elizabeth in his arms and called down a greeting.

Afraid to show her face until she knew the identity of the horsemen below, Sarah hung back where she could see without being seen.

There were two men. One, a Mexican, greeted Justin with a nod but said nothing. He wore a large straw hat and a colorful body blanket draped over the saddle in front of him. A cheroot hung out the side of his mouth.

The other rider touched the brim of his dark gray Stetson with a gauntlet gloved hand. "Howdy. Name's Wade Frazier. I'm a point rider for the Circle K ranch."

Sarah edged closer to Justin, and Frazier acknowledged her with a tip of his hat. He had a dark ruddy complexion and a sweeping mustache. He wore leather chaps over brown canvas pants, a pin-striped cotton shirt, a dark vest, and red bandana.

"You folks been traveling long?"

Justin nodded. "All the way from Boston."

Frazier pushed his hat back and stared at the baby in Justin's arms. "Boston?" He glanced at Sarah, then turned back to Justin. "Seems like a hard way for a family man to travel. You running from somethin'?"

"I'm Rocky Creek's new preacher."

"A preacher, eh? I reckon that accounts for it, then. Only a saint would attempt to travel across country on horseback with a wife and young'un in tow."

Justin made no effort to correct him.

"You and your family best stay off the trail till we get the herd through. It don't take much to spook 'em. We crossed the Red River four days ago, and already we've had two stampedes. Fortunately, we didn't lose any of 'em, but we lost time roundin' 'em up. Once they get in the habit of running, there's no stoppin' 'em."

"What do we do if there's a stampede?" Justin asked.

"They ain't much you can do. You got fifteen thousand tons of hide heading your way, you best give them a clear path. The trail narrows through these hills, so we're not gonna be able to circle 'em around until they hit the open range. You should be safe inside the cave. But if you wanna help, you can sing."

"I'm sorry?"

"Hearing a human voice helps keep them calm."

"Well, in that case, I hope they like hymns," Justin said.

Frazier tugged on the brim of his hat. "Lucky for you, Reverend, cattle ain't choosy about the lyrics." With that he rode off, the Mexican close behind.

Eighteen

Justin wasn't sure what woke him. He rolled on his back, eyes wide open. Something . . .

Leaving the comfort of his bedroll, he fumbled in the dark until he found the candle on the wooden table. He lit it and the flickering light sent shadows fleeing across the creviced walls, but all he could see was Sarah's empty cot.

His heart sank. She left—left without so much as a goodbye. Left never to be seen again. The very thought turned his blood cold. He could hardly breathe.

For weeks, he'd fought his feelings for Sarah, refusing to believe what his heart knew was true. Now that she was gone, all pretense left him. He covered his face with his hands but he couldn't hold back his anguished cry.

That's when he heard it—the voice of an angel.

Checking to make certain Elizabeth was still asleep, he rushed to the mouth of the cave and peered into the darkness. From the distance came the braying of cattle. No stars could be seen, but a glimmer of the waxing moon peeked through fast moving clouds.

Her voice was clear now. *Sarah's voice . . .*

Unable to see her, he reached for the lit candle, but a breeze blew it out, bringing with it the musty smell of damp earth. He grabbed a lantern that had been left by railroad workers and lit it with shaking hands. He held it up over his head, moving it back and forth until he could pick out her slight figure.

She stood on the rocky cliffs opposite the cave, singing. Though clear and sweet, her voice seemed at odds with the lyrics of an old Irish drinking song.

What was she doing? Why was she

standing atop a boulder in the middle of the night singing her heart out? But then he saw it, in the distance: lightning, followed by the low rumble of thunder. Recalling Frazier's warning about a possible stampede, a chill shot down his spine.

From behind the cave, Noah neighed and Blizzard whickered. Moses made a long rasping sound. Their animals were tethered high above the trail, out of harm's way, but obviously they, too, sensed danger.

Another bolt of lightning streaked across the sky, and the air crackled around him.

After a while, Sarah's voice stilled and he felt like he was in a wilderness with only the sky to keep him company.

He opened his mouth in song. "A . . . maz . . . ing grace . . ."

It had been so long since he'd sung, so long since he'd wanted to.

He wanted to sing now, not only because he hoped to avert a disaster, but because he wanted to reach across the chasm to where Sarah stood all alone.

His baritone voice floated between

them. After he'd sung the lyrics all the way through, he began again and this time she joined him. Her voice grew stronger as the words and tune became more familiar to her.

And he liked it. Liked the way their voices blended together. Like the music they made, the bond they created.

". . . How sweet the sound . . ."

A flash of light zigzagged across the sky, followed by a loud boom.

The ground shook. Rocks rained down from the upper cliffs, barely missing him. He quickly ducked beneath the overhang.

"Sarah!" he called, motioning her to safety, but it was too late. The first of the stampeding longhorns had arrived. The falling rocks forced him farther back into the cave.

Soon, a moving mass of panicked cattle swept through the canyon below. The heat of their bodies combined with swirling dust clouds made it nearly impossible to breathe.

The beeves didn't utter a sound, but the clash of horns and thumps of flying hooves bounced off the canyon walls with a deafening roar.

He glanced at Elizabeth's makeshift bed. The baby stirred and cried out, but there was no time to comfort her, not with Sarah's life in danger.

Sarah scrambled away from the edge of the cliff. She lost her footing and slid down the slick granite on her stomach.

Justin's breath caught in his throat, his body frozen in horror.

At the last possible moment, she grabbed hold of a slender tree. The sapling bent dangerously beneath her weight. Her feet dangled over the cliff, mere inches above the churning long horns. She searched for a foothold in the rocky cliff, her boots scrambling furiously against the granite wall.

"Hold on!" he shouted, "Hold on!" But the pounding hooves, claps of thunder, and blazing guns of cowhands trying to head the herd to safety all but drowned out his shouts.

Dust stung his eyes, and he coughed. Keeping his gaze glued on her, he covered his mouth with his neckerchief.

The stampede seemed to go on forever. Time stood still. At one point the dust was so thick, he could barely make out Sarah's slender form dangling helplessly from the side of the cliff.

Finally, finally, the ground grew still and the sound of beating hooves faded away.

He jumped to the ground and scrambled up the other side, crawling on hands and knees until he was able to grab Sarah's wrist and pull her to safety. The lantern he'd left at the dugout entrance provided a warm circle of light.

She was shaking so hard, it was all he could do to wrap his arms around her. Holding her tight, he buried his face in her hair. "If anything had happened to you—"

She lifted her face to him, her lips trembling.

Justin couldn't take his eyes off her. Something inside him broke loose. Some previously guarded part of him pulled free from its moorings and a feeling of wonder and amazement swept over him. Never before had he felt such overwhelming tenderness in his heart and he knew then, knew with every essence of his being, that nothing would ever be the same.

He lifted her chin. He stood so close to her that he could see the gold that tipped her eyelashes, count the freckles on her face.

Thunder sounded like marching soldiers followed by clashing swords of lightning. But no army could combat the temptation before him; no battle was fought harder.

"Sarah Prescott," he whispered in her ear. "I love you."

She stilled in his arms, then pulled away.

He laughed at her expression and reached out to her. "I do believe you're speechless."

She slapped his hand away. "What do you expect, you joshin' me like that?"

"I'm not joshing you. I mean what I say. I love you." He savored the feel of the words in his mouth, the sound in his ears. It wasn't new, this feeling. It had been there all along. Now that he had given it a name, he knew that pain would surely follow. He didn't care. No future misery could take away his present joy.

Her eyes round with disbelief, she stared at him. "You ain't got no business sayin' somethin' you don't mean," she said, sounding remarkably like her old self, considering her recent ordeal.

He pulled her close again and showered kisses across her forehead, down her cheek and jaw.

From inside the cave, Elizabeth's shrill cries could no longer be ignored. He stilled, then drew his mouth away from Sarah's. Kissing her nose and then her forehead, he reluctantly pulled away.

"Divine intervention," he said.

She laughed, and he thought he never heard a more beautiful sound.

Together they climbed down the rocky cliffs and hurried up the path leading to the cave. By the time they reached Elizabeth's side, she was fast asleep.

Shaking his head at the improbability of Elizabeth falling asleep before her late-night feeding, he lowered himself upon a cot.

Sarah watched him, the cool assessing look she gave him at odds with the soft curve of her mouth still swollen from his kisses. Her tousled hair fell to her shoulders in disheveled waves.

"What you said before," she began, her voice small and trembling.

"I meant every word."

A worried frown flitted across her forehead. "You can't love me. You're a preacher."

"Preachers can love," he said. "Nothing in the Bible says we can't."

The frown deepened. "But I'm an outlaw."

"Your brothers are outlaws, not you," he said. "You simply have the misfortune of being a Prescott."

She shook her head. "This ain't right. Look at me. I'm no lady. I don't even dress like one. You can't hitch a horse with a coyote."

He rose to his feet and started toward her.

Holding her hand up, palm out, she backed away from him. Instead of embracing his feelings, she looked trapped. "I don't even know the proper way to talk to God."

"God doesn't expect you to talk any special way."

"Don't—"

"Don't what?" he asked closing the distance between them. He grabbed her by the wrists and backed her against the granite wall where she couldn't escape. "You said you liked it when we kissed."

"You ain't talkin' about . . . no kissin'," she said. "You're talkin about lovin', and that's a leopard with stripes instead of spots. It ain't right."

"You don't want me to love you?" he asked.

She bit her lip and lowered her lashes. "It makes no sense to love someone you can't be with."

"Do you think I planned this?"

The eyes meeting his were filled with dismay.

"The truth is . . . Sarah, God knows I've fought the truth. I was just too stubborn to know my own heart. And . . . and . . . I—" He shook his head in frustration. "I'm no good at saying what I feel."

"I'd say you're doing a mighty fine job," she said.

He threaded his fingers through hers. "The truth is," he began again and this time his feelings flowed from him as easily as a song. "I loved you from the moment I first set eyes on you. I loved you when you were chin-deep in mire yelling your head off. I loved you when you were on hands and knees digging that marshal's grave. I loved you when you were swatting hoppers and singing to a bunch of crazy cows."

Her eyes filled with tears and she shook her head. "We can't do this," she said, her voice choked. She lowered her lashes. "I—I've got to leave. In two days."

"I know. I know." He cupped her chin in his hand and she lifted her eyes to his. "I just want to know . . . Do you . . . do you have feelings for me?"

"Oh, Justin," she cried. She flung her arms around his neck but just as quickly pulled away. "I don't think I'm ever gonna remember that a lady ain't supposed to throw herself at a man like that."

"Sometimes it's okay," Justin said. "In extraordinary circumstances."

"Like when a prayer is answered?" she whispered.

"Like when a man declares his love."

Not waiting for a second invitation, she flung her arms around him a second time. "Oh, Justin, I do love you. I do."

His mouth pressed against hers, her lips soft and yielding next to his own. Her skin felt warm and smooth and soft as fine velvet.

"Are you folks okay?"

At the sound of the cattle spotter's voice, Justin jumped back.

"Yes," he called back, his voice shaking. "We're . . . we're fine."

"We'd like you folks to join us at the chuck wagon for breakfast in the morning," Frazier said.

"Breakfast?" Justin mouthed and Sarah nodded. He called louder. "That's mighty generous of you."

"It's the least we can do for the trouble you folks had to put up with tonight. See you in the mornin'."

Justin waited for the sound of hooves to fade away, then turned to Sarah again. This time, he kept his arms to his side.

The longing in her eyes matched his own. Nonetheless, she shook her head. "I know. You're a preacher . . . a Christian."

"A Christian," he repeated out loud for his own benefit—a desperate attempt to quell the burning fires within.

Biting her lip, she nodded in agreement.

He watched the play of emotions on her face and her inner struggles mirrored his own. He felt a twinge of guilt for not validating her growing faith. In the face of temptation, it was often her strength more than his that saved him. Once he'd convinced her that her promise not to bother God again was invalid, she embraced her growing faith in God with childlike wonder.

At first, her short, simple prayers had startled Justin. "Keep her safe, God, You hear?" she'd say while holding Elizabeth, and that would be the extent of her prayer. Her prayers lacked formality but never substance. At times, he'd envied the simplicity of her faith. Her growing relationship with God was simple and pure. In contrast, his faith was often weakened by self-doubt.

"You're right," he said at last. "And I need to do the right thing. But not because of who I am. Because of who we both are."

He backed away but every inch that separated them added to his misery. "I'll . . . I'll check the horses." With that, he quickly turned and walked away. It was one of the most difficult things he'd ever had to do—and by far the most necessary.

He followed the path that led above the cave. Half walking, half running, he fought the temptation to turn back.

As far as he was concerned, he hadn't escaped fast enough. Holding Sarah in his arms, kissing her, hearing her declare her love for him had felt like paradise. No, torture. It had been torture because he wanted so much more. Had so much more to give her.

He walked faster.

He was a pastor, a man of the cloth, someone whom others looked up to and yet . . . He wanted to touch her, to fill her eyes with longing.

He walked faster, still.

He wanted her in every way that a man could want a woman. God forgive him.

This time, he broke into a full run.

At first he thought the campfire belonged to the cattlemen, but he realized his mistake the moment he stepped into the circle of light and found himself staring down the barrel of a gun.

"Hold it right there, mister," came a rough voice.

Justin stopped in his tracks, his hands held high. There were two of them, both dressed in black. The second man was younger, barely out of his teens. At first Justin thought he'd had the misfortune of meeting up with outlaws, but then he saw the silver badges.

Lawmen!

"Throw your weapons down."

"I'm not armed," Justin said. "I'm a preacher."

The man with the gun motioned for his partner to check Justin for weapons. The younger man stepped forward and

patted Justin down with quick effi-
ciency. He seemed overly eager, and
Justin guessed he was new on the job.

"No weapons," he announced.

Satisfied that Justin was unarmed,
the older lawman lowered his gun.

"Sorry to startle you," Justin said. "I
thought you were cattlemen."

"I reckon we wouldn't be sitting here
if we were," the lawman said. "We'd be
out chasing beeves." Even in the dim
light of the fire, Justin could feel the
man's scrutiny.

"You're out of breath. Hope you
weren't trying to outrun those cattle."

"Just out for a walk."

"Sit for a spell. Name's Marshal
Watson. This here is Deputy Marshal
Massey."

Justin nodded to both men and since
there didn't seem to be any way of
avoiding it, added, "Justin Wells. Reverend Justin Wells."

Marshal Watson eyed him curiously. A
rugged man whose craggy face looked
like it was carved out of the same granite as the surrounding hills, he spit a

stream of tobacco off to the side before sitting on a log.

"I reckon you'd either have to be a preacher or a fool to travel these parts unarmed."

Taking his cue, Justin sat on a tree stump opposite him. "Some people would say I'm both."

"Where you from?" Watson asked.

"Boston."

"Thought as much," Watson drawled.

Massey threw another log onto the fire. "You got yourself some accent, there."

"What are you doin' in these parts?" Watson asked.

"I'm on my way to Texas."

"Texas, eh? Any trouble on the trail?"

"Uh . . . no."

A less observant man might have missed the slight hesitation, but not Watson. The marshal's eyes sharpened as if to weigh its significance. "No one travels through these parts without trouble."

"If by trouble you mean weather problems, then I had plenty. I also ran into a swarm of locusts and some over-friendly Indians."

"You're lucky that's all you ran into," Watson said. "Some of our worst outlaws are hiding in Indian territory."

"We're working out of Judge Parker's court," Massey said proudly.

"Deputy Marshal Massey is a new recruit," Watson added in a tone that indicated he'd already grown weary of the younger man's enthusiasm.

"Judge Parker picked me hisself," Massey said, puffing out his chest. "Said my love of excitement and my desire to improve conditions made me a perfect man for the job."

Marshal Watson stuck a cheroot in his mouth, struck a match on the sole of his boot, and lit it. "We gotta telegram from Texas saying that one of our marshals has disappeared. He was bringing in a member of the Prescott gang."

Justin's mouth went dry. An icy chill shot down his spine and settled at the pit of his stomach. He wasn't good at deception. Had no idea whether to act surprised, indifferent, or merely interested.

Watson never took his eyes off him. "The marshal and his prisoner were supposed to catch a train to Texas from Kansas City but never showed up. You didn't happen to meet up with them, did you? A marshal with a woman prisoner? Stands yea tall." He held up his hand to indicate. "Red hair. Blue eyes. Name's Sarah Prescott."

Justin's mouth felt like it was stuffed with cotton, but he managed to keep a neutral expression. "Afraid I can't help you."

Watson shrugged. "Just thought I'd ask. Stranger things have happened."

"We're gonna get the Prescott gang," Massey said with a conviction that could only come with youth. "That will show the rest of them outlaws that we mean bus'ness."

Not wanting to draw suspicion, Justin endured the silence that followed. It started to rain, giving him an excuse to leave. "I better get back to camp."

"Maybe you could join us for break-fast at the chuck wagon," Watson said. "The cattlemen were kind enough to extend us an invite. Don't think they'd object to an extra mouth."

Justin's mind scrambled. "I plan to get an early start in the morning."

"Same here. But hittin' the trail is a lot more pleasant with some real grub under the belt."

"I'll think about it." To Massey, he said, "Good luck on your new job."

Justin turned and walked away, feeling Watson's eyes on him until he disappeared into the darkness.

Nineteen

For the longest while after Justin left, Sarah sat watching the lantern cast flickering shadows on the walls of the cave like uncontained laughter.

I love you, he'd said, and the words seemed to echo from the deepest part of her. She repeated his words over and over in her head until she was brave enough to believe that he actually had said them and it hadn't been just her imagination.

"I love you, too, Justin Wells," she whispered.

She leaned her head next to the jagged rock wall. So this is how love felt. This is what all those crazy feelings had been about. The quickening pulse. The sleepless nights. The longing. The quivering in the stomach. At first, she'd thought she was coming down with a fever or something. She blamed her physical ailments on her troubles with the law, afraid to believe that love was the culprit. Love didn't happen to people like her. At least, that's what she'd told herself.

"Sarah Prescott, you don't know beeswax from bull foot about love," she said aloud. Love was apparently somethin' that happened when you least expected it and there wasn't a dern thing a body could do about it.

Justin's declaration of love still ringing in her ears, she jumped to her feet and paced back and forth. Her thoughts dredged from a place beyond all reason and logic, she was almost ready to believe that anything was possible, even love between a preacher and a Prescott.

Justin loved her. There it was, plain and simple. She never understood why her brothers got all starry-eyed and crazy over the opposite sex. Everything suddenly made sense. Even Robert's mushy poems.

This can't be happening. She vowed never to make a fool of herself as her siblings had done. And yet . . .

Justin loved her.

Even though she wasn't a lady, he loved her.

And she loved him.

She was still reeling from the wonder of it all when Justin rushed into the cave, his tall, handsome form seeming to fill every inch of space. Rain rolled off his hat and clothes, forming a puddle at his feet, but it was the look on his face that alarmed her.

"Get Elizabeth ready. We're leaving. Now." His body tense, he grabbed one of the saddles.

She stared at him, not sure she'd heard right. Of all the things she imagined he would say when he returned, this was the least expected.

"You want to leave now?" She rose to her feet. "Because of what happened . . .?"

"It has nothing to do . . . with the two of us." His face darkened with a pained expression. "Two U.S. marshals are camped less than a half mile away."

Her mouth opened in dismay. Lawmen in the vicinity was cause for alarm, but it didn't explain Justin's sudden decision to leave. "It ain't the first time we've met up with marshals," she said.

"They asked me if I'd seen you. They haven't heard from Owen, so they suspect something happened."

Her jaw dropped. In that instant, she was jolted back to grim reality. One moment she was a woman loved and in love, the next an outlaw who could be neither of those things.

"Get ready," he urged.

Swallowing hard, she shook her head. "It ain't right to wake the baby," she said. "I'll leave. You stay with Elizabeth. I can make better time by myself."

"I'm not letting you travel alone. We're still in Indian territory."

"We ain't that far from Red River."

"I won't feel right until I put you on that stage myself."

She bit her lip. "Then let's stay here and wait till the marshals leave the area."

"They'll see the horses and know I'm not alone." He leaned forward, beseeching her. "Sarah . . . they described you. Your red hair and blue eyes. They know your name."

She took a deep breath. "I never meant to put you in such a picklement," she said.

He gave her a shadow of a smile. "I never expected to be in one."

"What . . . what did you say when they asked about me?" She hated to think he was forced to lie to protect her.

"I told them the truth," he said. "I told them I couldn't help them, which isn't a lie. I couldn't bring myself to tell them something that would put you in danger."

"Do you think they believed you?" she asked.

"I don't know." He thought for a moment as if going over the encounter again in his head. "I think so."

"They have to believe a preacher," she said with more confidence than she felt.

"Maybe. But Frazier has seen you, and there's no telling what he might say over breakfast. We need to go." Saddle in hand, he ducked out of the cave.

It took almost an hour to give Elizabeth her late-night feeding and make their way to the trail leading south.

Justin walked ahead, leading the little caravan around rocks and other debris that had fallen during the stampede. Elizabeth was asleep in her sling, her little head pressed against Sarah's chest. Holding the reins with a single hand, Sarah wrapped her free arm around the baby. Moses trotted behind, followed by Mira.

The storm had passed, and the air was thick with the smell of damp earth; the night was alive with sounds. Rain dripped from low-hanging branches. The blast of a cow-hand's gun echoed from the distance. An injured longhorn bellowed from a nearby ditch, sending chills down her spine.

Sarah and her brothers had ridden their share of hoot-owl trails, as they called them, a necessary precaution for outlaws. Even as a child, she hated it, hated being dragged from a warm bedroll in the middle of the night. Hated living in the shadows. But never before had she hated it as much as she did at that moment.

Nor had she ever been more afraid. Not for herself, but for the precious baby in her arms. For Justin, the man she loved more than she ever thought possible. They deserved so much better than having to sneak through the night like common thieves.

Like outlaws.

Like her.

A rustle in the bushes made her heart pound. "What's that?" she whispered as loud as she dared.

"Just a rabbit," Justin whispered back.

It wasn't until she felt a burning in her chest that she realized she had been holding her breath. She inhaled deeply, forcing air into her lungs, and tried to calm her nerves. But it was no use.

For her there was no escape, no matter what direction she traveled. No matter how fast or slow she rode. No matter if it were day or night, winter or summer, spring or fall, there was no escape.

She would always be a Prescott. And it nearly broke her heart to think about it.

They traveled the rest of the night and all the next day, stopping long enough only to care for Elizabeth, grab a quick bite to eat, and rest the horses.

Neither she nor Justin mentioned the words spoken in love, but the memory underscored every visual interchange, every moment they shared.

Sarah sensed urgency in everything they did. Even the most mundane tasks seemed more precious as their time together grew short.

During those last hours on the trail, she couldn't take her eyes off him. Like an artist painting a still life, she studied him, watched him, memorized his every move until his very essence was engraved in her heart, never to be forgotten.

They were close to the border, and even Moses seemed to sense a change in the wind, braying and pushing against Blizzard as if to get the horse to walk faster. Wild turkeys ran across their path taking cover in the nearby brush. The air vibrated with the grunts of wild boar and the deep lowing of cattle.

Golden rays of sunshine turned dew into teardrops that mirrored the ones Sarah dare not shed. She knew that if she ever lost control, she would never find the strength or courage to leave him.

In the heat of the afternoon, they rested in what little shade could be found and waited till the sun sank low in the sky before hitting the trail again, stopping only long enough to tend to the baby's needs.

On the morning of the second day, they followed the railroad tracks of the Missouri, Kansas, Texas railroad known as the Katy. The tracks looked like two streaks of rust. The train had stopped running since the bridge over the Red River was washed away in the late spring rains. A fingerboard reading Colbert's Ferry Straight Ahead pointed south. It was the ferry that would carry Justin across the Red River into Texas. Bullet holes riddled the sign, seeming to mirror the holes in her heart.

She and Justin sat side by side on

their horses, staring at the pointed finger as if it marked the end of the world.
All around them, the air rumbled with
the excited shouts of drovers.

"I reckon this is the end of the trail,"
she said. Unable to hold back her tears
any longer, she dug her heels into Blizzard's side and rode to the top of a hill
that overlooked the river.

The hill was dotted with several
graves marked by simple wooden
crosses, but Sarah knew the peaceful
scenario was deceiving. The river could
be treacherous, especially in the spring
when the waters ran high. Driftwood
hanging from tree branches and the
high water mark etched into the red
bluffs that formed its banks gave evidence of recent floods. Red River had
killed far more cattlemen through the
years than even the Indians had killed.

A steel cable stretched from bank to
bank, guiding the skiffs that helped control the herds. The river itself could not
be seen for the solid mass of hide moving across it. She'd heard tell that, at
times, a man could cross the river on

foot by simply walking on the backs of cattle.

On the opposite side of the river a distance away from the First and Last Chance store stood a white house with a veranda and two log houses. Behind was a red barn surrounded by livestock. From a short distance away came the hammering sounds of workers rebuilding the railroad bridge.

Sensing her need to be alone, Justin strolled from grave to grave, saying a prayer for the deceased. Then he rode down the road to check the time table at the stage station.

When he returned, his face was grim, his mouth set in a tight line. "The stage to Fort Smith is due to arrive here in the morning."

She bit her lip and looked away. "If you want to keep going, I'll be okay," she said. "I'll camp here for the night."

"I'll wait until you're on the stage," he said, his words seeming to be stuck in his throat.

"No need to bother."

"I'll wait."

Not wanting to spend what little time

they had left arguing, she gave a reluctant nod.

They camped that night a safe distance away from the river's edge and the trampling hooves of cattle. It was their last night together, but there was no time for sentiment. There was too much traffic and noise. Horses and cattle thundered along the trail leading northward. Buckboard wagons and other vehicles traveled the east-west trail.

Though they were ever on guard, no lawmen appeared. Yet there was a steady stream of travelers. Many stopped to chat and share news.

A former lamplighter was on the way to Texas seeking work. He described in great detail the new "electric candles" that lit the streets of his hometown of Wabash, Indiana.

"Four arc lights," he said, the resentment at losing his job tempered by his obvious amazement that such a feat was possible. "That's all it took, just four, and the town square was lit bright as day."

The next morning, the sound of rattling wheels and shouts heralded the arrival of the Wells Fargo stage heading for Fort Smith, and Sarah and Justin broke camp.

By the time they arrived at the ferry station, fresh horses had been harnessed to the stage, and the flat barge had already crossed from the Texas side. The ferry was some eighty feet long and sixteen feet wide. An older man and a young woman disembarked and headed for the stage, leaving the gray-haired ferry operator to haul their luggage on shore, his ebony skin glistening in the sun.

Then the operator led Noah, Blizzard, Moses, and the goat on board before loading the animals of other passengers.

The sign read twenty-five cents for man and horse. "I wonder how much they'll charge me for Elizabeth?" Justin said.

Sarah scoffed. "A pretty penny." Her brothers didn't have much regard for the Colbert brothers. The government now regulated the price ferries could charge, but that didn't stop ferry owners from taking advantage of travelers whenever possible. "I heard tell George Colbert charged General Jackson seventy-five thousand dollars to transport his troops 'cross the river."

"Maybe Colbert was on the side of the opposition," he said.

She grinned. "Or maybe he was just greedy."

He juggled Elizabeth in his arms and tapped her gently on the nose. "I'd say you're worth at least an arm and a leg. If he asks much more than that, we're in trouble."

Sarah smiled. She loved watching Justin with Elizabeth. No one would guess by looking at them that they weren't father and daughter.

He lifted his head and caught her staring at him. A world of emotion passed between them before they turned away: he to scan the river and she to battle tears.

Taking a bracing breath, she focused on Elizabeth. Her chest ached as she gazed at the child in his arms. After a strained silence, she said, "You take care of her, you hear?"

His gaze collided with hers. "You know I will."

"Find her a good home."

He nodded. "The best."

"Don't forget, she likes to have her forehead rubbed."

"I won't—"

"And she likes to be sung to when you're changin' her breeches."

"I don't know if I can remember all the words to that 'Little Brown Jug' song you sing."

"Don't you dare sing that to her," she said heatedly. Then seeing his teasing smile, she smiled too.

She bit her lip. She thought of all the things she wanted to say, but the words wouldn't come.

"Do you want to hold her one more time?" he asked.

She stepped back, hands by her side. "No." She couldn't. She didn't dare. If she took that precious child in her arms, she would never be able to let her go. She dug her fingers into her palms and fought for control.

He spread a blanket on the ground and lay Elizabeth on it. Then without warning, he spun around and crushed Sarah into his arms, sending her hat flying to the ground.

Oblivious to onlookers, he kissed her hard. His lips on hers made her heart pound till she could hardly breathe.

"Stay with me, Sarah," he said between kisses. "I won't let them hurt you, I won't. God will help us find a way. You have to believe that."

She was tempted—more tempted than she had ever been in her life—but her feelings for this man far outweighed any selfish notions she had.

She stared up at the face that she had come to know so well. Seeing the pain in his eyes was almost harder to bear than the anguish she felt.

"How would it look for a preacher to be hangin' out with a Prescott?"

The frown on his forehead deepened. Something seemed to die inside of him. "I don't know that I have much heart left for preaching," he said, feathering kisses on her forehead.

"That's crazy talk," she said, adding in a quieter but no less firm voice, "Preachin' is your life, your work."

"It's God's work, and he deserves someone who can give heart and soul to the job."

"And that someone is you," she said. "Don't go thinkin' it's not, you hear?"

He shook his head sadly, like a man who had seen his last dream fade away. "My heart won't be in it, Sarah. Not if you're gone." He hesitated. "I'm not even sure I'm cut out for the work anymore."

"Don't say that, Justin. Look how you helped that poor man who lost his wife and child. You even made a believer out of me."

He smiled at that. "I think you always believed. You just need to learn to trust God."

"I *do* trust Him," she said softly, "and I believe God means for you to be a preacher."

"Maybe in Boston, but not here. People out here are different. Do you know what women talk about in Boston? Fashions! They're obsessed with the latest Parisian fashions. And the men talk about the Red Caps."

She frowned, trying to understand

what he was telling her. "They talk about hats?'

"The Red Caps are a baseball team. The men come to church on Sunday and afterward they stand around and talk about a game. A ball game! But out here . . ." He gazed in the distance at a drover struggling to free a bogged cow. "I don't know what I can offer folks out here."

"I reckon they need God a whole lot more out here than those city folks do," she said.

"That may be true, but I don't think I'm the right person for the job. Don't you see? I've lived a relatively easy life. Before this trip, I never buried anyone with my own two hands."

"You lost your sisters," she said.

"Yes, but I didn't have to dig their graves and leave them in the wilderness. I never had to worry about Indians or stampedes . . . and I never knew what love was."

She blinked back the tears that threatened her resolve. "I s'pect you've always been a man of good leather," she said. "Now you're more experienced, is all. You got a lot more rings on your horns."

"Not enough," he said, his voice hoarse. He took her hand and held it in both of his. "I know how to talk about God to people who never have to worry about where their next meal is coming from. What can I possibly offer people who come face-to-face with death at every turn?"

"Your faith," she said, pulling her hand away.

He stared at her. "That's it?"

She nodded. "It's enough."

"I don't know—"

"It's enough," she said again.

The look he gave her reached into her very soul. "I don't know that I can find a better mother for Elizabeth than you."

"You and her . . . you deserve better than me. I'll be lookin' over my shoulder just like you said."

"I was wrong. You won't have to keep looking over your shoulder as I'll be watching your back every step of the way."

She bit her lip and took a deep breath. "It almost broke my heart to drag that baby out of bed in the middle of the night." Each word felt like broken glass in her mouth, but she forced herself to continue. "It ain't right. She deserves a ma she can count on. One who ain't afraid to show her face." Beseeching him, she lay a hand on his arm. "If only . . ."

He leaned toward her. "If only what?"

"It would make it easier if I knew you and Elizabeth were together."

He stared at her, his eyes wide with astonishment. "You want me to keep her?" He shook his head. "You know I can't . . . I have no idea what awaits me in Rocky Creek. Or even if I'm capable of doing the job I've been sent to do. How could I possibly care for a child?"

Regretting the additional burden she had placed on him, she reached up to smooth away the tortured shadow at his forehead. "You must give heart and soul to the Lord. For the first time in my life, I want to know that I've done right by Him."

He placed his hands on her shoulders. "Don't leave me, Sarah. Please don't go. God wouldn't bring us together only to tear us apart."

She pressed her hand against his roughened cheek, and the love she felt for him welled up inside until she thought her chest would rip open. "If that's true, then you can be sure there'll be a divine interruption."

"Intervention," he said softly. "Divine intervention."

She closed her eyes. It was a comforting but unrealistic thought. God had saved Elizabeth, and it seemed to her that a body didn't have a right to expect more than one miracle in a lifetime.

She pulled away and reached down for her hat. Then she fell on her knees and kissed Elizabeth on the forehead, the downy soft hair tickling her nose. She could no longer hold back her tears and quickly wiped away the one that fell on Elizabeth's round face. How was it possible for a heart to hurt so much?

She stood and slapped her hat against her leg before placing it on her head. She made a mistake by looking back at him. He was so tall and handsome, his eyes filled with both love and despair, but it was the noticeable sheen in his eyes that nearly tore her apart. If she lived to be a hundred, she would never forget his face on this day.

"God help me . . ." She shook her head. "I can't—"

"All aboard for Fort Smith." The rough voice of the stage coach driver sounded as final as a dirge.

Justin leaned forward. "Can't what, Sarah?"

She stared at him mutely and fought the impulse to rush into his arms. She pressed her hand one last time against his cheek, then quickly slipped away. It took every bit of strength she could muster to run the short distance to the waiting stage.

Twenty

The sun hung high in the sky by the time Justin finally reached the end of his journey and rode into the little town of Rocky Creek. His heart heavy, he felt all the anxiety and none of the joy of finally reaching his destination.

Not only did he question his reason for being there, he missed Sarah. Missed her more than he ever thought possible to miss another human being.

A lump rose in his throat, and he swallowed hard. He glanced down at the sleeping child in his sling. "You miss her too, don't you?"

Sarah denied knowing anything about babies, but she was far better than he at washing out baby clothes, milking that sorry excuse for a goat, and dressing the little one. The tiny buttons confounded him, and he could never seem to get the child's three-cornered breeches on right the first time. The goat was just plain ornery.

"Sarah, Sarah, Sarah. . . ." Whispering her name had become a habit with him. It was the first thing he did each morning, the last thing he did after his nightly prayer.

Heaving a sigh, he focused his attention on his surroundings. With Elizabeth nestled peacefully in her sling, he rode slowly through town.

Much to his dismay, Rocky Creek was every bit as wanting as Sarah had described. Main Street was narrow and deeply rutted by wagon wheels. Dismal false front buildings lined up on either side of the street like dejected wallflowers at a dance.

The street was deserted, the hot sun keeping everyone inside. Raucous laughter and loud voices drifted from the batwing doors of various saloons he passed.

He counted seven saloons in all. In addition there was a barbershop, town marshal's office, newspaper office, and dry goods store. A livery stable and blacksmith anchored the town at one end. A bank kept the town from toppling over in the other.

The Grand Hotel was located at the end of the street opposite the blacksmith. A ramshackle structure, it seemed to depend on the emporium next door for support. The only resemblance to its name was the size, twice that of the other buildings.

The desk clerk was a rail thin man with a sweeping mustache. His square-jawed face and fly-away ears resembled a squat sugar bowl.

"I need a room," Justin said.

The clerk scratched his head and stared at Elizabeth like he'd never seen a baby before. "All's I got is space in a three-man bed. I don't reckon the others will cotton much to sharin' their bed with a bawler."

Justin stared at the man, not sure he'd heard right. "Did I hear you say I'd have to share a bed?"

"Yep, you heard me all right."

"I'll pay you double for a private bed."

The clerk shook his head. "Hotel's full. Got a couple cattle companies here. You could try Ma Stevens's boarding house. It's located about a mile west of here. She's mighty particular 'bout who she takes in, but maybe she'll take pity on you."

Justin thanked him and left. His misgivings about the town and his ability to care for Elizabeth increased by the minute. If he had to depend on pity for accommodations, he was in worse shape than he thought.

Less than twenty minutes later, he spotted a sign on a fence post that simply said *Ma's.*

The well-kept clapboard house with its high-polished windows and full-blooming flower boxes looked as friendly as a puppy. He felt a flicker of hope.

"What do you think, Elizabeth? Think she'll take pity on us?"

The woman known as Ma opened the door to Justin's knock. Dressed in a bright floral dress, as wide as she was tall, she resembled a flower box herself—or would have, had she been lying down. Drying her pudgy hands on her ruffled starched apron, she greeted him warmly with a dimpled chin and a melting smile. Gazing tenderly at the small infant asleep in his arms, her buttery smile spread to her ears.

"Well, bless my soul. What have we here?"

Justin introduced himself and explained that he was the new pastor of the church.

"Come in, come in. You're just in time for some fresh berry pie." The woman hustled him through the neatly furnished drawing room to the sunny kitchen in back.

"Glory be!" she said, reaching for a padded potholder and opening the oven door. "At last we have a preacher to call our own. We saw the last one every six months if we were lucky, and he always preached the same sermon."

She set two pies on the windowsill to cool, then brushed a strand of white hair from her face. "Guess he figured after six months, no one would remember."

"You have my word that I'll preach a different sermon every week," Justin said. He glanced around, and the homey feel of the kitchen made him even more aware of his dismal future.

"Right now, though, I need a room for myself and the baby. I also have two horses, a mule, and a goat that need tending to."

She moved the blanket and peered down on the sleeping child. "What a dear sweet thing," the woman said. As if on cue, Elizabeth opened her eyes.

"Well, now, would you look at those big blue eyes!" Ma exclaimed. She made little clucking sounds with her mouth.

"Her name's Elizabeth," he said, introducing her with a sense of pride that surprised him.

Ma clapped her hands together. "I didn't know our new pastor was a family man."

"Oh, no, no, I'm not married. Her mother . . . I'm just taking care of her, and I need someone to watch her till I find her a permanent home."

"You think you're gonna find a good

home for this baby in Rocky Creek?" she said, shaking her head. "Not too many families around here willing to take on another mouth to feed."

"I'm counting on help from the Lord," he replied.

"Well, now." Ma lifted Elizabeth out of his arms and cuddled her close. "It's been a mighty long time since I've held a young'un. I would be happy to take care of her."

"That's very kind of you," Justin said. "I will, of course, compensate you."

"Nonsense. It's the least I can do to welcome our new pastor."

"Do you by any chance happen to know where Marshal Owen lives?" He wanted to fulfill his promise to the marshal as soon as possible.

"Follow that road out front and take a right at the fork. You'll see his house on the left." She gave him a questioning look. "But if you plan on paying them a visit, you best wait. The marshal's out of town on assignment, and his wife and their children are in Dallas visiting her sick mother."

"I see." He didn't want to tell anyone

about the marshal's death until he had a chance to talk to the widow.

"Do you know them?" she asked.

"I met the marshal." He purposely kept his answer vague. He dabbed at Elizabeth's cheek with a clean kerchief, hoping to discourage more questions.

She waited, but when he offered no further details, she shrugged in resignation. "Come along and I'll show you to your room. There's a barn in back. You'll find fresh hay and water and just 'bout anythin' else you need."

She led the way upstairs to the room at the end of the hall. It was sparsely furnished with a bed, a chest of drawers, and a single chair. A door led out to the balcony. It was more than he'd hoped for, and Ma offering to care for Elizabeth until he made other arrangements was an added blessing.

Later, Ma made a bed out of a little wooden crate, lining it with a handmade quilt. She gave the baby a bath, talking to her and making silly faces. "It feels mighty good to hold a baby again," she told Justin as Elizabeth stared at her.

Watching her, Justin knew that Elizabeth was in good hands, at least until he found her a permanent home. With this thought in mind, he walked outside to tend to the animals.

That night, he slept fitfully. Though the bed was soft and comfortable, he kept waking up. Each time he woke, he searched for Sarah's bedroll as he had done countless nights in the past, straining his eyes for a glimpse of her in the dark.

The following morning, after a hearty breakfast of bacon, eggs, and flapjacks that Ma prepared for him, he left Elizabeth in her care and headed for the barbershop.

The barber's name was Kip Barrel, a descriptive yet unfortunate name for the rotund man with a deep booming voice that shook the very rafters.

"A pastor, eh?" he said, after Justin introduced himself. "It seems that you and I have a lot in common."

Justin settled himself in the high barber chair. "Oh? What might that be?"

"You're a preacher and I sing opera, and the town has no use for either one of us. That's why I'm cutting hair." He laughed and motioned with his scissors. "I can teach you the trade. I could use another barber. Give you something to do."

Justin shook his head. "I think I'll stick to what I know." He watched Barrel in the mirror. "Shouldn't you be in San Francisco or New Orleans? Somewhere with an opera house?"

Barrel shook his head. "I suffer stage fright. As soon as I get up to sing in front of an audience, I squeal like a stuck pig. My big opening night at the French Opera House in New Orleans ended in disaster. I came here to lick my wounds and open a singing school. As long as I don't have to perform in public, I'm all right. The only client I had was a rancher who wanted to improve his singing skills for his cattle." Barrel shook his scissors dangerously close to Justin's ear. "I ask you, do I look like a man who wants to teach someone to sing to cattle?"

"Hardly," Justin said. Painful memories of the night he and Sarah sang together assailed him, and he gripped the arms of the chair for support.

He waited until Barrel's face had returned to its normal ruddy red color and he had calmly resumed cutting hair. "I could use a singer at the church. Would you be interested?"

Barrel shook his head so hard that his triple chins jiggled. "I'd have to sing in front of people, and that's something I can't do. God gave me this enormous talent, but He forgot to give me the courage to use it."

"I don't think God forgot," Justin said. "I think He simply gave you a challenge that you haven't yet conquered."

A short while later, Justin paid Barrel and left. No sooner had he walked outside than Barrel's strong tenor voice streamed out of the empty shop as smooth as liquid gold.

Justin stood outside and listened, recognizing *"La Donna é Mobil"* from *Rigoletto.* Justin had been to more operas than he cared to remember out of obligation to the church and its annual fundraiser. Not a fan by any means, he was nonetheless struck by Barrel's vibrant voice. The church could use a talent like that.

He walked to the hitching post and

grabbed the reins of his horse. "What do you say, Noah? Do you think we can persuade Mr. Barrel to switch from Verdi to Newton?"

No sooner were the words out of his mouth than he saw Sarah on a rock singing "Amazing Grace." So clear was the vision that he reached out to touch her only to find his hand pressed hard against Noah's neck.

Pushing his thoughts away, Justin mounted and followed Ma's directions along a winding dirt road leading to the church.

The square clapboard building sat upon a hilltop, affording a view of the town in the valley below. According to the sign in front, the place of worship dated back to shortly after Texas became a state in 1845. The structure had fallen in disrepair in recent years and the little cemetery in back was covered in weeds, except for the areas around newly dug graves.

The door hung from a single leather hinge, and a few jagged pieces of stained glass was all that remained of the window. Dry leaves covered the wooden plank floor and the potbellied stove was turned on its side. Sun poured through the sieve-like tin roof, and dust particles danced in the golden rays.

Someone had built a fire pit in the center aisle, and the remainder of a charred pew spilled over the blackened rocks.

Justin stared in dismay at the rubble, trash, and decay around him. The building bore no resemblance to the red brick church in Boston with its polished oak pews and stained glass windows. He hadn't expected such luxury, of course, in Rocky Creek, but never had he imagined anything quite so humble.

The church mirrored everything that was wrong with his life, and he had no idea where to start to make things right again. Without Sarah, he wasn't even sure if he could.

Twenty-one

The stage reached Fort Smith shortly after noon. Sarah stared out of the window with both a sense of relief that the journey was over and dread at having to return to a life she wanted to escape.

In the distance, lightning forked the angry clouds, followed by a clap of thunder.

It had been a long and difficult ride, requiring three overnight stays at crowded stage stop inns. The road was impossibly rutted, causing the coach to sway from side to side and bop up and down like a cork in water. Every last bit of space not taken by passengers was packed with bags of mail.

There were only three other travelers, one an older man who snored for the whole trip. A young woman was traveling with her father to Fort Smith for an arranged marriage. During the entire trip, her father sat with his arms wrapped around the suitcase on his lap, his face grim, while his daughter sobbed by his side.

Between snoring and hysterics, no one paid any attention to Sarah, and that was fine with her.

Her body cramped and her muscles throbbed, but the pain of leaving Justin was so great that no amount of physical discomfort could compare to her grief.

She dreaded reuniting with her brothers. By now, they must know she didn't go directly to Fort Smith, and she could well imagine George chewing iron over her disobedience. He was a firm believer in family loyalty, and every time she'd struck out on her own, trying to make a fresh start, she'd always wound up in trouble.

She found it increasingly difficult to go back to the family in recent years, but never more so than now. She'd stayed with Justin longer than she meant to, longer than was prudent.

Justin.

Just thinking his name made her heart ache anew. Waves of loneliness washed over her. She squeezed her eyes tight in an effort to forget the feel of his lips on hers. She dug her fingers into the palms of her hand and tried to erase the memory of him from her mind. But nothing she did could make her forget a single moment they'd spent together.

Nor could she stop thinking of Elizabeth. The sweet baby had managed in a very short time to steal her heart, leaving behind an aching hole that robbed her of her very breath.

Her thoughts scattered with the smell of burning wood. She moved aside the leather curtain and stuck her head out the window. The fresh air was a welcome change from the stale air inside the crowded stage, and she inhaled until her lungs were filled. Ahead, a thin gray smoke curled from the stone chimney of a two-story white wood house.

The single-lane road crossed over a wooden bridge, the horses' hooves beating hard against the wooden slats, the coach pushing its leather thongs to the limit.

Garrison Avenue was the main thoroughfare, stretching from the center of town all the way to the fort. It was a wide dirt road, deeply rutted in parts, and beaten into fine dust by hooves and wagon wheels. There were no gas lights, paved roads, or even boardwalks, which one would expect given a town of this size and notoriety.

Still, Fort Smith had its benefits. Crowded enough to provide anonymity, it was the sort of town her brother George favored. It was also progressive enough to provide ample means of escape should the need arise. Out of habit, she noted the location of docks and train station. George had taught her well.

The stage followed the stone wall of the old fort that gave the town its name. Overgrown with weeds and marred by the toppled walls of buildings destroyed by fire during the War Between the States, the fort could no longer guard anything more than its past. The garrison did however, house Judge Parker's courthouse, which was the only court with jurisdiction over Indian territory.

Spotting the sixteen-foot-high wall that hid the well-used gallows, Sarah shuddered and quickly looked away.

The fort overlooked both the Arkansas and Poteau Rivers. Ferry boats, Indian canoes, skiffs, and merchant ships battled for the right of way upon brown muddied waters. From the distance came a shrill whistle announcing the arrival of the train at the station on the far side of the river.

The stage turned off the main street before coming to a stop opposite the Ferris Hotel, where George told her to stay.

Sarah disembarked first. After stretching the kinks out of her neck and back, she glanced around anxiously before crossing the street and heading for the hotel entrance. George said this would be the last place anyone would think to find the Prescott gang, and she fervently hoped he was right.

In the distance, a dog barked. Music

drifted out of one of the many saloons that dotted the town.

An Indian dressed in buckskin pants and fringed shirt loaded crates filled with goods onto the back of a government issued wagon. A Mexican youth wearing loose cotton pants, shirt, and sombrero chased a squawking hen down the middle of the street. A lanky boy spun a ring with a stick. The scabless spots on his skin revealed a recent bout with measles.

Inside the hotel lobby, a clerk stood behind a high counter. He looked up as she approached, his brass-framed spectacles making his eyes appear larger than normal. His mustache twitched as she approached the desk.

"I'm looking for someone by the name of Cooper," she said. It was the name George used when checking into hotels.

The myopic clerk lowered his head until his beaklike nose practically touched the registration book. "No one by that name has checked in."

Surprised, she wondered if he could see enough to read the names even up close, but not wanting to offend him, she accepted his word. She wasn't all that anxious to deal with her brothers and was perfectly willing to wait till after she'd had a good night's sleep to do so.

She paid for a room and bath and signed herself in as Sarah Cooper. She dragged herself up the narrow stairway and found her room at the end of the hall.

A young Mexican chambermaid with long black hair and a shy smile brought her a tin bathtub and filled it with cold water. She handed Sarah a threadbare towel and a half bar of lye soap.

"Gracias," Sarah said.

The maid gave a quick smile and left.

Sarah scrubbed herself from head to toe, washing away every last bit of road dust until her skin was rosy pink. Then she washed out her clothes and arranged them over the windowsill to dry. Afterward, she threw herself on the bed and, despite the paper-thin mattress and rowdy noise rising from the street below, slept all night.

The next morning, she stopped at the desk to inquire about her brothers.

"No other Cooper has checked in,"

the clerk said, nose parked on the registration book.

Yesterday, she hadn't given the matter much thought, but in the light of day, their absence worried her. Following George's orders to lay low, she started for the stairs, but she was hungry and the thought of waiting in the stifling hot room for her brothers was more than she could bear.

She turned and headed back to the desk. "Where's the best place to eat?"

"Maude West's place is the best, but the whole building has been quarantined due to measles. You might try Mrs. Berry's Inn. It's right next door to the First National Bank."

Leaving the hotel, she walked to Garrison Street. Without boardwalks, it was all she could do to keep from being run over by the many carriages, shays, and buckboards that vied for space.

Dressed in baggy pants and shirt, her hat pulled low and hair tucked out of sight, she doubted that anyone would know she was a woman. Still, she wasn't about to get careless and her eyes were in constant motion. Some

businesses were closed, the black wreaths in the window indicating recent deaths in the family. Other shops had a sign on the door that read *Quarantined.*

On several occasions she thought she saw Justin, only to discover upon closer observation that each man in question looked nothing like him. By the time she reached the inn, she was shaking. She kept her identity as a woman hidden by pointing to the menu, but when her order came, she found she had little appetite.

Sitting by the wavy paned window, she watched a pale young woman walk by pushing an empty baby pram. Black ribbons fluttered from the handlebars and Sarah's heart ached. Thank God, Justin insisted upon keeping Elizabeth away from this town.

She saw a man lovingly helping a woman into the stagecoach, and it was all she could do to keep from bursting into tears.

Her spirits low, she started back toward the hotel. Hearing church bells, she thought of Justin. On impulse, she

followed the musical chimes to the Lost and Found Church.

The double doors were unlocked, so she peered inside. The church was empty except for a cat that ran between her legs and disappeared in nearby bushes when she opened the door.

On impulse, she entered the church. She hadn't been inside a place of worship since her mama's funeral. The church was similar to the one she remembered from her childhood. Surprised to find that the stained-glass windows and rigid pews seemed less intimidating to her now that she was an adult, she walked down the middle aisle.

A voice from behind startled her. "You know you're not supposed to be outside." She spun around to face the owner of the voice, an elderly man dressed in black, talking to a gray cat in his arms. Blue eyes regarded her from a wrinkled but kind face.

"I let the cat out," she said. "I'm sorry—"

"It's not your fault. The fool cat

doesn't know what's good for him. If he stayed in church, he would be safe. But he keeps wandering away, just like some people I know. Almost got run over by a wagon last week." He set the cat on the floor. "By the way, my name is Reverend Hotchkins," he said. "And you are?"

"Sarah . . . C-cooper," she stammered. Thinking there might be a rule about lying in church, she glanced up to make sure the ceiling and walls were still intact and not about to fall on her.

If the kindly preacher noticed her hesitation or suspected she was lying about her name, he kept it to himself.

"When a young woman comes to church between Sundays, it usually means one of two things. Either she wants to book the church for her wedding, or she's in a whole peck of trouble." He studied her. "I guess the latter. Am I right?"

She nodded.

"Want to talk about it?"

"I can't," she said.

"That bad, eh?"

"God and me . . . we ain't always been on friendly terms."

"Just because you wandered away from church is no reason to think God's not looking out for you. Isn't that right, Jeremiah?"

She smiled. "Your cat's name is in the Bible," she said.

The old preacher's eyes crinkled. "Maybe you aren't as lost as you think you are."

She stared at him in confusion. "I never said I was lost."

"I figured there was a reason you came to Lost and Found."

"I heard the church b-bells," she stammered. The preacher with his keen insights unnerved her. "I best be going." Anxious to make her escape, she started up the aisle.

Reverend Hotchkins scooped the cat up with one hand and stepped aside to let her pass. "Follow the signs," he called after her.

Her hand on the ornate handle of the heavy door, Sarah glanced over her shoulder. "Signs?"

"God is leading the way. You just have to follow the signs."

She paused outside the church, waiting for her eyes to adjust to the glare of the sun. Dodging around a horse-drawn hearse blocking the road, she headed for the hotel.

On the outer wall of a bank were colorful posters proclaiming the fall arrival of *Barnum's Greatest Show on Earth* and promising a "more extensive, expensive, and wonderful circus, hippodrome, and menagerie than has ever before been seen in this country."

Next to it a smaller poster announced the first Sebastian County Fair. The smaller print read: *The opening address will be given by Judge Parker.*

Just reading the name of the hanging judge sent shivers down her spine. Moving away from the bank, her eyes inadvertently lit upon a wanted poster tacked to a nearby post.

Stopping in her tracks, she stared at the yellow placard in horror. Bold, dark type read:
Wanted
Sarah Prescott

Reward: 500 dollars in gold coin.

Heart pounding, she glanced around. She'd seen wanted posters for her brothers but never one for herself.

Until today.

She ripped the notice away from its pinnings and read the small print at the bottom:

Suspect was last seen wearing canvas pants, slouch hat, and red leather boots.

The sketch wasn't a good likeness, but the description was accurate.

Whipping off her hat, she let her hair fall loosely to her shoulders. But there wasn't anything to be done about her pants or boots.

She crumpled the notice in her hands and stuffed it in her pocket. Suddenly it seemed that every man and woman was looking straight at her.

Though the sun beat down with unforgiving heat, she shivered. The busy street that had moments earlier wrapped her in anonymity now lurked with danger.

Could the man in a long black coat and gray pants be a Wells Fargo agent?

Were the two men dressed in brown and wearing plug hats Pinkerton detectives? And what about the tall, broad-shouldered man with the tawny mustache and goatee? Could that possibly be Judge Parker himself?

Feeling trapped, she glanced up and down the busy street. She spotted what surely was a marshal heading her way and quickly ducked through the door of the nearest open shop. A jangle of bells and the smell of sweet lavender greeted her.

Satisfied that no one had followed her, she glanced around the tiny, cramped shop. Rough wood shelves piled high with bolts of fabric lined the walls on both sides. On the back wall, spools of thread dangled from little wooden pegs, interspersed with trails of colorful ribbons and delicate lace.

A woman with hips wide as a depot stove bent over the counter, her graying hair a mass of spring-tight curls. A sign read Mrs. Springlock's Dry Goods. If the tightly curled hair was any indication, the woman could be no other than the proprietor herself.

"May I help you?" she mumbled through a mouth full of pins. Judging from the look of disapproval on her matronly face as she stared at Sarah's tousled red hair, she didn't much relish the thought.

Sarah stood behind a stack of fabric bolts to hide her canvas pants from the woman's prying eyes. "Just lookin'," she said.

Then she saw something that practically made her knees buckle beneath the heaviness of her heart. A dress similar to the one Justin had salvaged from the ill-fated wagon train hung from a nearby hook. But it was the color that tore at her soul and caused her heart to squeeze in anguish. It was the exact same blue as the dress ravished by locusts.

The sleeves were puffed at the shoulder and cuffs, and edged with blue satin ribbon. The pleats on the fitted bodice hid a row of fine china buttons.

She regretted not trying the first dress on for Justin. She regretted a lot of things.

She pulled the dress off the wooden

hanger and held it in front of her to hide her masculine attire from the woman in back. Her appearance in the mirror shocked her. For the longest while all she could do was stare at the unfamiliar image of herself. If this wasn't an answer to a prayer, she didn't know what was. The old preacher had told her to watch for signs.

But a wanted poster? A sign from God?

Shaken by the thought, she called, "Is this dress for sale?"

Mrs. Springlock hesitated as if to decide how she wanted to answer the question. "For a price," she said finally through stiffened lips. She pulled the pins one by one out of her mouth and jabbed them into the hem of a woolen cape.

"A price, eh?"

The shopkeeper pulled the last of the pins from her mouth. "I only sell to women of discriminating taste."

"Well, I'll be," Sarah said, unable to believe her good fortune. "Then I'm the person you're lookin' for. I'm 'bout as incriminatin' as you can get."

Sarah undid her gun belt and laid it next to a bolt of dark chambray. The woman's mouth fell open, and her face turned white as baker's dough.

Sarah, not wishing to frighten her, quickly tried to reassure her. "Don't you go worryin' none, you hear? I know how to use it. Why, I once shot a cigar out of a man's mouth from thirty yards away."

Mrs. Springlock's eyes bulged like the yolks of two fried eggs. Taking this as a sign that the seamstress was duly impressed with her skill as a marksman, Sarah pulled off her clothes right in the middle of the store. But before she had a chance to tug the dress down over her head, the proprietor rounded the counter and gasped.

"Oh my!" Mrs. Springlock exclaimed, her hands flying to her chest. Her curls bounced up and down like broken mattress springs. "What a disgrace. You should be ashamed of yourself."

At first Sarah thought the fool woman was still fretting over the gun, but then she noticed the seamstress staring openly at her unmentionables—or rather lack of them.

The way the women carried on, you'd think not wearing undergarments was as foolhardy as walking around without a weapon.

Ignoring the woman's scandalized gasps, Sarah slid the dress over her head and pushed her arms into the sleeves. She stood before the full-length mirror to work the tiny buttons into the holes. She viewed herself from every angle. Never before had she known the luxury of a full-length mirror.

"Will you look at that? I can see myself comin' and goin'." She lifted the hem of the skirt and wrinkled her brow. "I'd have to grow another coupla feet for this dress to fit. Are your incriminatin' customers really so tall?"

Mrs. Springlock gave a haughty sniff. "The skirt is designed to be worn over *three* petticoats."

"Three?" Sarah wasn't sure she heard right. It seemed like a waste to wear three of anything. "I ain't owned a single petticoat in my life," she admitted.

Robert had given her money, but she hadn't planned on purchasing anything so frivolous as a dress, let alone a petticoat. She didn't feel right about spending stolen money. The truth was that she never did. She hated watching her brothers throw money around on gambling and other vices. Though George offered to buy her pretty things, she never took one penny more than she needed for bare necessities. Now, however, it seemed like she had no other choice.

"Where money's concerned, I've always been a tight spitter," she explained, twisting and turning. She debated what to do. Finally, the vision of herself in the mirror was simply too much of a temptation to pass up.

"I'll take three of those there petticoats. If I'm gonna buy me a dress, I might as well go whole hog."

While Sarah worked the ruffled layers under her dress, the seamstress hovered nervously, wringing her hands and casting anxious glances at the door as if she feared the arrival of other customers.

"You don't understand. My dresses are designed for *ladies.*"

"Don't surprise me none," Sarah

replied. She stared at her reflection in the mirror, wishing with all her heart that a certain handsome preacher could see her now. "If this ain't a miracle!" she announced, feeling suddenly lighthearted. "I'm a full-fledged lady!"

The woman stood staring at her with hands placed firmly on her wide hips. "Not with that hair, you're not."

Sarah touched the unruly mass with her hand and frowned in dismay. "It's the only hair I've got."

Mrs. Springlock's face softened as if she suddenly felt sorry for her. "Come in back. I'll see what I can do."

Sarah followed her through a narrow door to a room that was even more cramped than the one in front. She stood before a beveled glass mirror while the proprietor brushed her hair back and created smooth curls with a flame-heated curling rod. After a while, the older woman stepped back and nodded approvingly at her own work.

"You clean up mighty nice," she said.

Sarah turned her head from side to another. "Looks like I've got me a head full of sausages," she said, grinning.

Mrs. Springlock smiled back at her.

Sarah walked around the room, testing the feel of soft fabric around her ankles. She never felt anything quite like it. "It's gonna take some gettin' used to."

"If you want to be a lady, you best stop walking like a man."

Sarah stopped midstep. "It's the only walk I got."

"Nonsense. You just need to work on it. Take small, dainty steps." Mrs. Springlock demonstrated, her bulky hips swaying like an old mule's rump.

Sarah tried her best to imitate the woman. "I feel like a hog on a saddle," she said, describing her discomfort.

The woman stared at Sarah's feet. "It would help if you wore decent footwear. Those boots—"

"I ain't parting with my boots," Sarah said. The hem of the dress nearly reached the floor, hiding most if not all of her boots.

Mrs. Springlock made a face. "If you want to be a lady, you must refrain from using the word 'ain't.' It's a contraction that should be avoided at all costs. The correct terms are 'am not,' 'is not,' 'have not,' or 'are not.'"

"Whoa!" Sarah's head spun. "That's a whole lot of 'nots' I'm gonna have to remember. If you need that many words to replace 'ain't,' then lady talk sure ain't . . . am not . . . efficient."

"Is not," Mrs. Springlock said sharply. "*Isn't* efficient."

Sarah sighed. She wasn't sure that she would ever learn to walk and talk like a lady, but she sure did look like one. Justin said that no one would hang a lady, and she wanted so much to believe he was right.

She stood staring at herself in the mirror for the longest while. Was the color of the dress purely coincidence— or something else?

Watch for signs, the old preacher had said. But what if she was reading them all wrong? Still . . .

She closed her eyes. Dare she take a chance? She'd told Justin that faith was enough for him, but would it be enough for her?

Heart pounding, she finally made up her mind. She pulled her wad of money out of her overall pocket with shaky hands and paid for the dress and unmentionables.

Then she buckled her gun belt around her middle.

Mrs. Springlock stared down her considerable nose. "A lady doesn't wear a gun belt," she sniffed.

"This lady does," Sarah said. Talking and walking like a lady was one thing, but giving up her weapon and boots was where she drew the line. She pushed the remaining money into the pocket of her dress.

"What's the fastest way to get to Rocky Creek?"

Mrs. Springlock put the cash into her money box and handed Sarah her change. "Take the ferry across the river and catch the train to Texarkana. From there you can take a stage to Texas."

Sarah thanked her, took a deep breath to brace herself, and left the shop.

Twenty-two

It took Justin a full day just to clear the rubble from inside the church and another day to rehang the door and replace the missing floorboards. The pews and piano were damaged beyond repair.

He worked long hours, but his heart wasn't in it. He questioned God's plan for him, questioned his ability to serve the people of Rocky Creek. Questioned why God brought Sarah into his life, only to take her away.

He tried to pray, but the words wouldn't come. Each night upon retiring, Elizabeth asleep at the foot of his bed in her little crate, he sought comfort from the Bible, but doubts and questions continued to plague him.

After another sleepless night, he sat at the kitchen table picking at the breakfast Ma had cooked for him. Since saying good-bye to Sarah even his appetite began to suffer.

He made a list of all the things that still had to be done to ready the church for worship. The list seemed endless. For every chore he crossed off, he thought of two more to take its place.

Next to him, Ma rocked Elizabeth in her arms. All rosy from her bath, the baby smelled like a flower garden after a spring shower.

He leaned over and tickled her under her little pink chin, and her bowlike mouth curved up.

He sat back in astonishment. "Look at that," he said, beaming. "She smiled at me."

"Just a little indigestion," Ma said.

Undaunted, he leaned forward again and made silly goo-goo sounds that would normally have made him feel like a fool. He was rewarded with another toothless grin. The softening in his heart pained him only because Sarah wasn't there to see Elizabeth smile.

Satisfied, he sat back. "See? What did I tell you?"

This time Ma didn't argue with him. "It's good to know that somethin' can put a smile on *your* face."

Elizabeth wrinkled up her little nose and started to fuss. "I think it's time for someone's nap," Ma said. She rose and placed Elizabeth in the little crate and carried it to the other room where it was quiet. She returned moments later and glanced at Justin's chore list.

"I think I can round up chairs for the church," she said. "How many do you need?"

Justin couldn't begin to guess. "A hundred?"

Ma looked dubious. "You'll be lucky if anyone shows up the first day."

Justin's disappointment must have shown, for she leaned forward and patted his arm. "A few will come out of curiosity, I suppose, you being a new preacher and all." In a more cheerful voice, she added, "If you want, you can move the piano from my parlor to the church. It's out of tune, but it's better than nothing."

He mopped up the runny egg yolks with a piece of bread. "I'm much obliged. Do you play?"

The question seemed to startle her. "Me? I play a little. Nothing religious, mind you. Our piano player Mrs. Kimble died last year, bless her soul. I'll ask around. There's bound to be someone else in town who can play."

Justin stared down at his list. "I don't know what I would have done without your help. I especially appreciate you taking care of Elizabeth. I haven't had time to look for a home for her."

It wasn't only time that kept him from searching for suitable parents. After losing Sarah, he simply didn't have the heart to part with Elizabeth too. After the smile she gave him that morning, he wondered if he ever would.

Ma sat down at the table opposite him. "I hope you don't judge our town by the condition of the church."

"I'm not here to judge," he said. Still, he couldn't help but think that had the citizens of Rocky Creek built fewer saloons, more time would have been left for the church. But he wasn't about to share that opinion with his kindhearted landlady.

"If you don't mind my saying so, you look like something the cat dragged in," she said.

Justin grunted. "I've not been sleeping well."

Ma gave a knowing nod. "She must have been some woman."

Justin looked up in surprise, his fork held in midair. "What makes you think it's a woman keeping me awake?"

"When a man spends half the night pacing the floor, it's generally because of some petticoat."

Justin smiled at her choice of words. *Petticoat* was hardly a word that came to mind when he thought of Sarah.

Ma folded her arms on the table. "Love is like a soft mattress. It's easy to fall into but near impossible to get out of."

Justin lay his fork on his plate and wiped his mouth on his napkin. "God called me to be a clergyman," he said, more for his own benefit than for his landlady's. *"That's* what I need to think about. God's work."

Ma gave him a tender, motherly look. "Seems to me like you're putting the cart before the horse."

Justin raised a questioning brow. "I'm sorry?"

"All I'm saying is, God made you a man before He made you a preacher."

Twenty-three

Sarah stepped out of the stagecoach in the center of Rocky Creek and felt a surge of panic. The town looked exactly as she remembered it, arousing the same old fears.

Memories of the trial and verdict assailed her. The last time she'd left town, she was on a fast horse and dodging bullets. She'd hoped never to see Rocky Creek again, but here she was of her own free will and shaking like a quivering bow.

Main Street was deserted, the residents inside away from the hot August sun. Hugged on three sides by rolling hills, the town appeared serene, but she knew better.

She wondered where Justin was. She didn't want to see him yet, not while her future looked so bleak. She was taking a big chance on coming here, and she desperately wanted to believe that she hadn't misread the signs. She told herself that if Justin was right about the town not hanging a lady, then she had nothing to worry about. Maybe then she could clear her name and have a chance for a normal life.

Oh, Justin, please be right.

Just thinking of Justin gave her back the courage that had near deserted her. She could do this. She *must* do this. For his sake as well as her own.

The town marshal's office was located directly across from the stage stop. She stepped off the wooden boardwalk, her pounding heart as erratic as an unbroken horse.

Since the town was deserted, she abandoned the confining ladylike steps she'd tried to emulate. Instead, she kicked up her boots in high-steppin' strides and crossed Main Street.

Before entering the office, she raised her eyes to heaven and braced herself with prayer. "God, I know I've asked for Your help a lot lately. I'm sure You got a lot of other people to help, and I don't want to take unfair advantage or anythin'. But if You have another one of those miracles lyin' around that You don't need, I'd be much obliged if You'd send it my way. Amen."

She took a deep breath and went over the words she had copied down from a newspaper on the train ride to Texarkana and practiced in her head. Pressing against the butterflies in her stomach with one hand, she threw open the door with the other.

Marshal Briggs sat behind his desk, his feet propped up, a hole centered on the sole of each boot. At sight of her, he quickly dropped his feet to the wooden floor with a thump and looked her up and down like a man buying livestock.

"May I help you, ma'am?"

Ma'am. No lawman had ever addressed her with such regard before. Encouraged, Sarah closed the door behind her. Standing proper as she imagined a lady to stand, hands folded demurely in front, she said, "I wish to turn myself in."

The marshal's bushy gray eyebrows rose so high that only his receding hairline kept them from disappearing altogether. His eyes then crinkled as if he was privy to a joke.

"And what crime are you guilty of, ma'am?" he asked, his voice edged with sarcasm. "Failing to do your wifely duties?" He winked. "Spreading vicious gossip?"

The law man's mocking tone was downright insulting, and she could feel her anger beginning to flare. Her future was on the line, and she was in no mood for snide remarks. She threw back her head and nailed him with a scathing look that was more characteristic of her true nature than her earlier demeanor had been.

"My name is Sarah Prescott."

The smile slid off his face as quickly as a greenhorn off a bucking horse. This time, he not only looked shocked, his eyes practically popped out of his head.

"You're the Prescott woman?" he sputtered.

"I am," she said, keeping her voice steady.

He rubbed his chin. "You don't look like her."

"I'm her, all right," she said. "Since I'm now a lady, I demand all charges be dropped." Pleased that she had remembered the exact words she'd practiced, she gave herself a silent pat on the back.

Marshal Briggs scratched his head. "I don't follow. What does one have to do with the other?"

It was a question she hadn't expected and she wasn't sure how best to answer it. "I've heard it on good authority that no one hangs a lady."

"You don't say?"

"It's not right."

He rubbed his chin. "And who might that authority be?"

She hesitated. "I . . ." Drats! She couldn't remember the word Mrs. Springlock used to describe the word *ain't*. Contraption? Conception? Contraction? Yes, that was it, contraction.

"I is not—" She stopped and tried again. "I are not—" The marshal frowned and she sighed. This could take all day.

Choosing clarity over proper English, she blurted out, "I *ain't* at liberty to say."

If Briggs noticed her lapse in grammar, he didn't show it. "In that case, I'm gonna have to carry out the judge's orders."

"But I'm innocent, and you have no right to hang me."

"You're a Prescott," he said as if that were explanation enough.

"You can't hang me 'cuz of my family name."

He pawed through a pile of papers. Finding what he was looking for, he waved a wrinkled document in the air. "I've got an order here that says I can." He tossed the paper aside.

He scrutinized her. "Speaking of family, where's my brother-in-law? He sent a wire saying he'd captured you and was bringin' you in."

"Y-your b-brother-in-law?" she stammered. She felt her hopes sink.

"U.S. Marshal Owen is married to my sister."

She bit her lip, her mind scrambling.

"Well?" he said impatiently.

Since there didn't seem to be any nice way of wording it, she decided to come right out and say it. "I-I'm sorry to tell you, but he's dead. Died in Missouri from a bullet wound, he did."

The marshal's face turned beet red and the veins in his neck stood out in thick blue cords. "You killed him!" He rose to his feet, sending his chair flying backward.

Startled by the unexpected accusation, she was momentarily speechless. She stared at him in disbelief. It had never occurred to her that she would be blamed for the marshal's death.

"I did no such thing," she shot back, "and don't you go sayin' I did, you hear?"

Hands on his desk he leaned forward. "The only reason he left Texas was because of you. In my book, that makes you responsible for his death."

Panicking, she spun around and frantically tried to escape. Her fancy sleeve caught on the door latch, and before she could pull herself free, the marshal was on her like a hawk on a snake.

She fought him off with everything she had, kicking and screaming all the while. Papers scattered, hats flew off nails, and the potbellied stove tilted to one side.

She could have escaped had it not been for all the layers of lace and silk beneath her dress, which slowed her down.

After much fumbling, Briggs finally managed to slam her up against the wall and snap handcuffs around her wrists. He was clearly winded, and he slumped against the wall next to her, trying to catch his breath.

"What a pity I can only hang you once," he gasped.

Not wanting to give him the satisfaction of thinking he had the upper hand, she lifted her head in open defiance. "I reckon that gives me the advantage."

His gaze sharpened. "How do you mean? Advantage?"

"There ain't no limit on how many times a person can escape."

The marshal somewhat recovered, grabbed hold of her arm. "There isn't gonna be any escaping. Not this time!"

Twenty-four

Justin hammered the last nail in place and stood the pulpit upright. He wiggled it back and forth. It seemed sturdy enough, though it needed paint.

He stood behind it and gazed at the mismatched chairs that his landlady had rounded up. He imagined the church filled with people. Families with small children. Older folks. Young. He thought of the couples he would join together in holy matrimony, the babies he would baptize.

Maybe once he started preaching again, the aching loneliness and despair would go away, and he would better understand God's plan for him. Maybe then he could sleep again and stop thinking about Sarah.

Today, as always whenever he thought of her, he said a silent prayer, ending with the plea, *Lord, keep her safe.*

He forced his troubling thoughts away. Not now, not here. Today, his thoughts didn't belong to Sarah. Couldn't. Today he had to concentrate on spreading God's Word to the citizens of Rocky Creek.

He donned his black frock coat that Ma had cleaned and ironed for him, picked up the Bible, and waited as he had so often waited on Sunday morning.

It was almost 10 a.m. Soon worshippers would fill the church—and yet he felt none of the eager anticipation he normally felt on Sunday mornings.

He closed his eyes and imagined himself back in Boston, back in the church he loved so much. He could practically smell the polished wood pews and waxy scent of burning candles. Hear the resonating chords of the organ.

From his distant memory came the

rattle of carriage wheels on cobble-
stones. He could almost hear the rustle
of silken gowns and feathered hats, the
tapping sound of high-buttoned shoes
on white marble floors.

Feeling the familiar sense of joy and
expectancy return, he smiled broadly
and opened his eyes. He walked to the
door to greet the first arrivals and stared
outside. Much to his surprise, not a single soul could be seen. Ma had warned
him that few if any townsfolk would
show, but he had refused to believe it.

He'd tacked posters around town and
was confident that at least some worshippers would attend service, if for no
other reason than curiosity. He pulled
his watch from his waistcoat pocket and
checked the time. It was almost ten fifteen.

Outside, the dirt road leading up the
hill was deserted. Neither horse nor
wagon headed his way.

He walked to the end of the narrow
dirt path. Loud voices, laughter, and
music floated up from the saloons
along Main Street. The revelers never
stopped, but today was Sunday, the

Lord's Day. Justin noted with surprise that these people treated the Sabbath like any other day of the week.

Never would he have imagined such a thing in Boston. There, blue laws required saloons and other businesses to remain closed on the Sabbath.

He stood on the hill overlooking the town and felt utterly alone and disheartened. "What am I doing here?" he shouted to the sky. "Why me? I don't understand these people. What could I possibly give them?"

In the stillness of his troubled mind, he thought he heard a voice—her voice—seeming to come out of nowhere. "Your faith."

He spun around, knowing even as he scanned the surrounding hillside, she was lost to him.

Shaken, he turned back to the town. It was then that an idea came to him: *If they won't come to me, then I will go to them.*

The idea surprised, shocked him. Never did he have to seek out worshippers in Boston. Never, for that matter, did he have to do much more than stand behind a pulpit to spread God's Word. His ministry seldom went beyond the church walls, except for an occasional visitation. His convictions had been strong, but he had never really put his faith in action. Saddened by his past failures as a pastor, he resolved to do things differently here in Rocky Creek.

Feeling more vitalized than he'd felt in ages, he hurried back into the church and grabbed his hat. With his Bible still in hand, he dashed back outside.

Moments later, he rode down the center of Main Street and tethered his horse in front of Jake's Saloon, by far the noisiest saloon of the lot. The place was packed.

Justin stood outside the batwing doors and almost lost his nerve. *"Faith,"* Sarah had said. *"You can offer them your faith."*

An old man sat in a rocking chair in front of the saloon smoking his pipe. "The last stranger who walked in there without a gun was carried out feetfirst."

"Thank you, sir, but I don't need a gun. I have something better."

With that, he walked in and stood by

the door until his eyes adjusted to the dim light. At first, no one paid attention to him.

Men squeezed around square faro tables placing their bets. Others stood at the bar downing whiskey like water. Women in garish gowns flitted from one man to another, coyly smiling from behind feathered fans.

Justin walked toward the bar. He was taller than most of the other men, and dressed in his dark trousers and frock coat, he stood out like an elephant in a herd of cows.

The room suddenly grew quiet as all eyes turned in his direction.

"Gentlemen," he said, tipping his hat. "And ladies. As I'm sure you've heard, I'm your new pastor." He glanced around the room. "Reverend Justin Wells at your service. I would like to welcome you all on this glorious day that the Lord has made."

Silence followed his announcement. No one seemed to know what to make of the preacher's presence.

Finally, Link Haskell, whom Justin recognized as the blacksmith who had welded metal door hinges for the church, raised his shot glass. "Welcome, preacher. Why don't you belly up to the bar and join us in a toast?"

"Thank you, kindly, but I don't imbibe. Especially when I'm working."

"You working?" someone slurred.

"That I am," Justin said. "Preachers are allowed to work on the Sabbath. Now, then. If you will kindly bow your head in prayer, we'll begin."

Stunned silence followed his proclamation. Mouths rounded in disbelief. Jaws dropped. One jowly man rolled his eyes. A drunk raised his head from a table, saliva dribbling from the corner of his mouth. Women in low-cut gowns peered at him from painted faces, their feathered fans beating what little air was left in the room.

Finally, a pale-faced man stood. "I ain't listenin' to no Bible thumper." He started toward the door, and others stood to follow.

"Hold it right there!" The voice belonged to a tall, bearded man wearing a rebel kepi cap. His long hair tied back, he walked with a limp. He held a rifle pointed in such a way that no one doubted he meant business.

Justin didn't know if it was the kind of rifle that required skill or luck, but no one in the room seemed willing to find out—he least of all. One by one, the men sat down again and the women backed up against the wall.

His finger on the trigger, the gunman tipped his hat to Justin and introduced himself. "Everyone 'round here calls me Timber Joe on account of my wooden leg. So go ahead, Preacher, and do what you came to do." To emphasize his words, Timber Joe pointed the rifle at Justin momentarily before leveling it around the room.

"Uh . . ." Justin cleared his throat and brushed the back of his hand across his damp forehead. He'd heard of shotgun weddings, but this was the first he'd heard of a shotgun sermon.

"Please join me in prayer."

He looked at each face in return and was greeted with eyes full of resentment and, in some cases, downright hostility.

Timber Joe limped around the room, the thumping sound of his wooden limb muffled by the sawdust on the floor. He nudged any slacker with the barrel of his rifle and soon, even the most stubborn of men had complied. Satisfied, Timber Joe spun around, pointing his gun straight at Justin.

Justin cleared his voice, lowered his head, and hastily began, "Dear heavenly Father . . ."

Sarah called him long-winded, but today called for as much wind as he could muster. God didn't need to hear his prayer as much as the townsfolk did. Judging by what little he knew of the town, there was a lot to pray for.

"Amen," he said at last and a sigh of relief circled the room. Anyone who so much as shifted in his chair found himself staring down the barrel of the gunman's rifle.

Timber Joe glanced around the room and, apparently satisfied, nodded. "It's all yours, preacher."

Justin opened his Bible to Exodus 20:8 and read the verse aloud. "'Remember the sabbath day, to keep it holy.'"

While he read, Jake's customers

sat attentively. If anyone so much as scratched his nose, Timber Joe's rifle swung into action.

After a while, Justin closed the Bible. "How many of you consider yourselves honest?"

Hands shot up all around the room. A homemade faro cheating device fell to the floor, but no one moved to pick it up.

"I see we didn't need Timber Joe's help with that one," Justin said with a wry smile.

A few brave souls laughed, but most remained stoic, bodies rigid, ready to escape at the first opportunity.

Justin continued, "So what we have here is a room full of honest people stealing a day that belongs to God." It felt good to be preaching again. Never did he preach to a more attentive audience, thanks to Timber Joe, and he made the most of it.

Dead silence followed his sermon. Justin pulled off his hat. "God gives freely, and it's now our chance to give freely back. The church is in dire need of windows and pews. And I'm sure there are many in this town in need of your kind generosity."

He passed his hat to the nearest person, a skinny man with a sweeping mustache and bobbing Adam's apple. The man stared down into the crown, then passed it to the man next to him. "I ain't got no money."

Timber Joe was on him in a flash, rifle leveled at the man's throat. "Look again, Moe."

Moe started to argue, then apparently thought better of it. He reached into the pocket of his pants and produced a shiny gold coin. With more prodding from Timber Joe, he reached over and dropped it into the empty crown.

By the time Justin's hat made its way back to him, it was overflowing. He gave the benediction. In Boston, people knew to leave following the blessing, but here no one made a move. All eyes watched Timber Joe.

Taking the hint, Joe slipped the rifle strap over his shoulder. No other invitation was needed. Every patron jumped up and made a mad dash for the door, knocking over tables and chairs in their haste to escape.

Timber Joe nodded in satisfaction and tugged on the beak of his gray kepi hat. "You sure do know how to empty a saloon," he drawled. "We could have used you in the war."

Justin grinned. "You think my sermon was that good, huh?"

Timber Joe nodded. "I'd say it was good enough to torture a whole roomful of Yankee prisoners."

Justin's smile died.

Timber Joe slapped him on the back. "You might consider hiring me permanently. That way, it won't matter if you preach good or bad. They'll listen either way."

"I prefer to use more gentle persuasion," Justin said as tactfully as he could. Not wanting to sound ungrateful, Justin thanked him.

"My pleasure." Timber Joe touched the visor of his cap in a salute. "Let me know if you change your mind." He limped out of the saloon, leaving only Justin and Jake, the bar's proprietor, behind.

Jake spit a yellow stream into a tarnished brass spittoon. He then wiped the bar down with a dirty rag, watching Justin with a disapproving frown. A heavy-set man with squinty eyes, a pointed chin and drooping mustache, he clearly did not appreciate Justin's turning his saloon into a place of worship.

"The man's crazy," the bartender muttered. "The war did somethin' to his brain. He acts like he's still fightin' them Yankees."

"I guess we're all fighting our own private wars," Justin said.

He stared down at his overflowing hat. He still didn't believe how much money he'd collected. Not even Christmas services in Boston commanded so much generosity. Nor, for that matter, had he ever known a more attentive audience. As much as he hated to admit it, there was something to be said for Timber Joe's unorthodox methods.

Justin stuffed his pockets with the collection, placed his hat on his head, thanked Jake for his hospitality, and walked outside.

He was greeted by the same old man on his rocking chair. "You're still alive."

"Yeah," Justin said. "I guess I am."

"Hank Applegate's the name." Squinting beneath the brim of his old leather hat, he clamped down on his jaw, letting his toothless gums grind against each other. "That was some preachin' job you did, young man."

Justin tipped his hat. "Much obliged." Justin eyed the saloon across the street. If he cut his sermon down, he could probably empty the remaining six saloons by suppertime.

Applegate studied him from watery eyes. "Don't go judgin' this here town too harshly."

Justin looked the man square in the face. "I'm not here to judge. That's God's job."

"Reckon I know judgin' when I sees it. You're askin' yourself what kind of town neglects its church?"

Justin rubbed his chin and felt a pang of guilt. "I'm afraid the thought did cross my mind," he admitted.

Applegate gave a sage nod. "The folks around here have had some mighty tough times. Kind of makes you lose faith, you know what I mean? We lost a bunch of boys in the war. Cattle ranches went bankrupt after an outbreak of Texas fever. Entire families were wiped out by a smallpox epidemic. A tornado ripped through here three years ago. Then there was the flood year before last. Water swept down Main Street like nobody's bus'ness. Before that, there was all that Indian trouble."

Justin didn't know what to say. People in Boston had problems, of course, but their problems seemed mild compared to what this little town had gone through.

He gazed up and down the street, seeing things in a different light. Instead of saloons, he saw buildings where hurting people went to drown their sorrows. He was reminded of his own careless youth following the death of his sisters.

All at once, he knew why God had sent him to that town. Who better to lead the way out of the darkness than someone who had traveled that very same route?

What he didn't know was how to go about restoring the town's faith.

"I'm not judging the town," Justin said again, and this time he meant it.

"Well if you ain't now, you will be." Applegate rocked his chair and it squeaked beneath his weight. "Day after tomorrow, Rocky Creek is gonna hang a woman."

Justin stared at him. "A . . . A woman, did you say?"

Applegate nodded and ground his gums together. "Don't look so shocked, Reverend. Some say the woman's only gittin' what's comin' to her. She's a member of the Prescott gang, and—"

Justin didn't wait to hear the rest.

Twenty-five

At first Justin thought someone had made a mistake. The woman's face was hidden in the shadows, but he could see the ruffled hem of her skirt. It wasn't Sarah!

With a sense of relief, he moved closer to the tiny jail cell, thinking that whoever she was, she could probably use some spiritual counseling.

He squinted to get a better look. The narrow band of light that streamed through the square cut high in the gray stone wall failed to reach the cot.

"Hello," he called softly. "My name is Reverend Wells."

The shadow on the cot moved. "Justin?"

His heart skipped a beat. "Sarah!"

Battling yards of ruffles and lace, Sarah jumped to her feet, rushed across the tiny cell, and grabbed hold of the iron bars. Under normal circumstances, he would have laughed at the feminine fussiness that weighed her down. Today he could only gaze at her, absorbing every detail of the face he had dreamed about since the day they parted.

He reached through the bars to grab hold of her hands, and they both started talking at once.

"I—"

"I—"

He fell silent, and for the longest while, he could only gaze at her. "I never thought I'd see you again," he whispered at last, his voice hoarse.

"I missed you so much."

Suddenly, neither one of them could get their words out fast enough.

"I couldn't stop thinking about you," he said.

"I ain't hardly slept."

"I should never have let you go."

"How did you know I was here?"

"It's a small town," he replied. "News travels fast."

"Knowing you, you probably think this is some sort of divine intervention," she said.

"Interruption," he said, correcting her out of habit. Realizing his error, he laughed.

She laughed too. "I've been practicin' my words. Tryin' to talk like a lady."

She wore a pretty blue frock the very same color as her eyes. The dress swept around her in gentle folds, the fabric whispering each time she moved. He noticed now that she still wore her red boots. The sight of scuffed toes beneath the ruffles of her dress made him smile.

"You've always been a lady to me," he said, aching with a need to hold her in his arms. Even her hair was different, falling gracefully down her back in silken strands of gleaming red curls. He lifted his hand to her cheek. "You're so beautiful."

"And you're so handsome," she whispered back, pressing both her hands against his.

"Are . . . are you all right?"

"I've seen better days." She searched his face. "Elizabeth?" He could see the pain it caused her to say the baby's name. "Did you . . . find her a good family?"

He shook his head. "Not yet. My landlady is taking care of her. Wait till you see her. She smiled at me."

"Oh!" Tears sprang to her eyes. "I wish I could—"

"You will," he said. "You will."

She dropped her hands to her side and shook her head. "It's bad, Justin. It's really, really bad."

He pulled his hand away. "I don't understand. How did you get here? I thought you were in Fort Smith with your brothers. I thought you were safe."

A shadow clouded her face. "They ain't in Fort Smith. I don't know what happened to them. I'm really worried."

"But this still doesn't explain how you got here."

"I turned myself in."

"What?" He gaped at her. Sarah was

impulsive, but never did he imagine she would do something so foolhardy. "Why . . . why would you do that?"

"I couldn't stand bein' away from you. And you said that no one would hang a lady."

He moaned and slapped his forehead. "This is all my fault."

"Don't go thinkin' that, you hear? That fool marshal's to blame, not you." She pinched the fabric of her skirt and held it out. "I'm all gussied up. Even put on *three* petticoats. But that don't make no difference to the marshal. I'm tellin' you, the man don't know dung from honey."

"Sarah, if anything happens to you—" Never did he think they would actually *hang* a woman. Such a thing would not happen in Boston, but Texas was a horse of a different breed, one that he obviously knew nothing about.

"Don't go blamin' yourself, you hear? It's my own fool fault that I'm in this mess. I didn't read the signs right."

"Signs? What signs?"

Ignoring his question, she continued. "I'm trying to put my trust in God, just like you said I should."

He nodded his head. "That's good, Sarah."

She looked at him long and hard. "No matter what happens, it was worth seein' your face again." Her voice broke. "Do . . . do you think I can see Elizabeth before they . . . ?"

"I'll bring her, but . . . they aren't going to—" He couldn't bring himself to say it. He pressed his forehead against an iron bar. "Remember, you said you were going to put your trust in God."

"I'm tryin'—I really am. I don't know if even He can save me." Her voice faltered. "I don't know if anyone can. The marshal's plumb got his heart set on tyin' a bow around my neck. Said I killed his brother-in-law."

Justin lifted his head. "His brother-in-law?"

"U.S. Marshal Owen was hitched to Marshal Briggs' sister."

A knot tightened in the pit of his stomach. This was worse than he'd thought. "But you didn't kill him. You tried to save his life." His thoughts raced. "How does he know about the marshal's death?"

"I told him," she said. "He asked me where Owen was and I told him."

He reached through the bars and gently brushed his fingers against her cool pale cheek.

"God will help us find a way to save you. Elizabeth needs you."

A shadow creased her forehead, and her lips trembled. "I told you, she needs someone better to be her ma. She don't need the likes of—"

"*I* need you," he said. "I love you."

She glanced over his shoulder to make sure that no one had heard. "Shh. If they know the town's new preacher takes a fancy to an outlaw, there ain't no tellin' what they'll do."

"I don't care," he said.

"I do," she whispered, and her eyes filled with tears.

"Sarah," Justin pleaded. "Please don't cry."

She pulled her hand away from his. "See what happens when you dress like a lady? I'm as leaky as an old water pump."

He dug through all the bills and coins in his coat pocket for his neatly folded handkerchief and then wiped away her tears. "I promise, with God's help, I'll find a way to get you out of this."

She managed a wan smile. "I reckon it's gonna take a miracle to get me out of this mess."

"Miracles happen," he said.

She wiped away the last of her tears, and her smile widened. A look of shining hope had replaced the earlier fear. "You wouldn't be pullin' my leg now, would you?"

He shook his head. "Miracles happen. You know they do. Mira the goat is living proof of that. Remember the ten plagues of Egypt and the parting of the Red Sea?"

"Don't forget the eighty-year-old woman havin' a baby."

Grinning, he squeezed her hand. Suddenly, something occurred to him.

"Sarah, you've just given me an idea. I think there might be a way to save you."

Anxious to put his plan into action, he spun around and called for the marshal to let him out, rattling the bars on the outer door with impatience.

"Wait!" she called after him, hands on her hips. "You can't say somethin' like that and take off, you hear? How do you expect to save me?"

He turned. "It's easy," he said with a grin. "All I need is God's help—and a quick tongue." He laughed at the expression on her face. "I'm not sure about the quick tongue, but I'll give it my best shot."

Twenty-six

Marshal Briggs sat with his feet on the desk, his hands folded across the generous mound of his stomach. Tapping his fingers together, he stared at Justin like a cat trying to decide whether a mouse was worthy of attention.

Briggs had permitted Justin to visit the prisoner out of respect for the church, but his disapproval of the preacher's visit was etched in every pore of his sunbaked skin. His mustache twitching, he indicated the ladder-back chair in front of his desk with a nod of his head.

"Did you get a confession from her, Reverend? Did she tell you how she killed my sister's husband in cold blood?"

Justin sat down and balanced his hat on his knee. He gave the marshal careful regard before responding. After what happened in Boston, he wasn't eager to divulge having spent all that time alone with Sarah. It wasn't only his own reputation that worried him; he hoped to prove Sarah's innocence and, for that, he needed credibility. Any scandalous gossip about the two of them could only hurt his cause.

"I'm sorry about the death of your brother-in-law, and my sympathies are with your sister." Briggs said nothing, and Justin continued, "Miss Prescott had nothing to do with Owen's death. The two of them were ambushed, and Owen was shot in the shoulder. Sarah . . . Miss Prescott did everything in her power to save him."

"That's what she told you, eh?" Briggs dropped his feet to the floor and he hit the desk with his fist. "My brother-in-law left Texas for one purpose and one purpose alone, to track down Sarah Prescott. I don't care who fired the actual bullet. I hold the Prescott family personally responsible for his death."

"While the real killer goes free?"

The marshal's eyes glittered. "I'll have them all before I'm through, don't you worry none about that."

Justin fingered his hat. "Revenge is a poor excuse for justice."

The lawman's mouth twitched as if he fought to control his anger. "It would be to your advantage to stick to preachin' and let me worry about the likes of Sarah Prescott."

"I don't know about Texas, but in Boston, that would be considered a threat."

"Call it what you want," Briggs said, his mouth twisted in contempt. "Owen was a fine man. He was also a husband and father," Briggs said. "Thanks to that . . . that woman, my sister is a widow and his children orphans."

Justin chose his words carefully. He didn't want to say anything that could be used against Sarah. "Miss Prescott hasn't been charged with Owen's death."

"More's the pity." Briggs picked up a

paper from his desk and waved it. "This here is a proclamation signed by the Honorable Judge Fassbender himself, ordering Sarah Prescott to hang for the death of a Wells Fargo passenger during the course of a robbery. I'll just have to be satisfied with hanging her once."

"What if I prove that Miss Prescott was wrongly accused?"

"You're beginning to sound more like one of those fancy Boston lawyers than a preacher."

Ignoring the mockery in the marshal's voice, Justin persisted, "She's guilty of no crime."

"She's a Prescott. Around these parts, that's crime enough."

"The real crime is hanging a woman without a fair trial."

"She had a trial, Reverend. When I took the oath of office, I vowed to uphold law and order. I have the full support and approval of the folks in this town."

"The full support, huh? Well, I guess we can't argue with popular opinion, can we?"

Justin stood and walked casually

toward the door. His hand on the tarnished brass doorknob, he looked over his shoulder and regarded the marshal thoughtfully.

"One more thing, Marshal. I'll be bringing Miss Prescott's . . ." He hesitated and cleared his throat. "Her daughter to see her later today." It wasn't exactly a lie as Sarah was, in fact, Elizabeth's *god*mother. More than that, she was the only mother Elizabeth had.

Briggs sat back in surprise. "Miss Prescott has a daughter?" he sputtered.

"Her name's Elizabeth. She's still a baby. It sure is going to be tough on her, growing up without a mother."

The lawman rubbed his chin. It was obvious from his dark expression that this was not welcome news. "I didn't know she was . . ." He caught himself. "That's not my problem."

"Maybe. Maybe not," Justin drawled. "Of course when word gets out that you're stringing up an infant's mother, the folks around here might take issue with the way you carry out justice. You just never know, do you? The public can be so fickle at times. Especially during an election year."

Justin glanced at the *Vote for Briggs for County Sheriff* sign in the window. Similar signs were plastered all around town. Briggs had his eye on bigger and better things, but according to Ma, he was fast losing ground to his opponent. Briggs obviously counted on a Prescott hanging to turn the tide in his favor.

Justin placed his hat on his head and opened the door. "Good day, Marshal."

Twenty-seven

Ma had just finished feeding Elizabeth when Justin returned to the boarding-house.

"She's a little angel," she declared, shifting the sleeping baby onto her shoulder and patting her on the back.

Justin ran a knuckle along the baby's cheek. "That she is." He turned a chair around, straddled it, and folded his arms on top of the ladder back.

"Do you know anything about the county sheriff? I believe his name is Bockoven."

Ma heaved a sigh. "At one time, he was the best. He helped us through all that terrible Indian trouble." Ma told him about Rocky Creek's Indian war and how her husband had been killed while defending the town against a raid. The Comanches were finally moved to a reservation in Indian territory, thus effectively ending their Indian troubles and making the fort outside of town obsolete.

"The sheriff took an arrow to the back during that raid. He recovered, but he was never the same and got worse over time. It's like the arrow poison kept eating away at his brain or something. They tried to hide it, but old man Thompkins rode out to see him recently. Though he and the sheriff have been friends for years, the sheriff didn't even know who he was."

"That's too bad," Justin said. Abandoning any hope of getting Bockoven to intervene on Sarah's behalf, he decided to put his second plan into action. "Tell me, if I wanted the whole town to know something important, how would I go about spreading the word?"

Ma lay Elizabeth in her tiny crate before answering. "If you want it spread accurately, you could tell the Society for the Prevention of People Being Buried Alive."

"Is that still a problem?" he asked, surprised. Boston's medical community had come a long way in preventing such tragedies.

"Not so much anymore. Doc Myers is up on all the latest medical advancements. If he declares you're dead, you better believe that you are." She hesitated a moment. "Speaking of the doctor, it might not be a bad idea to take the baby to see him. He has this instrument that can administer smallpox vaccinations with hardly any pain."

He hadn't thought about taking Elizabeth to a doctor and he felt a surge of guilt. "Yes, that's a good idea. I'll take her." Anxious to get back to the original topic, he leaned forward. "I'm not so much interested in accuracy as I am in speed. Who would I go to if I wanted news spread fast?"

Ma's yellow-toothed grin looked like ripe corn. "In that case, Reverend, you tell the ladies of the Rocky Creek Quilting Bee."

"The quilting bee, eh?" He sat back

and smiled to himself. Well, what do you know? Texas wasn't all that different from Boston, after all.

~

The ladies of the Rocky Creek Quilting Bee met in the widow Mrs. Taylor's home two afternoons a week and just happened to be meeting that very next day. According to Ma, no marriage, birth, or death was considered official until a quilt marking the occasion was made and presented to the family with great fanfare by the group's leader.

Following Ma's directions, he found Mrs. Taylor's clapboard house and knocked on the widow's door. The door flew open on its own, but the ladies inside were too busy chatting to hear his knocks.

He stepped into the cool parlor that opened to a dining room. The quilters sat around a long, narrow table covered with colorful fabric scraps.

No one noticed Justin standing in the doorway, Elizabeth in his arms. She was dressed for the occasion in a pretty blue frock that Ma had whipped up on her hand-cranked sewing machine.

Justin waited politely for an opening in the conversation to introduce himself. But the longer he stood, the more he feared he would never get a word in edgewise.

Their nimble fingers were hardly able to keep up with the latest gossip that flowed around the table like rising floodwaters.

"If you ask me," one older woman sniffed, "Sarah Prescott is getting exactly what she deserves."

A young woman who was obviously with child shook her head. "It doesn't seem right to me. A woman can't vote, but she can be strung up like some common horse thief just because she's a Prescott."

"It's not just because she's a Prescott," another quilter argued. "She and her brothers shot that passenger in cold blood. The marshal says she's also responsible for Marshal Owen's death."

A woman with a sharp, pointed nose rose to her feet. "If that's true, she deserves her fate!"

Everyone talked at once until a matronly woman wearing a big feathered hat spotted Justin. She clapped her hands together until the room grew silent, then turned to him. "May we help, help you?"

Justin introduced himself. "I'm Reverend Wells, the new pastor of the church, and this is Elizabeth."

The woman who appeared to be the leader of the group rose and swept toward him, apologizing profusely. "Oh, yes, yes, I heard you arrived. It's about time Rocky Creek had a pastor of its own." While most of the other women wore unadorned bonnets, the leader's outlandish hat looked like a flock of birds about to take flight.

"Welcome to Rocky Creek. Rocky Creek. I'm Mrs. Hitchcock." Quickly, she introduced him to each woman in the room, repeating everyone's name twice.

Justin smiled politely at each woman in turn. Altogether there were eight of them. Some gave him full attention, others merely lifted their eyes momentarily before returning to their stitchery.

The last woman she introduced was

Mrs. Maddie Thomson. "This is our soon-to-be mother."

Maddie snipped a piece of thread with her scissors. "Really, Marcy. You've embarrassed Reverend Wells."

Justin smiled at her. "I look forward to baptizing your little one," he said, then added, "I was hoping to see you ladies at church on Sunday."

The women exchanged guilty looks.

"Oh dear, oh dear," Mrs. Hitchcock exclaimed. "We're just so out of practice. God knows how long it's been since we've had a pastor."

The woman who had been introduced as Mrs. Cranston stabbed her needle into one of the fabric squares. "We recently moved here and didn't know what the rules were for attending church."

"Rules?" Justin asked.

"The church back in Austin required that you be Republican to attend," she explained.

Justin knew about racial discrimination in churches, but this was the first he'd heard of political bigotry. "Everyone is welcome to attend our church," he assured her.

"Really?" Mrs. Cranston sounded dubious. "How democratic."

"I planned to go," the woman who had been introduced as Mrs. Emma Fields announced with a conciliatory air. She was a birdlike woman who wore her brown hair in a nest-like bun on top of her head. "But this old hip of mine was aching something fierce. I figure there would be plenty of time to hear your sermon."

"Just so you know, I preach a different sermon every week," he said.

Several women's eyebrows shot up.

"A different one. Really?" Maddie said.

"What a quaint idea," Mrs. Fields exclaimed.

Mrs. Hitchcock walked over to him, her ample hips swaying like a boat on high seas. She stuck her face in Elizabeth's and made an odd little cooing sound. Elizabeth stared at her with big round eyes.

"I had no idea you were a family man. A family man," Mrs. Hitchcock said.

"Actually, I'm not," he explained. "The baby's father was killed during an Indian attack."

"How awful," Mrs. Fields exclaimed and all the women nodded in solemn agreement.

"I'm taking care of baby Elizabeth here for her mother," he said. "Perhaps you've heard of her?"

He cast a casual glance around the room, meeting the curious gaze of each woman in turn. "Her name is Sarah Prescott."

A stunned silence followed his announcement. Mouths dropped open, eyes rounded, needles froze in midair.

Mrs. Hitchcock was the first to break the strained silence. "Oh, that poor, poor baby. Poor baby," she gasped, hands on her ample bosom.

The expectant mother rubbed her belly and exclaimed. "That sweet child's mother doesn't deserve to die." She glanced at each woman in turn. "I don't care what any of you say."

"I couldn't agree more," Justin said. "Especially since she tried to save the marshal's life." He then explained how

Sarah had removed Marshal Owen's bullet with her skillful surgery.

Miss Monica Freeman waved her quilting needle. "If you ask me, this whole debacle is a miscarriage of justice. The woman was condemned even before that farce of a trial."

Mrs. Hitchcock leaned over and whispered in his ear. "Miss Freeman is the schoolteacher, schoolteacher." As if the woman needed further endorsement, she added, "And she reads books, books." Her eyes rounded. "Thick, thick books."

Everyone started to talk at once. Two of the ladies maintained that Sarah deserved her fate but changed their minds when Elizabeth broke into a broad smile.

"She's as sweet as a gumdrop," Mrs. Hitchcock purred.

Mrs. Fields nodded. "One look at that face, and you just know she's from good stock."

The schoolteacher frowned. "That's ridiculous. You can't tell that by looking at a baby's face."

"I can!" Mrs. Fields said heatedly.

"So can I," Maddie Thomson added, hand on her swollen belly.

After much discussion, the members of the Rocky Creek Quilting Bee decided two things: Elizabeth's mother didn't deserve to die, and Sarah Prescott's dear, sweet baby would be the recipient of the next quilt.

Satisfied, Justin thanked the ladies and took his leave. He walked down the flower-lined path and parked himself next to the gate. It was near Elizabeth's feeding time and she began to fuss. He jostled her, hoping he wouldn't have to wait long.

He didn't. Almost at once, the front door flew open and the exodus began.

The ladies of the Rocky Creek Quilting Bee apparently hadn't even bothered to wait for their president to declare the meeting over before making a mad dash for the door. He could hear Mrs. Hitchcock's objections from inside the house. "Ladies, ladies . . . Come back, come back!"

It was only by pure luck that Justin wasn't knocked off his feet in the mad rush that followed. The women apologized profusely for nearly barreling over him, made clucking sounds at Elizabeth, then scattered in different directions like hens trying to outrun a hatchet-wielding farmer.

They spread the news so fast following Justin's startling announcement that he barely had time to return to the boardinghouse to feed Elizabeth before he noted a number of carriages and buggies barreling past the house.

Arriving in town on horseback with Elizabeth slung against his chest, he smiled in satisfaction at the group of outraged citizens gathered outside the marshal's office to protest the hanging of baby Elizabeth's mother.

Tethering his horse on a hitching post, he leaned against a post in front of Fairbanks General Merchandise and watched, one hand cradling the baby's weight. Women of all shapes and sizes packed the street, carrying hastily made signs protesting Sarah's fate.

Things got so loud that Briggs was finally forced to step outside his office to control the crowd. Holding his palms outward, he pleaded with the women. "Now calm down. All of you."

Mrs. Hitchcock stepped forward. "We'll calm down, calm down, when you let that baby's mother go," she said, repeating herself twice more for good measure.

Marshal Briggs' face grew a worrisome shade of red, but he nonetheless appeared to waver until a starched woman dressed in black walked up to him. An uneasy silence settled over the crowd. Even so, Justin had to strain his ears to hear the woman's soft voice.

"Do I need to remind you all that my husband is dead because of that . . . that woman?" she asked. "My children are without a father. What kind of brother are you to deny me justice?"

Justin was surprised to see her there. He didn't know Owen's widow had returned from her trip. He felt remiss for failing to pay his respects and fulfill his promise to Owen. Listening to her continue to rant, his heart sank. He hadn't counted on Owen's sister making a plea on her husband's behalf. Poor woman.

She was so distraught. Who could blame her?

Briggs glanced at his widowed sister, then at the crowd. If Justin guessed right, the marshal's thoughts were on the upcoming election and his chances of becoming sheriff. He was caught between a rock and a hard place, and he knew it. Justin knew it. His brother's widow wanted one thing; the town, another.

Justin pressed his lips against Elizabeth's head. "So what do you think, little one? Will he choose the election or family?" Women, of course, didn't have a vote, but they did influence the men in their lives. A man seeking office would be foolish to discount popular female opinion.

Justin didn't have to wait long for his answer.

Briggs raised his voice to address the crowd. "Bring me Miss Prescott's outlaw brothers, and she's free to go."

Justin was caught by surprise. Since the sheriff was out of the picture, the most he expected was to force Briggs to talk to the judge. What kind of place was this that a mere town marshal had the power to decide a prisoner's fate?

The crowd cheered, but Owen's widow stomped away angrily.

The marshal's gaze followed her all the way to her horse and buggy before he turned his attention back to the town's womenfolk. "You've got three days." Briggs turned away from the crowd.

Justin followed the marshal into his office, slamming the door shut behind him.

The marshal spun around to face Justin, his eyes flashing with impatience. "What do you want?"

"I can't find her brothers in three days," Justin said, anger creeping into his voice.

"What do you want me to do about it?"

"Talk to the judge. Demand another trial." Justin's gaze held the marshal's.

The marshal made a face. "It'll take longer than three days to sober him up."

"Then give me ten days," Justin said,

though he had no idea if he could find her brothers in even that length of time.

Briggs practically sputtered. "Do you have any idea how much trouble that woman has caused? It ain't proper to jail men and women together. I had to release thirteen prisoners to make room for her. I've got killers and thieves walkin' around town just so I could put one woman in jail."

"Eight days," Justin persisted, and to sweeten the deal, he added, "Three Prescotts for one."

He could see the wheels turning in the marshal's head. Hanging a woman would give him notoriety, but capturing her three brothers would win the election.

"Five, and that's my last offer. Now get so I can work."

Justin's mind worked furiously. "Not until I see the prisoner."

The marshal narrowed his eyes. "Again?"

"You wouldn't deny a mother a chance to see her baby, now would you?"

Briggs glanced down at Elizabeth but said nothing. Instead, he stood and plucked a ring of keys from a rusty nail. Turning, he led the way to the cells in back, the keys jingling in his hand.

Twenty-eight

Fearing the commotion outside signaled a lynch party in her honor, Sarah's heart pounded and her knees trembled. The sound of a key in the lock of the outer door struck terror in her, and she backed into a corner.

When Justin walked up to her cell, she almost fainted with relief. He pulled Elizabeth out of her sling and held her up.

She rushed forward. "Oh, Justin . . . If you ain't a sight for sore eyes." Hands on her chest, she gazed at Elizabeth and tears stung her eyes. "I reckon there ain't anythin' more beautiful."

"Just like her mother," he said. She

opened her mouth to protest, but before she could say a word, he added, "Her *god*mother."

She reached through the bars and stroked the baby's soft pink cheek. Elizabeth's little bow mouth curved upward.

Justin beamed with pride. He settled the baby in the curve of his arm. "See? What did I tell you?" All too soon the smile left his face.

She studied him, searching for the least sign of good news. Much to her dismay, he looked dead serious, her fate plainly written in the fine lines creasing the corners of his eyes and mouth. She felt her heart sink like a rock in a river.

"Oh, Justin . . . If . . . Promise me, you'll take care of her."

"Sarah—"

"Make sure she learns her contraptions."

"What?"

"I mean . . . Conception."

He stared at her. "I don't think we should rush things."

She brightened. "No, no, I mean contractions. That's it. Make sure she learns her contractions so she can talk like a lady."

"Sarah—" His voice was hoarse with emotion.

"Don't you go stretching the blanket, none, you hear? I want the truth. They're fixing to lynch me, right?"

"The marshal has granted you a five-day reprieve."

She frowned. "Is that good?"

"The good news is that he has agreed to spare your life altogether providing . . . uh . . . certain conditions are met."

Something in his voice made her mouth go dry. "What . . . what conditions?"

Justin hesitated.

"Justin Wells, you tell me ev'rythin', you hear? What conditions?"

He shifted Elizabeth from one arm to the other. "He says he will spare your neck if your brothers turn themselves in."

She took a deep breath. "I reckon my goose is cooked, then."

"Don't say that, Sarah. We haven't even begun to fight."

"We ain't got but five days."

"God doesn't need that much time," he said. "Just think, in only three days He went from Good Friday to Easter Sunday."

Though she didn't feel much like smiling, her lips curved upward. "You always know how to make me feel better."

"Help me, Sarah. I need your help to find your brothers."

She shook her head sadly. "It's not going to work. My brothers ain't gonna hand themselves over on a silver platter to no marshal."

He reached through the bars with his one free arm and caressed her cheek. "I only met your brothers once, but it was enough to tell me how much they care about you. They won't let anything happen to you."

Her lips quivered and her knees felt weak. "They will if they don't know I'm in trouble."

"I've got to find them."

"You only have five days," she reminded him.

"Maybe they're in Fort Smith looking

for you. That's where George told you to meet them. If I send a telegram—"

"No!" She shook her head. "No, that could be dangerous. We never use—" She stopped but not soon enough, for it was obvious from the look on his face that he had figured out what she had been about to say.

He drew back. "You communicate with one another using a false name." He nodded. "That makes sense. What name do you use when you need to contact your brothers? Tell me. If not for your sake, then do it for Elizabeth."

She stared down at the baby in his arms, the baby she now realized she would do anything to protect. "They'll never turn themselves in."

"Maybe they'll think of another way to save you."

She bit her lip. "I don't know—"

"Please, Sarah, tell me the name."

"If I tell you, it could put my brothers in danger, Justin. If you say that I'm going to hang, the telegrapher will know—"

"Sarah, I've been around you long enough to know how to confuse words.

I guarantee that no one but your brothers will have a clue as to what I'm talking about."

Her shoulder pressed against the bars, she gently stroked his face. "You're so good," she whispered. "I don't know what you see in the likes of me."

He closed his fingers around her wrist. He wasn't about to be distracted. "The name."

She lowered her eyes to Elizabeth, and her arms ached to hold her.

"She needs a mother," Justin said. "She needs you."

"Cooper," she whispered at last. She pulled her hand away from him and covered her face. She would never forgive herself if her brothers were caught, and she prayed that George would know what to do. She dropped her hands to her side and clenched her fists in attempt to hold on to what little control she had left. "George Cooper."

Justin turned to leave, but she stopped him. "Justin, wait." She dug into the pocket of her dress and pulled out a wad of money. Hard as it was to believe, Marshal Briggs was too much of a gentleman to search her, though he did take her gun.

"This is the money left over from what Robert gave me." She held her hand through the bars. "It's not much, but I want you to give it to Owen's widow."

Justin took the money from her and stuffed it into his own pocket. "I love you, Sarah Prescott."

She reached out for his hand and drew it up to her lips. "I love you, Justin Wells." She gazed up at him, at the baby in his arms, and her heart swelled until she thought it might burst.

"Do you think God's got a miracle in store for us?"

An easy smile slid over his features, all but melting away the lines of worry and fatigue. "I would say conditions have never been more right for a miracle than they are at this moment."

"You ain't just sayin' that, are you? To make me feel better? I know I'm knee-deep in dung here, but—"

"That's one of the conditions for a miracle," Justin reassured her. "To be knee-deep in, uh . . . trouble."

She flashed him a teasing smile. "Then I guess you could say I'm one lucky lady."

Justin left the jailhouse and hurried toward the recently opened telegraph office next to a half-built railroad station. Rocky Creek would soon be a railroad town, and the clanging sound of Chinese workers spiking down tin plates echoed from the distance.

The telegraph operator's name was Mason Smith, a young man in his teens. Tapping the telegraph key rapidly, Smith's head bobbed with each click as if the Morse code corresponded to some inner tune.

Shifting Elizabeth into his left arm to free his right hand, Justin stood at the counter to compose his message and realized he hadn't the slightest idea what to say.

He was more worried than he let on with Sarah. It was true that her brothers loved her, but he wasn't so naive to think they would turn themselves in.

Still, they had the right to know that their sister was in trouble.

He glanced up. The operator was too intent upon sending his message to pay him much heed. With a heavy sigh, he lowered his head and closed his eyes. *Heavenly Father . . . help me get the words right.*

He stared down at the blank paper. A voice from the past filled his head, surprising him with its clarity. *Write the vision.* It was his father's voice. Justin couldn't help but smile. How often had he heard those very same words whenever he was stuck on his schoolwork? And how many times had he turned to his father for advice only to hear him say, *My son, if your heart is wise, my heart will rejoice?*

An agent for the American Bible Society, his father traveled from door to door to make his sales. A stoic man of few words, Justin never thought of him as religious. It wasn't until he attended seminary that Justin discovered his father's oft repeated phrases were really quotes from the Bible.

On his deathbed, his father uttered

his last five words, not to the family members who surrounded him, but to God.

It was these last five words that rang in Justin's head as he wrote *Psalm 38:22*. Praying that his heart was wise, he signed his name.

Twenty-nine

The following morning, Justin rode out to the Owens' house. The town marshal's sister, Claudia Owen, lived in a stone house with a slate roof and wrap-around porch.

Hat in hand, Justin stood on Claudia's porch and knocked on the door. The tidy flower garden in front was surrounded by a white picket fence.

A black mourning ribbon fluttered from the front gate. That and the tightly closed draperies were the only outward signs of Owen's death.

Justin visited the homes of congregation members in Boston. Nowhere near as many as he should have, he now realized, but some. He had grown accustomed to odd reactions whenever he appeared unannounced on the doorsteps. On several occasions he had been kept waiting on the porch, even in the dead of winter, until all alcohol or tobacco had been hidden. Dime novels were whisked off tabletops and replaced by open Bibles. Immoral paintings were turned over to reveal pastoral or religious scenes.

Children's faces were scrubbed, husbands duly warned, and the house made to look chaste as a nunnery before he would be invited inside.

The U.S. Marshal's widow, however, made no such effort to impress him. Instead, she opened the door and stared at him as one would stare at an unwanted salesman. Her skin pale, she was dressed in black, her brown hair pulled into a tight bun at the nape of her neck.

Evidently guessing who he was from his frock coat and dark trousers, she scowled. "What are you doing here? I heard you were helping that murderer."

"I'm returning your husband's horse."

She craned her neck to glance over his shoulder at Blizzard tethered in front next to Noah. She looked momentarily confused. "How . . . how do you happen to have my husband's horse?"

"I ran into your husband in Missouri. He had been shot. Miss Prescott and I—"

At mention of Sarah's name, the widow tried to close the door, but he stopped her with a well placed foot.

"Please, Mrs. Owen. Hear me out."

Claudia's face twisted into despair. "I have nothing to say to you. My brother said you were helping *her*."

"I promised your husband I would help *you*. It's not easy for a woman alone to raise three children."

A small, freckled-faced boy peered from behind his mother's skirts, his eyes round with curiosity.

Justin stooped and extended his hand to the child. "And what is your name, young man?"

The boy glanced at Justin's hand but made no move to grasp it. "David."

"I'm pleased to meet you, David." Justin pulled his hand back. "Did you know that there was a boy named David in the Bible?"

The boy's eyes grew wider, but he didn't answer.

"He was so brave," Justin continued, "that he fought a giant all by himself."

The boy glanced up at his mother before asking, "Did he win?"

"Not only did he win," Justin said with a wink, "but he grew up to be a king."

The boy giggled and vanished inside the house.

Justin straightened. His exchange with her son did nothing to lessen the dislike on Claudia's face. "As I was saying earlier, I promised your husband to help—"

"I don't want your help," she retorted.

He drew the wad of money from his pocket. "Some of this is from the church, and the rest is from Miss Prescott."

"I don't want her money," she said, spitting out the words like hard-driven nails. "I want nothing to do with her."

"Please," he forced the money into her hand. "Take it for the children's sake."

"I'd rather my children go hungry than accept charity from an outlaw." With that, she threw the money onto the porch next to his feet.

He made no move to pick it up. "Sarah did everything she could to save your husband's life."

She stared at him, her face hard and unyielding. "So what do you expect from me? Gratitude?"

"All I ask is that you talk to your brother. A word from you could save her life."

She tossed back her head and glared. "Because of that woman, my husband is dead."

"Sarah didn't put that bullet in him," he said. Claudia flinched and he regretted his choice of words. "Nor did she kill that passenger. And if she hangs, a baby will be without a mother."

"My children are without a father."

"For that I am deeply sorry." Justin knew if he hoped to gain her sympathy he would have to make her understand the full extent of Sarah's efforts to save her husband.

"What I said about Sarah helping him

is true. She removed the bullet from his shoulder. Worked night and day to keep the infection at bay. When he died, she found a spot on top of a hill overlooking the river and helped dig his grave. If it's any comfort, we gave your husband a proper funeral."

Claudia lifted her chin, her eyes hard as two black pebbles. "If you're asking me to return the favor by digging her grave, that I will gladly do. But don't ask me to try and save her neck."

She slammed the door shut with a bang that shattered what little hope he had that she would talk to her brother-in-law on Sarah's behalf.

Leaving the money on the porch, he left, his heart heavy. Before mounting his horse, he glanced back at the house. David peered at him from an upstairs window. Justin waved and the boy waved back.

He patted Noah on the neck. "It looks like we made a friend." With one more glance at the house, he mounted and rode into town intent upon tracking down Judge Fassbender.

If anyone knew where he could be

found, it had to be Hank Applegate, who watched the town's coming and goings like an old hound.

Hank was at his usual place in front of Jake's saloon, his head circled in smoke from his corncob pipe.

Justin didn't even bother dismounting. "Do you know where I can find Judge Fassbender?" he called.

Hank removed the pipe from his mouth, cupping it by the bowl. "Last I saw him, he was headin' for Al's Saloon at the end of town."

Justin tipped his hat. "Thank you."

"If he's not there, you might try The Gold Coin or Stan's. He might even be at The Blue Bull or—" He rattled off the other saloons in town.

Justin thanked him again and rode off.

Starting at the end of town, he began to check the saloons one by one, recognizing many of the patrons from Jake's. He greeted each familiar face with a tip of the hat, only to be met with glaring looks and hasty departures. A saloon packed when he walked in was nearly empty by the time he walked out.

"Don't worry," he said lightly, walking into the Blue Bull. "I'm not going to preach. I only work on Sundays." It was an old joke among preachers, who rarely got credit for the many hours they ministered.

No one looked amused at his comment, and his attempt at humor did nothing to stop the mass exit.

He found the judge in the Silver Bell, the fourth place he searched. The bartender pointed to a man slumped at a corner table. He turned to look, but all he could see were men scrambling to make their escape, pushing and shoving their way outside.

By the time he walked to the corner table, most everyone had left. The only evidence of the hasty departure was overturned chairs and the swinging of bat-wing doors.

The man reeked of alcohol and sweat and appeared to be out cold. "Judge Fassbender?"

No response.

Justin shook him. The judge groaned but didn't open his eyes. Drool rolled down his unshaven chin. He wore black pants, a waistcoat, and scuffed boots. A tangle of uncombed hair more gray than black fell to his shoulders.

Justin shook him again, harder this time, and the judge lifted his head, his eyes red and unfocused.

Justin lifted his arm to catch the bartender's attention. "Do you have any Arbuckle's?"

The man scoffed and spit out a yellow stream of tobacco. "This ain't no Harvey House, and I ain't no Harvey girl."

Without coffee, Justin had no idea how to bring the judge out of his stupor. Maybe some fresh air. He tried lifting the judge out of the chair, but the man flopped forward, knocking over a half empty bottle of whiskey. Justin quickly uprighted the bottle, but not soon enough to prevent the contents from getting in Fassbender's face.

Justin jerked on the judge's collar, lifting his head off the table. He drew a handkerchief from his coat pocket and dabbed at the man's wet cheek.

The judge twisted his head from side to side, his tongue hanging out of his mouth. His eyes opened, but all Justin could see were the whites.

The judge sat back in his chair under his own power, staring at Justin through slotted eyes. "W-hat . . . what are you trying to do to me?"

"You have my heartfelt apologies."

Fassbender shook his head as if trying to clear it. "Who are you?" he slurred.

"Reverend Justin Wells. I'm the new pastor."

"You have no right b-baptizing people without their thaythoo," he stammered.

"Don't worry," Justin said. "Your sins are safe. Baptism by whiskey doesn't count." He pulled out a chair and sat down. "I need to talk to you."

The judge flinched. "Don't yell," he said, though Justin spoke in a normal voice.

Justin leaned forward. "Does the name Sarah Prescott ring a bell?" he asked.

Fassbender gawked at Justin with bloodshot eyes and shook his head.

"You sentenced her to hang," Justin said, forgetting to lower his voice.

The judge looked confused. "Bres—?"

"Prescott. Sarah Prescott."

Fassbender waved his hand in the air. "Killed . . . someone."

"No, she didn't." Justin moved closer.

"Killed someone," Fassbender repeated. The man's eyes cleared and he almost looked lucid.

"She didn't kill anyone," Justin said.

Fassbender combed his fingers through his hair. "How do you know she didn't?"

It was a fair question for which Justin had no real answer. He believed Sarah, but her word alone wasn't likely to impress the judge. "How do you know she did? Were there any witnesses? What about the other passengers? The driver? What did they say?"

The judge looked confused by all the questions. His eyes rolled, and he slumped forward again, his head on the table.

Frustrated, Justin slapped a fist against his palm. This was a waste of time and he had so little to spare. He stood, pushed in his chair and started to walk away. The judge's voice made him stop.

Justin whirled around to face him. "What did you say?"

"I said, have you ever asked yourself why . . . why bother?" Fassbender's words were muffled. He lifted his eyes to Justin. "How many people have you saved, Reverend?"

"I-I don't know," Justin said, surprised by the question. After all, God saved. All Justin did was help pave the way. He sat down again. "It's not something I keep track of."

The judge lifted his head but held on to the table with both hands. "Oh, you keep track," he said in a low monotone voice. "We all do. It's our n-nature." He gazed across the empty room. His words garbled, he began to talk about his father.

"Did you say your father was shot?" Justin asked.

Fassbender nodded. "Horse thieves . . . I was ten years old when he died in my arms."

"I'm sorry," Justin said. "Losing a parent at such a young age . . . I can't imagine how hard it must have been for you." He thought of Sarah and her brothers. Of countless others he'd ministered to through the years. Lost childhoods often led to broken adults.

Fassbender wiped his chin with the back of his hand. He straightened as if talking about his dead father had a sobering effect on him.

"I vowed to go into law and bring every blasted cr-crimi-nal to justice. I got myself elected sh-sheriff." Fassbender's words were less garbled, but his voice was still thick from the effects of alcohol. "I figured that one or more of them would turn out to be my f-father's killers." Fassbender scratched his unshaven chin and grimaced. "Most of the ones I arrested got off scot-free. So I became a . . . judge."

Elbow on the table, Fassbender lifted his arm and shook an unsteady finger. "That's when I found out that fighting bribed witnesses and fancy lawyers was a losing battle. The only way I could see any sort of justice was to ban witnesses from my courtroom and rule everyone guilty."

Shocked, Justin stared at him. "What about the innocent?"

"The innocent don't have a chance either way. They can't afford bribes or lawyers, and they don't know how to work the system." Fassbender shuddered and wagged his head as if trying to clear his thoughts. "Tell me you've never been discouraged in your line of work. Tell me you've never wanted to give up when someone you save reverts back to old ways."

It was all Justin could do to choke back his anger. He stood and leaned over the judge, glowering at him. "Yes, I've been discouraged. Yes, I've seen more people walk away from God than come to Him, and yes, I've been tempted to give up. But I've never forgotten why I went into ministry in the first place."

"It's easy for you to judge—"

"I don't have to," Justin said. "By the looks of you, I'd say you're doing a good job of judging yourself."

Fassbender said nothing. Instead, he

stared at the now empty whiskey bottle as if that alone would save him.

Sickened, Justin turned and walked away.

His next stop was the office of the *Rocky Creek Gazette.* The man sitting behind the cluttered desk stroked the orange cat on his lap. The eyes behind steel-rimmed spectacles were wide with curiosity. A neatly trimmed mustache twitched beneath a bulbous red nose. An ugly red scar ran along the side of his face. "What can I do for you?"

"I'm looking for the editor."

"That's me," the man said. "Jacoby Barnes at your service. And this here," he said pointing to the cat with an ink-stained finger, "is Extra."

Justin introduced himself. "I'm the new pastor." He wasted no time getting to the point of his visit. "I thought you might be interested in some facts about Sarah Prescott for your newspaper."

Barnes looked skeptical. "I have nothing against facts. As long as they correspond with my opinion."

Justin sat down and told him what he

knew about Sarah Prescott—or at least the facts as they pertained to her plight.

When he finished, the editor chased Extra off his lap and sat forward. "This is all very interesting, and I'll be happy to include it in Friday's paper."

"Friday?" Justin said in alarm. "That will be too late."

"That's when the paper comes out. That's two weeks ahead of schedule. I figured everyone would want to read about the hanging."

Justin rubbed his chin. "What will it take to put out a special edition tomorrow?"

Barnes pursed out his lips. "A lot of work."

"I'm willing to pay your expenses." By Boston standards, his church salary had been modest but more than enough to cover his meager living expenses. Half his savings was left, and he would gladly spend every last penny if it meant saving Sarah's life.

Justin could see the man's mind working. Barnes tapped his jaw with broad fingers, leaving a smudge of ink on his chin. "It could get expensive. I'd have to walk down to the jail and all."

Justin couldn't imagine how walking to the jail two doors away could result in additional expenses, but he didn't have time to argue. "I can give you ten dollars now and pay the rest later."

The editor afforded him a triumphant smile. "Reverend Wells, I believe you've got yourself a deal."

Thirty

Justin left the newspaper office feeling more depressed than encouraged. It had been a difficult morning. A hammering came from the direction of the livery stable, and his stomach tightened. Four men were putting the portable gallows in place.

Sickened by the sight, he turned toward the marshal's office. He was frustrated by his reception at the saloon, his talk with Fassbender, and the lack of progress on Sarah's behalf. The gallows only added to his torment.

As if to guess at his state of mind, Sarah greeted him with a bright smile, but she didn't fool him a bit. She could

hide her anxiety behind a lively demeanor, but she couldn't hide her pale
cheeks and the dark shadows under her
eyes.

She insisted he tell her all about Elizabeth, even though it had only been
yesterday that she saw her.

"Let's see," he said, trying to match
her light manner. "In the last twenty-four
hours, she's grown a whole foot and
she's ready for music lessons."

"Justin Wells, I do believe you're
joshin' me."

He reached through the bars and took
both her hands in his.

She looked up at him, and all pretense between them fell away. Her eyes
filled with tears and her lower lip quivered. "Anything?" she asked.

"Not yet," he whispered, his voice
hoarse. He dropped to his knees, forcing her down with him. "Pray with me."

She nodded. "You go first."

Still holding her hands, he lowered his
head. "Dear heavenly Father, Almighty
God, Creator of heaven and earth . . ."
He pressed his head against a steel bar.

He was so close to her, he could feel her warm breath. "You go," he whispered.

She gazed up at him for moment before lowering her head again. "God, I ain't meanin' to bother You . . ." After a moment of silence, she whispered, "Your turn."

"My strength and my salvation."

"And I sure do appreciate everythin' You done for me . . ."

She showed none of her earlier shyness in praying out loud, and for this he was grateful.

"Show us the way, Lord. Show us the way . . ." he continued.

"I ain't seein' no signs, God. If you could please make them a little more noticeable, I'd be much obliged."

"Amen." He squeezed her hands.

"Amen," she said, squeezing back.

Warned by the rattling sound behind him, he pulled away and stood just before the outer door flew open.

"Time's up," Marshal Briggs said.

"I'll see you tomorrow," Justin said, trying to keep his voice sufficiently reserved. His back to the marshal, he lifted his eyes upward. "Hold on to

God," he said softly. There was so much more he wanted to say but couldn't. Not with the marshal watching his every move.

He walked past the marshal, through the front office, and out the door without looking back.

An hour and a half after leaving the jail, Justin was ushered into Dr. Myers's parlor, Elizabeth tucked into the sling at his chest. Soon, he would have to find another way of transporting her as she had just about outgrown her carrier.

The doctor was young by Boston standards, somewhere in his early forties. Only a couple of inches shorter than Justin, he wore tweed trousers and a matching waistcoat, his white shirt rolled up at the sleeves. His dark hair was cut short as was the style, and it was parted in the middle. He was clean shaven except for his mutton-chop sideburns.

The doctor's most intriguing feature was his eyes. One iris was blue and the other brown, and Justin couldn't help but stare.

Dr. Myers glanced at the cluttered

parlor as if seeing it for the first time, then led Justin to an equally cluttered dining room.

Used to the relatively sterile medical offices in Boston, Justin felt a tremor of apprehension. He only hoped that Ma's confidence in the doctor wasn't overly optimistic.

After clearing a stack of books off the dining room table, the doctor spread a blanket on the mahogany surface, talking all the while. "I heard about Miss Prescott," he said. "If you ask me, hanging a woman is a crime." Myers shook his head and motioned for Justin to lay Elizabeth on the table.

Justin sensed an ally in the doctor. "Miss Prescott is one of the reasons I came here today. She's not been sleeping well. I wonder if you would be kind enough to look in on her? Perhaps you can give her something to help her sleep."

Myers nodded. "I'd be happy to."

"I'll pay you in advance if you prefer."

Myers waved his hand. "If you can't trust a man of God, there isn't much hope, is there?" He rubbed his chin. "Any chance the lady won't hang?"

Justin released Elizabeth from the fabric confines. "Do you believe in miracles, doctor?"

"Any doctor who doesn't believe in miracles is a fool," Myers replied. "God heals, and we doctors accept the praise,"

Justin chuckled. "Same with us preachers. God saves, and we take the credit."

"Ah, see? You know what I'm talking about." The doctor rubbed his hands together as if anxious to get started. "Let's take a look at this little one."

Cradling the baby in his arms, Justin hesitated.

The doctor studied him from beneath a knitted brow. "I'm not used to patients coming here," he said. "I'm what you call a horse-and-buggy doctor."

"We still have those in the east," Justin said. "Mostly in the rural areas."

The doctor gave a knowing look. "Last year, I attended a medical convention in Boston and had the opportunity to tour a doctor's office." He shook his head. "I fear the practice of having patients come to an office will one day be the norm."

"You don't think it's a good idea?" Justin asked, surprised. Boston doctors could now see more patients in a single day than they ever could in their traveling days.

The doctor gestured in disgust. "I can tell more about a patient's health by stepping into his home than all the medical equipment in the world can tell me." Pausing briefly, he continued, "Not long ago, I had a lethargic little boy and I couldn't for the life of me figure out what his problem was. One day, I noticed him eating chipped paint off a hobby horse. I don't know what was in that paint, but I figured it couldn't be doing him any good. I had his parents remove the horse and the boy recovered"—he snapped his fingers—"just like that. Do you think a doctor sitting in his fancy office would have solved the problem? I doubt it. Just as I doubt, you could do much good if you sat in church all day."

Justin felt a stab of guilt. In Boston, that's exactly what he did most days. He

sat in the church office waiting for people to come to him rather than reaching
out to them.

"If it will make you feel any better . . ."
the doctor added. He pointed to the
framed document on the wall over the
paneled sideboard. "I graduated from
the Jefferson Medical College in Phila-
delphia."

"I've heard of that college," Justin
said. He was acting like an overprotec-
tive father, again, but he couldn't seem
to help himself. "It's a fine college."
Without further ado, he lay Elizabeth
down and undressed her while Myers
washed his hands in the kitchen.

The doctor returned, drying his hands
on a towel. He then examined Elizabeth
carefully, and she rewarded him with a
wide toothless smile. "When was she
born?" the doctor asked, grinning back
at her.

"I'm not sure," Justin said. "I'm
guessing sometime in March or April."

The doctor nodded. "That would
make her four or five months old. That
sounds about right. It looks like she's
about to pop her first tooth."

"Really?" Justin leaned forward for a closer look. A speck of white showed beneath her lower pink gum. *Wait till Sarah hears about this.*

While the doctor wrote in a leather-bound notebook, Justin dressed Elizabeth. It was time for her nap, and she started to fuss.

"If you like, I can give her a smallpox vaccination," the doctor said.

"What about measles?" Justin asked, thinking of his sisters. "Is there any way to protect her against measles?"

"Not unless you plan to keep her locked in a room somewhere."

Justin wished he could. "Will she have a reaction to the vaccination?"

"Yes, but very mild. She'll probably run a fever."

Justin grimaced. The last thing he needed right now was a sick baby.

As if to guess his thoughts, the doctor said, "We can wait if you like. There's no immediate danger of her getting small-pox. We haven't had a case in more than nine months."

Justin nodded in relief. "I'll bring her back at a later date."

"If it's all the same to you, I'd rather see her in her normal surroundings," the doctor said.

Justin nodded. "Right now, I'm staying at Ma's Boardinghouse."

The doctor's eyes twinkled. "She'll take good care of you both. She's the next best thing to a preacher and a doctor."

Promising to look in on Sarah that very afternoon, Myers walked him to the door.

For the next two days, Justin worked like a madman, pleading Sarah's case to anyone who would listen. In the past he accepted everything that happened as God's will—even having to leave Boston in disgrace. He never fought the charges against him, never stood up for himself, never really stood up for anything. It wasn't until he thought that Indian woman meant to harm Elizabeth that he even knew he had a fighting spirit.

It shocked him to look back and realize how passive his faith had been. Convinced that God wouldn't bring Sarah into his life only to snatch her away, he was ready to fight like he'd never fought before. He now knew what it meant to put faith into action. Oddly enough, the more he battled to save Sarah, the closer he felt to God.

He dashed off telegram after telegram addressed to Governor Roberts in Austin, and President Hayes at the White House.

He went door to door asking citizens to intervene, only to find that Owen's widow had already tried to rally the townsfolk to her side. Talking to Claudia Owen had obviously been a mistake. It only strengthened her resolve to place the blame for her husband's death squarely on Sarah's shoulders.

He checked the telegraph office several times a day, hoping for a telegram from the president, the governor, or George. He pleaded for God's help on bended knee. But the clock kept ticking, the world kept turning, and nothing he did produced any positive results.

Sarah lay on her cot wide awake. It was pitch black except for the single star that shone through the barred window high above her head.

Hold on to God, Justin told her. She tried, she really did try, but it was so hard. Doubts kept creeping in. What if God meant for her to die?

Something scraped against the outside wall. She sat up and listened.

Thinking it was a mouse or rat, she let out her breath. Then the sound came again, followed by a hushed voice.

"Sarah?"

Her heart leaped. "George?"

"Shh."

Arms crossed in front, she closed her eyes. *Thank You, God.* She had been so afraid she wouldn't have a chance to say a final good-bye to her brothers.

"Now listen and listen good," George said, his voice rough. "I want you to go to the opposite side of the cell and cover your face. We're gonna blow a hole in this here wall."

She covered her mouth with both hands, her eyes filled with tears. She should have known that her brother would come to her rescue. She slid off the cot and backed away from the wall.

Crouching by the bars of her cell, she covered her face.

Thoughts of Justin and Elizabeth filled her head. Knowing she would never see them again was more than she could bear. Was this really the answer to her prayer? To spend the rest of her life with her outlaw brothers? Was this what God wanted for her?

Justin's voice spoke to her in the darkness. *"Hold on to God."*

"Oh, Justin," she whispered, tears rolling down her cheeks. "I'm tryin' to."

Brushing the moisture from her cheeks with the palms of her hands, she rushed across the cell to her cot. "George," she called.

"Hush. What's the matter with you? I told you to move away from the wall."

"Wait. I ain't wantin' to be an outlaw anymore. I don't want you robbin' no more stages."

"This ain't no time to argue. Now do as I told you, move away—"

"No," she said. "Not until you promise to give up robbin'."

"I ain't promisin' nothin'. Now get away from the wall."

Hold on to God. Her fingers curved into two tight fists, she gasped for air to brace herself. "No," she repeated.

He cursed. "We only got twelve hours to your lynchin' party. There ain't no time to argue."

But argue they did. Sarah tried pleading with him, but the more she begged him to give up his life of crime, the more he resisted.

"All this talk about God," he spit out. "What has God ever done for us? Except take our ma and pa."

"He didn't take them," she said quietly. "He received them."

"Now you sound like that preacher of yours. I'm telling you God's done nothin' for us."

She bit her lip. Justin once told her that God always sent the right people when you needed them and she needed to know if that were true. "After . . . after our parents died, did anyone offer to help?"

"What difference does it make? That was years ago."

"I need to know," she said.

"There was Mrs. Bonheimer. She wanted to adopt you."

Her thoughts traveled back in time. Mrs. Bonheimer always gave Sarah candy whenever she and Mama entered the store, and once even gave her a doll made out of straw and scraps of fabric. Her life would have been very different today had George taken her up on the offer.

"Any more?" she asked. *Please let there be more.*

His answer came slow. "There were job offers. Mrs. Bonheimer wanted me to work in her husband's shop."

"Why didn't you?" she asked.

"We didn't need no charity," he said. "Besides, I wasn't about to let the people who killed our parents off scot-free."

Shivering against the hatred in his voice, she ran her hands up and down her arms. So Justin was right. God *did* send the right people when you needed them. Knowing that didn't make her any more willing to go along with George's plan. He wasn't the right person. She didn't know how she knew this; she just did. Maybe, he never had been the right person.

"We're wasting time," he said, his voice thick with impatience. "Now move."

"No," she said. "I druther take my chances on a miracle."

He kicked the wall so hard, she feared the bricks would come tumbling down on top of her. "What's all this crazy talk about a miracle? It's that preacher, ain't it? He's the one who put all these crazy ideas in your head."

Before she could answer, Jed's voice called from the distance. "Someone's coming. Looks like the marshal."

George's curses were followed by the sound of running feet. More shouts. Then silence.

Thirty-one

Justin fell exhausted onto the bed without even bothering to undress. He covered his face with both hands.

He had run out of time. Less than twelve hours away at high noon, Sarah was scheduled to hang. The thought cut through him like a knife.

Now, he turned over and gave his pillow a thump. He'd hardly slept since learning of Sarah's incarceration, and he knew another long sleepless night awaited him. He dreaded dawn, dreaded the thought of losing the woman he loved, dreaded the thought of facing a future without her.

Never had he felt so utterly and completely helpless, so utterly alone. Had God really deserted him? Did his prayers fall on deaf ears?

Around midnight, something, the softest of sounds, jolted him upright. He swung his legs over the edge of the bed and strained his eyes in the darkness. Nothing.

Thinking perhaps he'd heard the baby stir in the crate next to his bed, he was just about to lie down again when a creaking floorboard made his heart pound.

"Who's there?"

A voice floated out of the darkness. "It's me."

Thinking he recognized the voice, Justin's heart skipped a beat. "George?"

"Jed."

Justin fumbled in the dark to light a candle. He checked Elizabeth, covering her with a blanket. Then he led Sarah's brother to the balcony where they could talk without waking the baby. Outside he set the candle on the railing.

Overhead, the stars that seemed to shine so bright whenever he and Sarah had been together had lost their luster. It was as if her absence had drained the world of its sparkle and color.

He spun around to face Jed. "It's about time you got here. Sarah is scheduled to hang tomorrow."

"We got here as fast as we could, no thanks to you."

"What are you talking about? I sent a telegram. What else could I have done?"

"You sent that cryptic message, and we didn't have no Bible. So we tried to rent us a hotel room to avail ourselves of a free one. But that Garfield fella was in town campaignin' for the presidency, and there weren't no rooms to be found."

Berating himself for not sending a message that could be more easily interpreted, Justin asked, "What did you do then?"

"We broke into the Lost and Found Church."

Justin stepped back. "You broke into a church?"

"There weren't no way around it," Jed

said. "Robert read from the Bible, and it said, 'Make haste to help me.' I figured you were in trouble and, no offense, Preacher, but I wasn't 'bout to put myself at risk to help you. Then Robert said maybe it was Sarah who was in trouble.

"We were just 'bout to leave the church when we got caught by the preacher. Accused us of lettin' his cat out when we broke in. Guess that's why the door was locked. In any case, since we were reading the Bible when he found us, he figured we wanted to be saved or found or somethin' and he insisted on baptizin' us. He dunked our heads in water, he did."

Justin laughed. He would loved to have seen the expression on George's face when his head came out of the baptismal font. He grew serious again. "Thank God you're here. You're an answer to my prayers."

Jed's brows shot up in surprise. "Never thought to be an answer to anyone's prayers," he said, adding in a more serious tone, "We're here to spring our little sister free."

Justin stiffened. "You aren't going to give yourselves up?"

Jed frowned. "Now why would we go and do a dumb thing like that?"

"The marshal agreed to let Sarah go if the three of you give yourselves up."

Jed shook his head. "How dumb do you think we is? We're here to spring Sarah, not put our own necks on the line. Only thing is, we need your help."

"My help?"

"It seems Sarah's got other ideas."

"You've talked to Sarah?"

"Not me. George. He snuck into the alley behind the jailhouse. T'wasn't easy. That marshal's got eyes in the back of his head. Accordin' to George, Sarah said you have some miracle tucked up your sleeve."

Justin's mouth went dry. "A miracle?"

"That's what she said. Said she druther wait for the miracle."

"The marshal is adamant. Unless you and your brothers give yourselves up—"

"We ain't doin' no such thing," Jed said loud enough to wake Elizabeth.

Justin hurried inside to rock her back to sleep.

Jed was still waiting on the balcony when Justin returned.

"We're not givin' ourselves up." This time Jed spoke in a hoarse, though no less firm, whisper. "Now, you're gonna have to talk some sense into my little sister. Tell her you know nothin' about no miracles. Tell her whatever you want, but make her forget this fool notion of hers that you're some kind of miracle worker."

Justin turned and rested his hands on the railing. He didn't like the way her brothers operated, but if he didn't help them, Sarah would hang sure as night followed day. "How do you plan to free her?"

"I reckon that's our business. All I can tell you is you better stay out of the way."

Justin turned. "It's too dangerous. Someone could get hurt. Sarah could get hurt."

"You don't think it's gonna hurt when they tie that rope around her neck?"

"There's got to be another way. Take me to the others."

Jed thought for a moment. "George ain't gonna like it. He's already hopping mad at Sarah. Said if she did what he told her to do, she wouldn't be in this mess."

"Let me talk to George."

Jed hesitated. "What about the baby?"

"I'll let my landlady know I'm leaving." He scrutinized Sarah's brother closely, sensing the private battle that raged within. "Trust me," he urged. "I want to save Sarah as much as you do, and we don't have much time."

Jed scratched his head. "George ain't gonna like it, but if you insist."

Justin tapped on the door of Ma's room to tell her he was leaving, then hurried downstairs to the barn to saddle his horse. He then followed Jed to a deserted fort outside of town.

Inside the building, he faced the three grizzled men in the light of a single candle and explained what had to be done.

"That's it?" George asked, his voice

thick with impatience. "That's your miracle? You want us to turn ourselves in?"

"I never said anything to you about a miracle," Justin said. "We're talking about doing what's right by your sister."

Jed's gaze darted between Justin and George. "Tomorrow night at this time, Sarah and us will be far away. That's doing what's right."

"No," Justin said, frustrated. "Someone is bound to get hurt."

George glared at him. "We sprung Sarah out of jail before and no one got hurt. We'd have done the same thing tonight if she weren't so determined to wait for a miracle. We almost got caught arguin' with her. Now they've got the town blocked off at both ends. There's no way we can get our horses near the jail. We got to wait till tomorrow. You better hope that she forgets about a miracle and cooperates with us."

Justin regarded each of the three men in turn. "The marshal blames her for his brother-in-law's death. He's out for revenge and is determined to do everything in his power to stop you. He's got a lot riding on this, and he isn't about to let you waltz out of town a second time. I've heard that he's deputized extra men to keep watch tomorrow. It could be war."

George folded his arms across his chest. "Since you know so much, you tell me what choice we have."

Justin fought to keep his anger in check. "I told you. Your choice is to turn yourselves in."

George's dark eyes blazed. "You think you've got all the answers, don't you?" He flashed a look of disdain. "You stand there looking all righteous. Well let me tell you somethin'. You don't know nothin' 'bout us."

Justin glanced at Robert. Out of the three, Robert was the most likely to do right by his sister, but his face remained passive.

Justin turned his attention back to George. "Sarah told me what happened to your parents."

George's lips curled upright. "Wells Fargo took everything from us. Do you hear me? *Everything.*"

Justin shook his head. "That's where you're wrong. Your integrity, your good name, a chance for a normal life . . . those you threw away yourself."

A crack seemed to show in George's armor, a look of uncertainty crossed his face. Justin felt encouraged, but the moment, if indeed there had been a moment, soon passed and Justin's hopes were dashed.

George backed away as if to distance himself from the truth of Justin's words. He turned his back, throwing his hands upward in exasperation. "Take him back to town."

Justin quickly switched tactics. "Please. Hear me out." He waited until he had George's full attention again before continuing. "Sarah tells me that none of you ever hurt anyone."

"That's true," Jed said. "What they said about us killin' that passenger is a downright lie."

"If it's true that you've never hurt anyone, then maybe . . . I know a lawyer in Boston who—"

George spat in disgust. "Once the

marshal gets his hands on us, we're as good as bear meat. We ain't gonna be around long enough to wait for no fancy lawyer from Boston."

"There's got to be another way." Justin beseeched each man in turn. "In the name of God, I beg you to do the right thing. For once in your lives, think about what your actions will do to Sarah."

George wagged his finger in Justin's face. "We've always put our sister's needs first."

Jed nodded in agreement. "Everything we've done we've done for her. We even put her in that there orphanage when she was twelve so she'd have a proper home."

"For all the good it did us," George scoffed. "She wasn't there a week when she ran away. It took us three months to track her down. She was always running away. We never knew what trouble she was gonna get into next."

Jed gave an emphatic nod. "You won't find more carin' folks than the three of us."

Justin was tempted to argue the point but decided it would only make her brothers more obstinate than they already were. "Sarah would stop running away if she had a more normal life. You can give it to her. All of you. Just turn yourselves in, and—"

George kicked an empty water bucket across the room. "If you're so anxious to help Sarah, then get over to the jail and tell her to cooperate with us."

Justin stared hard at George. "I can't do that."

George cursed and pointed to the door. "Then get out of here and don't come back."

⁂

"Psst."

Sarah heard the sound and her heart pounded. *Not George again. Please don't let it be George.* He'd been furious with her, and the last thing she wanted was to get into another heated argument with him.

"Sarah!"

"Justin?" Relief flooded through her. The window was too high for her to see out, but she pressed herself against the wall beneath it. "What are you doing here?"

"I can't stay long," he said, his voice hushed. "They have the town blocked on both sides. I had to climb over a roof to get here. I just saw George."

"Then you know what he wants to do," she whispered back.

He hesitated before answering her. "It might be the only way."

She took a deep breath. The wall between them was only a few inches thick, but he seemed so far away. She closed her eyes and visualized his face. "Remember when you told me that God sends the right people when we need them?"

"I remember," he said.

"All these years, I thought God didn't care a hill o' beans about me. But tonight I asked George if anyone tried to help us after Ma and Papa died, and you know what he told me? Ol' Mrs. Bonheimer offered to let him work in her husband's store. She also wanted to adopt me. Said she'd give me a good home."

"And he turned her down?"

Sarah nodded. "He said we didn't need no charity."

"I'm not sure—"

"You were right," she said, a tad too loud. Then remembering to lower her voice, she added, "All these years, I thought God had turned His back on us, but that ain't true. It was George who refused to accept God's help. Then God sent you, then Elizabeth, and He sent that goat, and—"

"See? What did I tell you? God loves you. And *I* love you," he whispered. His words made her smile.

"I love you too," she said, squeezing back tears.

"We're running out of time." His voice grew more urgent. "Sarah, I hate to say this, but . . . Your brothers may be your only chance."

She searched his face. "You ain't giving up on God, now, are you?"

"Of c-course not," he stammered. "And don't you give up on Him either."

"I ain't planning to."

"I've got to go. Someone's coming."

"Who's there?" a male voice shouted and, after that, all she heard was the sound of running feet.

Thirty-two

The sun rode high in the sky, and the air shimmered with oppressive heat. Only two women had been hanged in all of Texas, both convicted of murder. Sarah would be the first woman to hang in Rocky Creek.

Folks traveled from miles around to witness history in the making. They came on horseback and on foot. They came in buckboards, shays, and surreys. A long line of vehicles extended far beyond the town limits, blocking Main Street in both directions.

Merchants closed their shops. Even the Chinese railroad workers abandoned their sledgehammers and walked the five miles to town to gather around the rough wood gallows erected next to the livery stables.

One man left the barbershop half-shaved, the right side of his face still covered with shaving cream.

Justin stared at the faces in the crowd. Some he recognized, but most he didn't. He spotted Barrel, the singing barber; Jake the saloon owner; Dr. Myers.

The feathers on Mrs. Hitchcock's hat bobbed up and down like a washday plunger as she fought her way through the crowd. Even Hank Applegate thought the occasion momentous enough to leave his rocking chair.

Justin wondered if he would have the heart to minister to these people after today.

He craned his neck looking for Sarah's brothers. *Where were they?* At first, he'd hoped they would do what was right to save their sister and turn themselves in. Now, he just wanted them to save her however they saw fit.

Justin was horrified to spot Ma in the crowd, Elizabeth in her arms. He'd given her explicit instructions to stay away. Heart pounding, he waved in an effort to catch her attention with no success. Shouldering his way through the mob of people, he reached her side.

"What are you doing here?" he demanded.

Ma didn't look the least bit apologetic. "Now, Reverend, this could be the last time that poor mama can see her baby."

"It's dangerous," Justin said. "You must leave."

Ma's eyes widened. "Dangerous how?"

A buzz among the spectators signaled Sarah's appearance. Justin glanced in the direction of the jailhouse, then turned back to Ma. "I don't have time to explain. Just go."

"But—"

The marshal could be heard above the loud clamors. "Step aside! Step aside!"

The mob crowded the boardwalk and pressed closer to the buildings to leave an opening down the center of Main Street for the marshal and his men to pass. Sarah walked in the middle of the group, her hands shackled behind her back, her face pale.

The ladies of the Rocky Creek Quilting Bee had provided Sarah with a clean frock and fixed her hair. The paisley striped linen dress was trimmed in brown velvet and gathered in back with just a hint of a bustle. The brown and beige dress offered a startling, though no less pleasing, contrast to Sarah's red hair and boots. In Justin's eyes, she looked beautiful as always.

Justin made his way through the crowd and stepped in front of her. Briggs shielded his prisoner with a protective arm.

Sarah smiled at Justin. Her eyes were filled with such complete trust, his own lack of faith felt like a heavy weight on his shoulders. *What if George fails to help her escape? What if something goes wrong? God, please don't let anyone get hurt.*

Marshal Briggs glared at him. "Move out of the way, Reverend."

"The prisoner has the right to spiritual counsel."

Briggs hesitated. "All right, then. But make it quick." He motioned to his men to step away from the prisoner.

Justin moved to Sarah's side. Her face was pale, but her eyes were as wide and blue as the noontime sky.

"Are you okay?" he whispered.

She rolled her eyes upward. "You don't suppose God forgot about me, do you?"

The question pained him. Last night, her faith had been the guarding light that kept him going. Now even she was having doubts.

"Not a chance," he said with a confidence that belied his own misgivings.

Her face lit up. "I've been praying hard."

"That's good."

"I even prayed a long-winded one for good measure."

"I'm impressed."

Justin glanced at the mob of people surrounding them, but there was still no sign of Sarah's brothers.

"Hurry it up, Preacher," Briggs called, scanning the crowd, one hand on the gun at his side.

Justin raised his hand to indicate he needed another minute or two. "Close your eyes, Sarah."

"What?"

"Close your eyes and look like you're praying."

"I am prayin'," she said. "Like I told you, I've been prayin' up a storm."

Justin lowered his head. "Now listen to me. Everything's going to be okay. When the time comes, you'll know what to do."

Her lashes flew up. "That must be some kind of miracle you're expectin'." She eyed him with a suspicious gleam. "It ain't gonna be locusts, is it?" she asked with an anxious glance at the sky. "You know I can't stand those things."

"Shh. Close your eyes." He glanced at Briggs, who was busy giving orders to the hangman marshal. The marshal was a youth of no more than seventeen or eighteen. Face drawn, he appeared to be almost as scared as Justin felt. Obviously, this was his first official duty.

"I'm sure it won't be locusts," Justin said.

The hangman lifted the hinged trapdoor, checked the iron lock, and then let the door fall with a bang.

Sarah jumped and her eyes flew open.

"It's okay," Justin whispered.

Marshal Briggs moved to her side. "Okay, that's enough praying for one day." He pulled a watch from the pocket of his waistcoat and signaled for the hangman to escort Sarah up the steps leading to the platform.

Sarah sought Justin's eyes, her trusting gaze ludicrous in light of her situation. "I'm not all that fond of snakes either," she shouted to be heard over the crowd.

"I'll pass on the message," he called back.

He turned and scanned the throng of people. What was taking so long for George to make his move? As much as he hated violence, he couldn't think of any other way to save her. None of his own efforts had worked. Now it was up to George. He prayed a silent prayer.

"Psst."

Justin turned and spotted Sarah's brother Jed frantically gesturing with his hand. Feeling a sense of dread, Justin pushed his way through the mob of people to join him.

"We have a problem," Jed whispered. "We can't get our horses through. The road in and out of town is blocked with wagons. We need more time."

"We don't have more time," Justin said sharply.

"Think of somethin'," Jed said. "And hurry!" With that, he turned and disappeared through the crowd.

Justin spun around and frantically pushed his way toward the gallows.

A hush fell over the spectators as the hanging marshal positioned Sarah directly below the gibbet and pulled a black hood out of a wooden box.

Marshal Briggs walked up the steps and stood in front of Sarah. He unrolled a parchment death warrant and read it aloud. She was charged as an accessory to the killing of one Matthew Jenkins, an innocent passenger on a Wells Fargo stage. After reading the warrant, he rolled it up again and handed it to one of the men by his side.

Justin moved forward. "Marshal, the prisoner has made one last request."

Briggs faced Justin, his expression dark with impatience. "This is a hanging, Reverend, not a general store. Request denied."

"She's entitled to one last request!" someone shouted, and Justin thought he recognized Jed's voice.

The crowd began to hiss and boo, and Briggs quickly relented. "All right, but make it quick."

Justin looked around for Ma, thinking he could buy time by having Sarah hold Elizabeth. Apparently, she'd done what he'd told her to and taken the baby home.

Now what? Then he spotted Barrel a short distance away and an idea clicked in his mind.

"Miss Prescott has an affinity for the hymn 'Amazing Grace,'" he said. "And Mr. Barrel has graciously agreed to sing for her."

Barrel's face turned a shocking red. He shook his head, both chins trembling, and backed away. "No, no, no," he protested. He moved away, his arms windmilling as he fought his way through the crowd.

Before he could escape, Timber Joe stopped him. "Hold it right there, mister." His rifle pointed at the big man's chest. "We can't have ourselves a hanging till the fat man sings," he drawled. "If you know what's good for you, you'll start howling like a lovesick hound."

Ignoring Barrel's pleas, Timber Joe nudged him with his rifle and forced him to walk toward the gallows. All eyes followed the two men up the steps. The stairs sagged and creaked beneath Barrel's considerable weight. The barber stood next to Sarah sweating bullets. A passing stranger might easily mistake Barrel for the one to be hung instead of Sarah, who looked remarkably calm by comparison.

Barrel pulled a handkerchief from his pocket and mopped his forehead.

"Sing!" Timber Joe ordered, thrusting the muzzle into Barrel's back.

Barrel opened his mouth, emitting an awful screeching sound. Somewhere in the distance a dog protested with a wailing howl.

Sarah's mouth dropped open, her eyes wide in disbelief. Briggs fell back as if shot, his hands clamped firmly over his ears. Men and women alike scrambled about in an effort to escape. Horses nickered and pawed the ground.

A look of pure agony crossed Timber Joe's face, but he stubbornly kept his rifle in place.

Looking sorry for the man, Sarah glanced at Justin, then back at Barrel. She then surprised Justin by joining Barrel in song, her voice sweet and clear. Justin was so touched that she remembered the words to his favorite hymn, it took him awhile to notice Barrel had stopped screeching. The tenor's tone was now strong and vibrant, each note resonating with depth and power. Barrel couldn't sing solo in front of a crowd, but he could sing a glorious duet.

Slowly, the spectators began to move in closer, and even Marshal Briggs seemed affected by what he heard, a wistful look having replaced his usual scowl.

Justin couldn't resist lifting his voice

in song, too, and soon others joined in. Even Timber Joe lowered his rifle and began to sing.

At the end of the hymn, a waiting silence hung in the air.

All too soon, the marshal raised a megaphone to his mouth. "The Prescott brothers have exactly sixty seconds to turn themselves in. If they fail to do so, Sarah Prescott will meet her Maker. May her soul rest in peace."

Justin glanced around but the street was still blocked, and there was no sign of Sarah's brothers.

Once again, Briggs reached for his pocket watch. "The countdown begins . . . now!"

Thirty-three

"Forty-six, forty-five, forty-four—"

Sarah kept her eyes focused on Justin. The man looked as nervous as a gunslinger without his weapons. She forced a smile, hoping to relieve his mind. *God performs miracles. Isn't that what Justin always says?*

"Thirty-five, thirty-four, thirty-three—"

Her faith got her through the night, but it was hard to hold on to God's hand with a rope hanging over your head. A chilling reality hit her: time was running out. With nothing left to hold on to, she began to panic.

Her mouth dry, her body trembled so hard that her handcuffs rattled. What if she'd run out of miracles? Like her papa. Like her ma.

"Seventeen, sixteen, fifteen—"

Her mind muddled with fear, the last bit of hope faded away. She glanced up at the sky. *God, I plumb hope You know what You're doin'.*

"Zero!" Briggs shouted, and a hushed silence followed. The only sound that Sarah could hear was the pounding of her own heart.

The marshal held up his hand, and no one moved. "This is the last chance to save Sarah Prescott. If her brothers are here, now is the time to step forward."

She stared hard at Justin and mouthed the words, *"I love you."* Never again would she be able to feel his arms around her.

Briggs signaled with his hand, and the hanging marshal moved toward her, slowly, refusing to look at her. He lifted the hood upward. Sarah closed her eyes.

"No!" Justin cried.

Her eyes flew open.

Briggs pointed a threatening finger at

Justin. "You come one stop closer, and I'll arrest you for obstructin' justice."

Justin took another step.

"Arrest him!" Briggs yelled.

"No, don't, please," Sarah begged, but no one paid her the least bit of heed.

Two of his deputies hastened down the steps, but before they reached Justin's side, a man who was vaguely familiar broke through the crowd, his face flushed as if he'd been running.

"I canna tell a lie. I'm the lassie's brother," he called with a wave of his hand.

Confused, Sarah stared at him. Had she heard right? She suddenly recognized him as the Scottish drummer they'd met on the trail and who had sold them baby bottles. But identifying the man raised more questions than it answered. Why would the hawker say something that was not true? Something that was bound to land him in hot water?

Stunned silence followed the peddler's announcement, followed by thunderous applause led by Barrel, the singing barber. The deputies bypassed Justin and started for the drummer.

Then a second man stepped forward and introduced himself as a Prescott. Sarah had never seen the man before in her life. Judging by the look of confusion on Justin's face, neither had he.

This time, the crowd went wild. Several moments passed before the clapping and hooting stopped. The instant it grew quiet, another stranger stepped forward. "I'm Sarah's brother."

Sarah glanced at the marshal, who stood rubbing his hands together and practically licking his chops. "We got the Prescott brothers," he announced to the crowd. "You can be certain that at long last, justice will be served."

At that very moment, shouts sounded from a short distance away. Three men forced their horses along the boardwalk, yelling and waving their weapons until the gawkers scrambled out of their way. The leader, a short stocky man wearing an eye patch, slid off his horse and walked up to the marshal on bowed legs.

"Thought we'd never get through," he

said. "We're Miss Prescott's brothers," he announced, his thumbs hooked onto his belt. "Now you let that girl go, you hear?"

Briggs looked downright befuddled. "I didn't know there were *six* Prescott brothers," he said.

Sarah was even more perplexed than before. She glanced at Justin, who shrugged his shoulders in bewilderment.

Just then, a tall man with a sweeping mustache stood on the rooftop of the livery and introduced himself as a Prescott. "Sorry, Marshal," he shouted, "but me and my two brothers couldn't get through Main Street."

Much to Sarah's surprise, Jed stepped from the crowd. "I'm Sarah's brother, and so is he." He pointed at Robert.

Sarah gasped in dismay. She never meant for her brothers to sacrifice their safety on her behalf.

By the time it was over, some twenty "brothers" had turned themselves in. The deputy marshals practically ran around in circles, not knowing who to arrest first.

Justin ran up the wooden steps and quickly strode up to Briggs. "You've got what you wanted, Marshal. A deal's a deal."

"Now you hold your horses," Briggs bellowed. "You're not gonna get away with this!" He turned to all the men claiming to be Prescotts. "You're imposters, all of you! Get out of here, before I run you all in." He pulled out his gun and fired it into the air, sending the men running for cover. "Go!"

Briggs holstered his gun and shouted to the hanging marshal, "String her up!"

Thirty-four

Justin lurched forward, but he was stayed by two deputy marshals, each grabbing an arm.

The crowd booed. Seeing Sarah standing beneath the gibbet apparently had a sobering effect on even the most revengeful spectator. Even Owen's widow seemed to have second thoughts.

"Let her go," she said to her brother, before turning and disappearing through the crowd.

The cries grew louder and fists pounded the air. "Let her go! Let her go!"

Briggs showed no sign of backing down. The townsfolk had made a fool of him, and his eyes glittered with the need to reassert his power.

The hanging marshal started to lower the black hood over Sarah's head, but she refused it. With a shrug, he tossed the hood aside and reached for the knotted rope. The shouts had died down, and only a few sobs could be heard. A couple of spectators fell to their knees in prayer.

Justin fought to free himself, but the deputy marshals held tight.

A single voice shattered the hushed silence. "Release Miss Prescott at once." The speaker's commanding voice attracted attention, and all eyes turned to a man who stood in the shadows of a doorway. From where he stood, Justin was unable to get a good look at the speaker and didn't recognize the voice.

Even Briggs seemed puzzled at first by the man's identity. "By whose authority?" he sneered.

The man stepped out of the shadows, and a murmur rippled through the crowd. "By the authority vested in me by the state of Texas, I order you to release this prisoner."

Justin's mouth dropped open. The dignified man was none other than Judge Fassbender. The judge didn't look or sound anything like the drunk man Justin had previously encountered.

Briggs still couldn't see him clear enough to recognize him. "Only the governor can stay a hanging, and I've not heard from Governor Roberts."

Under less grim circumstances, Justin might have laughed. Suddenly, the town marshal was concerned with protocol.

Fassbender pushed his way through the throng and stood in front of the gallows. "I'm not staying the execution. I'm overturning it."

Surprise registered on Briggs's face. "You're—"

"Judge Fassbender." He turned to the crowd and tipped his hat. "I just received a telegram from a witness who disputes the claim that the Prescott gang was responsible for the death of a Wells Fargo passenger. It seems that the stagecoach victim's abused wife decided to shoot her husband during the holdup and let the robbers take the blame."

Shocked gasps rose from the crowd.

Briggs looked like a man about to be pushed over a cliff. His face red, he stammered a denial. "Since when did you give a witness any heed?"

"Since I was soundly reminded why I became a judge in the first place. And it wasn't to hang innocent people." He glanced at Justin before pointing to Sarah. "Since Miss Prescott has not been charged with any other crime, she is to be released at once."

Cheers drowned out the rest of his sentence.

The hanging marshal quickly unlocked her handcuffs, and the crowd broke into applause.

The instant her hands were free, Sarah ran down the stairs and into Justin's arms.

Justin held her tight. He couldn't believe their good fortune. If it hadn't been for the Scottish peddler, Jed, and all the rest, Sarah might have been hanged before the judge arrived.

"You didn't tell me you had so many brothers," he said softly in her ear.

"I didn't know myself," she whispered back. "I guess it's what you call a plague of brothers."

Justin laughed. "That's exactly what it was," he said. "A plague of brothers! God really does work in wondrous ways."

Wanting to thank the judge, he searched the crowd, but Fassbender was gone.

Mrs. Hitchcock saddled up to Justin and nudged him with her elbow. "Cost me a bundle to hire them," she said and then promptly repeated herself.

Justin stared at her. "*You* hired those men to say they were Sarah's brothers?"

"Not all of them," she said, her voice shrill with uncertainty. "We only hired three."

"That's the God's honest truth," added another woman. "I know what you're thinking, Pastor. They can prove their real identity, so there was no chance of them being hanged or anything."

Mrs. Hitchcock nodded. "We couldn't let that precious child's mother hang, now could we? Could we?"

"None of us could," Ma added, joining the little circle that had gathered around Justin and Sarah.

"I thought I told you to leave," Justin said.

"I couldn't leave," Ma replied. "My dray is boxed in with all those other vehicles."

Sarah clapped her hands together in delight upon seeing Elizabeth.

"Don't tell me," Justin said, eyeing his landlady. "You arranged for Sarah's 'brothers' to show up too."

Ma refused to admit it, but she didn't deny it either. Instead, she handed Elizabeth over to Sarah, a conspiratorial smile on her face.

Sarah held the infant in the circle of her arms, tears glistening. "You're the dearest, sweetest baby in the whole wide world."

Elizabeth stared at Sarah with unblinking eyes and her mouth twitched upward.

"Would you look at that?" Sarah said "If that ain't the most beautiful smile."

Justin grinned like a proud papa. Ma and the other ladies walked away, leaving him and Sarah alone with Elizabeth.

"She's cutting a tooth," he said.

"Oh, Justin . . ." She looked up, her eyes swimming in tears of happiness.

"Come on," he said. "Let's go home."

"Wait," she said. She lay Elizabeth in his arms. "I need to talk to my brothers."

He glanced at the end of the street where George, Jed, and Robert sat on their horses waiting with a saddled horse for Sarah. Justin glanced back at the marshal. The lawman was in a heated argument with Judge Fassbender and not paying any attention to them.

He shifted Elizabeth onto his shoulder. "Sarah, if the marshal finds out that they're the real Prescotts—"

She squeezed his arm. "I won't be long."

"Let me go with you."

"I need to talk to them alone."

He didn't want her to go, didn't want

to let her out of his sight. "If anything happens to you—"

"It won't," she promised.

"Hurry before Briggs realizes who they are. Meet me at Ma's house." He gave her directions and kissed her on the forehead.

She lifted her skirts higher than any lady should and ran down the street to her three waiting brothers.

Thirty-five

George led the way to the deserted fort outside of town, riding hard. By the time Sarah dismounted and tethered her horse to the railing in front of one of the old buildings, George and Jed were already in a heated argument.

"Of all the foolhardy things to do!" George shouted. "What if the marshal had recognized us as the real brothers?"

"He didn't," Jed said defensively.

"He could have!"

"Okay, so I made a mistake," Jed said. "I didn't like all those other men claimin' to be Sarah's brothers when they ain't."

Sarah walked over to Jed and hugged him. "I'll never forget what you did," she said, knowing his heart was in the right place.

George shrugged in disgust. "We ride out tonight." He spun around and stalked away. Sarah called after him. He stopped and waited for her to catch up to him.

"George . . ." She bit her lip. "I love you. I truly do. After Ma and Papa died, you took care of us. Done kept us all together, you did." It might have worked better had he accepted Mrs. Bonheimer's help. But she had no heart to blame him at this late date. Right or wrong, he did what he thought best.

The anger left his face and his eyes softened. "I'll always take care of you, Sarah. You gotta stop runnin' off all the time and doing the first fool thing that pops into your head."

"I'm not a little girl anymore," she said.

George looked surprised, as if suddenly forced to confront something outside his range of experience. "I-I can see that. You . . . uh . . . look mighty pretty in that frock. But you're still a woman, and you need a man to take care of you."

She lifted her chin. "Not the way you see fit."

A muscle twitched at his jaw. "What's that supposed to mean?"

With a pang she realized her mistake in looking up to him. As a child, she thought George could do no wrong. Now she wondered if he was capable of doing what was right.

"Today I almost got my neck in a noose—"

"And you almost took us down with you," he said, his voice harsh as thunder. "Now maybe you'll listen to me!"

She shook her head. "I can't listen to you anymore, George."

"You have no choice." He pointed to his chest with his thumb. "I'm your brother. Without me, you'd have nothing!"

"I still have nothing," she argued. "I don't have a home. I don't have a future. What kind of life is that?"

George frowned with impatience. "I don't have time for this."

"Robbing stages is wrong," she continued.

George's eyes glittered. "That Bible thumper has you brainwashed."

Refusing to allow herself to be intimidated by him any longer, she threw back her head and met his eyes without flinching. "It's wrong, and our ma and papa would turn over in their graves if they knew their children were outlaws. We're stealing, and ain't nothing you say gonna change that."

"You call it what you want, little sister. I don't want to hear about it."

"I'm not your *little* sister," she said evenly. "I'm all grown up. I don't have to do what you tell me anymore."

His jaw tightened. "You ain't got no choice. I'm the head of the family." He turned and stalked away, his fists held tight at his side.

Having no intention of giving up so easily, she called after him, "George, I'm begging you. No more robberies."

He stopped, his back toward her. "We

pull out tonight. Be here." With that he stomped up the wooden steps and walked into the log outbuilding.

She turned to find Jed and Robert staring at her. Without a word, she ran to her horse and rode back to town.

Thirty-six

Her heart heavy, she searched the road ahead for Ma's Boardinghouse. She was a free woman and no longer had to worry about being hanged, but as long as her brothers continued with their outlaw ways, her future looked as bleak as a coal mine.

She would always be worried about the next holdup, the next wanted poster, the next newspaper headline. She feared that her brothers' outlaw ways would hamper Justin's work. Even more worrisome was the thought of Elizabeth being subjected to the taunts of other children—and possible danger from those who might take revenge on the Prescott brothers by harming her.

Dark clouds gathered behind the distant hills. The wind had picked up, and the trees bowed like performers onstage.

Spotting the sign on the fence, she tethered her horse next to Justin's. Noah moved his head up and down and nuzzled her with his nose. She stroked his forehead. "Hi there, fella. It's been awhile."

Moments later, Justin greeted her at the door with a tender kiss, then pulled her through the house and into Ma's cozy kitchen.

Glancing at the neat counters, crisp curtains, and steaming kettle, Sarah was assaulted with regrets. She remembered her mama's kitchen and suddenly realized how much she had missed through the years. Missed having a home. Since her parents' death, she and her brothers had moved from town to town, taking shelter in abandoned buildings, shoddy hotels, and, on occasion, cold, drafty caves.

The smell of freshly baked cookies

wafted through the air. Sarah recalled helping her mother roll out pastry dough. She could hardly remember her mother's face, yet she could remember every detail of that long-ago day.

Such a sense of longing and loss washed over her, it was all she could do to breathe. What would it feel like to live a normal life again? To follow recipes instead of stagecoach routes? To wield a rolling pin instead of a gun?

"You okay?" Justin asked, as if he sensed her anguish.

Before she could answer, Ma spoke up. "Of course she's okay. She's just dazed from all that's happened. Sit down and I'll fix you somethin' to eat."

Sarah sat at the table across from Justin. Ma fixed them bowls of hot vegetable soup with homemade muffins.

Justin led them in prayer. There was a lot to thank God for, and Justin didn't leave a single thing out.

"Mercy me," Ma said, when he ended the prayer. "I do believe the soup has gone cold."

Sarah giggled.

Ma added more hot soup to their

bowls. "Folks out here don't have a mind to sit around listening to a lot of talk," she said kindly.

Justin regarded her thoughtfully. "So what you're saying is I better stop being so wordy."

Ma gave an approving nod. She leaned closer to Sarah. "He catches on fast."

Sarah smiled. It was one of the things she loved about Justin. If only George was as eager to change his ways, how much happier she would be.

"I'll leave you two to enjoy your lunch in peace," Ma said. Wiping her hands on her apron, Ma left the room, leaving the two of them alone.

Justin studied her thoughtfully as if he sensed something amiss. "I'm curious . . . Why did Jed turn himself in?"

"He told me he didn't like all those strangers claimin' to be my brothers when they weren't," Sarah explained.

Justin laughed. "If Briggs only knew that he let the real Prescott brothers go, he'd have a fit."

After lunch, he stood and pulled her

to her feet. "Come, I want to show you something." He called to Ma in the other room. "Do you mind watching Elizabeth for a while? I want to show Sarah the church."

"You two run along," Ma called back. "That sweet baby and I will be just fine."

A short while later, Justin led Sarah by the hand through the double doors of the church.

"What do you think?" he asked, his eyes dancing with joy.

Not wanting to hurt his feelings, Sarah didn't know what to say. The rusted tin roof had more holes than a bucket after target practice. The windows were broken. Floorboards warped. The church was as battered as a war-weary soldier.

None of this seemed to matter to Justin. "What do you think?" he repeated impatiently, his face split in a wide grin. Never had she seen him look so happy. This was truly where he belonged.

"It's . . . really something," she managed, and his smile grew wider.

Lifting her eyes, she followed the waning rays of sun all the way to the rafters. There was as much sky as roof. Storm clouds blotted out the bright light, casting moving shadows upon the church floor.

"It looks like the inside of your church is about to be baptized," she said.

He laughed. "If you think it's bad now, you should have seen it before. How are you with a hammer and nails?"

She smiled. "I reckon I can hold my own."

His grin practically reached both ears. "Good. I wouldn't want it to rain on our wedding."

She choked back a sob and turned away.

He lay a hand on her shoulder. "Sarah?"

She closed her eyes against the pain that welled up inside her. She wanted so much to put her past behind her and build a new life with Justin. But wishing didn't make it so, and being a Prescott made it impossible.

While they traveled across country, Justin had been in her world and their dissimilarities seemed not to matter. But now that she was in his world, their differences seemed insurmountable.

"I don't belong here," she whispered. She turned to face him. "I have to go."

Justin stiffened, the blood seeming to drain from his face. "I don't understand . . . I thought once your legal problems were over, we could be together. I thought that's what you wanted."

"I do," she whispered. "I do."

"Then why, Sarah? Why can't you stay?"

She swallowed the sob that rose to her throat. "You belong here. I don't."

"You belong with me," he said, reaching for her.

She backed away. She couldn't do what was right by him if he touched her. Her resolve was far too fragile, her heart far too self-serving.

"My . . . my brothers . . . I . . . We're leaving tonight."

He stared at her dumbfounded. "You're going with your brothers?"

"What choice do I have?" she asked. "They're my family."

Something seemed to die in his eyes, an inner light dimmed like an extinguished candle. "What about me? Elizabeth? We're your family."

She felt a twisting, searing pain in her heart, and she was nearly overwhelmed with anguish. But she didn't dare allow herself to give in to despair. Too much was at stake.

"Why are you doing this to me?" she cried. "Why?"

His face clouded in confusion. "Doing what?"

"Making it so difficult."

"I want us to be together. What's so difficult about that?"

"How can you say that? I'm a Prescott. Just like my brothers."

"You're not like your brothers, Sarah. How they choose to live their lives has nothing to do with you."

"That's a fool thing to say, and you know it. My brothers ain't exactly pickin' grapes off the Lord's grapevine. They're thieves. What they do reflects on me."

"They have their lives, and you have yours."

She loved him even more for believing the way he did, but she knew from painful experience that people judged families as a whole.

"When they pull off their next robbery, the wanted posters will have my name on it," she said. "The name I was born with. How will your church feel about us then?"

"Sarah, please, we'll work this out."

She shook her head. "My reputation will follow you and Elizabeth for the rest of your born days. All the pretty words in the world ain't gonna change that. I can't do this to the two of you. I . . ." Her voice faltered. "I love you too much."

"Sarah, listen to me. When I lost my church in Boston, I thought my life was over. I had no idea why God turned against me. But thinking back, I realize that it was all part of His master plan to bring the two of us together."

"Some master plan," she said. "I ain't been nothin' but trouble to you from the first day we met. Don't go sayin' otherwise, you hear?"

"I wouldn't have wanted it any other

way," he said with such heartfelt meaning, he took her breath away. "More than that, you believe in miracles."

Sarah held on to what little resolve she had left. She had to make him understand how she could only hurt him in the future, hurt the church he loved so dearly, hurt the child that had come to mean so much to both of them.

She lifted her lashes to him. "It seems to me that a person is only entitled to so many miracles in a lifetime. I'm afraid I've run through my allotment in the last few weeks."

"Sarah—"

"Don't, Justin." She cast her eyes downward. "It's killin' me to do this, but I ain't got a choice."

She spun around and ran down the aisle. Her red boots hammered the warped wooden floor like nails in a coffin.

He chased her down the aisle and out the double doors. "Sarah . . . please don't go. Talk to me."

Without so much as a backward glance, she mounted the horse George bought for her and raced out of town.

A bolt of lightning zagged across the sky, followed by the low rumble of thunder and large drops of rain.

Looking over her shoulder to make sure no one trailed behind, she veered off the road and into the woods.

Though the trail leading to her brother's hideout was hidden by overgrown brush, she found it again without any difficulty.

Shoving two fingers into her mouth she whistled, signaling her arrival, and slid off her horse. The door swung open and Jed motioned her in with a wave of his hand.

She tethered her horse next to the others. Ducking her head against the rain, she ran inside.

Jed greeted her. "It's 'bout time you got back. George is havin' a conniption."

George stood staring at an old cannon, probably left there following the War Between the States, his hands behind his back. He didn't even look at her when he spoke.

"Are you sure you weren't followed?"

"I'm sure," she said.

He turned. "We should have been long gone by now. It's only a matter of time before the marshal figures out that he let the real Prescotts go, if he don't already know."

Robert filled a tin cup with coffee and handed it to her. "Relax, all of you. The marshal won't want anyone to know he had us in the palm of his hand and let us get away."

"Shh . . . someone's coming," Jed said, peering out of one of the dirty windows.

"Who is it?" Sarah asked.

His back to the wall, Jed quickly glanced outside. "Drats! It's the preacher."

George glared at her. "You ain't nothin' but trouble."

Sarah's knees almost caved beneath her. "I don't want to see him," she whispered. "Tell him to go away."

Her three brothers exchanged looks before George started for the door. "I'll talk to him."

"No, not you," Sarah said. "Let

Robert talk to him." She knew that of her three brothers, Robert would be the most gentle and kind. "Please, George."

George nodded to Robert. "Tell him to get lost. And make it quick."

Thirty-seven

Justin didn't know what he'd hoped to accomplish, but he couldn't just let Sarah walk out of his life. Not without a fight. He'd hoped that she'd had time to reconsider, but the moment he saw Robert emerge from the dilapidated log building, his hopes all but vanished.

Robert wasted no time getting to the point. "She doesn't want to talk to you."

Justin glanced at the old fort building, both heartened and dismayed by the small movement in the window. She was so close, yet so very far away.

"I'm not leaving till she does."

Robert moved to the guard station out of the rain, and Justin followed suit.

For several moments the two men stood in silence, oblivious to the puddle of water that formed around their feet.

Robert was the first to speak. "What's goin' on with you two? When Sarah left earlier, I was sure she would never come back."

Hands on his hips, Justin glanced down at the little river of water that ran past his boots. "I want to marry Sarah."

"I thought as much."

Justin nodded. "I love her."

"I know."

"She turned me down."

"Because of our outlawing ways?" Robert asked.

"Yes."

Robert gazed into the distance as if seeing something in the distant past.

"I once asked a girl to marry me," Robert began slowly, his face soft with sadness. "Prettiest girl you ever did see. Blonde hair. Big blue eyes. Her mother was a schoolteacher, her father a cabinet maker. She came from a real family, and I wanted what she had. A home. A profession I could be proud of. Children.

"She turned me down even after I swore to go straight. Said that whatever my family did would haunt us for the rest of our lives."

Justin gave a brief nod. "Sarah said practically the same thing."

Robert rubbed a hand over his unshaven chin. "She's right, you know. You being a preacher and all."

"There's a baby who needs a mother, and Sarah . . . she's great with her. She's everything we both need, Elizabeth and me." Justin studied Robert's face, sensing both a tortured soul and a sympathetic ear.

Robert stared back, his forehead furrowed. "She's a Prescott."

Grimacing, Justin took a moment to gather his thoughts before meeting Robert's troubled eyes again. "Sarah always said nice things about you. She said you taught her how to read and write. Seems to me of all her brothers, you've shown her the most concern."

Robert's eyes darkened with emotion. "George believes he's doing right by us."

"Believing doesn't make it so."

For the longest while, Robert didn't say a word. He just kept staring at some distant memory. Heaving a sigh, he stepped from beneath the overhang. He paused for a moment, rain beading his head and trickling down his face. Finally, he turned toward the fort. "Stay here."

"Let me go with you," Justin called after him.

Robert's steps faltered. "Stay right where you are, Reverend. You've got a whole lot of prayin' to do."

As soon as she heard Robert's footfall, Sarah spun around to face the door. Robert walked inside and took his time wiping the mud off his boots though the scruffy wood floor was already covered with dust, dried leaves, and animal droppings.

Sarah took one look at his grim face and her heart sank. His encounter with Justin must have been even more difficult than she imagined. "Is . . . is Justin—"

Instead of answering her question,

Robert surprised her by talking about a girl named Laurie Anne. She never knew the girl's name. The only reason she knew about her at all was because she had followed Robert one night to find out why he was acting so secretive. Sarah had only been sixteen at the time and Robert eighteen, but it was obvious he was in love. She questioned him about the gir later, but he refused to tell her anything and made her promise not to say a word to George and Jed. Now, he went into great detail.

"Her smile was as bright as the sun," he said.

Sarah had never heard Robert talk with such passion, seen such fire in his eyes. This was how he wrote, not how he usually spoke. Sarah always thought that his literary voice was far stronger than his actual voice, but today he proved her wrong.

"What's gotten into you, Robert?" Jed asked, shrugging with impatience. "You're acting like a lovesick coon."

Ignoring him, Robert continued. "She loved reading my stories."

Sarah stared at him in surprise. "You let her read your work?"

Robert nodded. "I figured if I'm gonna ask a girl to marry me, she had the right to know what she was gettin' herself into."

His two brothers gaped at him as if he'd lost his mind. Neither George nor Jed had much patience with his scribblings.

Sarah squeezed his arm. That's wonderful," she said. She frowned. "Isn't it?"

Robert covered her hand with his own. "Sarah, you found a good man out there. He loves you and wants to take care of you. It's what we always wanted for you. What *I* always wanted for you."

Sarah tried to pull her hand away, but he held on tight. She glared up at him. "A man like him can't be married to the likes of me. Don't you understand? He's a preacher. A man of God, and I ain't nothin' but a—"

"He loves you," Robert said with firm conviction, as if that alone were enough.

Sarah felt what fragile control was left begin to falter. "And I love him." She struggled to keep her voice steady. "But that don't change nothin'."

George shoved a chair aside. "What is this? We've got more important things to worry about. Wells Fargo is moving a big shipment of gold. If we don't hit the trail, we're gonna be out of luck."

Her stomach knotted, and a sick feeling came over her. She swallowed the bile that burned her throat. More shipments, more gold. Would it ever stop?

Releasing her hand, Robert turned and faced his brother. "There isn't going to be any gold."

George leveled him a glowering look. "What kind of crazy talk is that?"

Robert didn't so much as blink. "We're done. The robberies, the holdups, they end now, in this room."

Sarah stared at Robert in disbelief. *Dear God, let it be true . . .*

George's eyes bulged. "Have you gone plain loco? What we're doing . . . It's only right that they should pay after what they did to our parents. Our family."

"And Wells Fargo did pay, George.

For sixteen years they've been paying. But so has Sarah. So have the rest of us. We take the bank's money, and the bank robs us of any sort of a decent life. Do we really want to spend the rest of our lives on the run?"

"Robert has a point," Jed said, his voice wavering. "We almost ended up with a noose around our necks tryin' to save Sarah. Next time, we might not be so lucky."

George jabbed his finger against Jed's chest. "If we were in any danger, it's only 'cuz you had to go and announce to the world who we are."

"Jed did a very brave thing," Sarah said. She never thought Jed had the backbone to act so bold. She could only imagine what it must have cost him to stand up in front of the marshal and confess to being a Prescott.

George's face turned a bright red. "What's wrong with you all?" he exploded. "Gone soft, have you?"

"Not soft," Robert said quietly, his measured voice a startling contrast to George's thunderous roar. "We just got smart, is all."

It was three to one and George looked trapped. His eyes grew wild. His gaze swept from one to the other, as if to search for the weakest link among his united siblings.

"George," Sarah pleaded. "I love you, and I'll always be grateful to you for takin' care of us after our parents died. But Robert is right. There's a wonderful life waitin' for us. One that we can be proud of. One that our dear ma and papa would want us to have."

George leaned toward her. His face dark with cold fury. "Every time you leave the family, you get into trouble and come runnin' back."

"That's 'cuz I never really *leave* the family," she said. "How can I? Our reputation follows me wherever I go. There's no gettin' away from it."

"It's that preacher." George all but spit out the words. "He's the one who put all these fancy ideas into your fool head."

Refusing to let her anguish overcome her control, she lifted her chin and forced herself to stand her ground. "I've always wanted to live a normal life. I wanted to find me a husband. Have children. Justin didn't put those ideas in my head. All he did was make me realize that wantin' those things ain't—isn't wrong."

George glanced from one to another like a cornered animal, and Sarah could only guess what was going through his mind. As the oldest, George had exerted his rightful place as head of the family. His brothers rarely argued with him and all through her growing-up years, she never even questioned his authority. But today, his younger siblings stood united and he looked like the wind had been knocked out of him.

He staggered around like he had too much to drink. Placing both hands on a wooden table, he hung his head low. A tall man, he suddenly seemed to shrink, every curve of his body spelling defeat.

For the longest while, no one spoke. The only sound that could be heard was rain beating against the roof and windows.

Finally, George straightened. "If marriage and children are what you want,

Sarah, then marry your preacher." His voice was low and hollow, sounding nothing like the brother who had ruled the family all these years. He turned to face her. "I won't stop you."

"She can't," Robert said. "Not as long as the Prescotts are in business."

George threw up his hands. "Then there's no helpin' it."

"Yes, there is," Robert said in a deadly calm voice that gave Sarah goose bumps. "I'm out. I'm no longer riding with you."

George glared at him, and Sarah feared they would come to blows. But then an amazing thing happened. Jed stepped between them and turned to face George.

"Count me out too," he said. "I want what's right for Sarah. It's 'bout time she got herself a husband. It's over, George. The Prescott gang is done."

"We can't quit just like that," George argued.

"Sure we can," Jed said. "That preacher in Fort Smith done baptized us. That means that in God's eyes we got what you might call a clean slate. It's the perfect time to quit. All we gotta do is change our names and the way we dress. If what they say 'bout clothes makin' the man is true, then maybe plaid sack suits would make us look like respect'able citizens."

George's face was pale with shock and disbelief. He stared at Jed, the follower, the one who was most likely to see things George's way.

"Robert writes and can work for a newspaper. But what about you? What skills do you have?" His voice was harsh, almost cruel. "I'll tell you what you have. You have nothin'. You ain't got a blasted thing!"

To his credit, Jed didn't back down, revealing a strength of character not previously shown. "Robbin' stages ain't no longer practical. Most money is being transported by railroads nowadays, and we'd be competin' with Jesse's gang. The real money today is in cattle."

George made a dismissive gesture with his arm. "The cattle business ain't gonna last forever."

"Maybe not," Jed said, "at least it'll make honest bus'nessmen out of us."

Robert nodded. "Jed's right. Cattle are pulling in some seventy dollars a head."

Encouraged by Robert's approval, Jed's voice grew stronger. "I say we take what money we have left and invest in cattle."

Without waiting for George to respond, Robert turned to Sarah. "Laurie Anne married someone else," he said. "So it's too late for me. But it's not too late for you, little sister. You have my word: the Prescott gang is no more."

Sarah's eyes filled with tears. She tried to speak but the words wouldn't come. The end of the Prescott gang was nothing short of a miracle.

Robert pointed outside. "Don't just stand there, Sarah. Go! There's someone waiting."

"You mean Justin is still here?" Sarah practically flew across the room and ripped open the door. She picked up her skirts and ran down the steps, her feet slipping and sliding on the rain-soaked ground, and threw herself into his waiting arms.

Gazing up at him, she frowned. "I

know a lady's not supposed to throw herself at a man, but—"

His lips prevented her from completing her sentence. She stood on her toes and kissed him back.

When at last he released her, he searched her face. "Does this mean . . .?"

She nodded. "There ain't—isn't—gonna be no more robberies."

"Sarah, that's great news but . . ." His face grew serious. "Going straight doesn't make up for all the crimes they committed in the past."

"I know," she said softly. "But I reckon it's a start. Maybe God will find a way to make some good come out of this."

"I believe God already has," Justin said, his voice tender.

She smiled. "You just wait and see. I'm gonna be as respectable as an old maid."

He threw back his head and laughed. "You an old maid? This I've got to see."

"Maybe not an old maid," she conceded. "But I will be a lady if it kills me."

He tilted his head to the side. "Not too much of a lady, I hope."

She thought a moment. "There ain't—isn't—much chance of that. I don't think I can keep from throwin' myself at you like a lasso around a calf."

He grinned.

"And don't go expectin' me to wear one of these sausage-stuffing corsets."

His grin inched wider.

She suddenly grew serious and pulled away from him. "Oh, Justin. I don't want to cause you any trouble with your church. I'm still a Prescott."

"I know how to fix that," he said.

"You do? How?"

"By changing your name to Mrs. Justin Wells," he said.

Her heart filled with happiness. She gave herself a pinch to make sure she wasn't dreaming. "Is . . . is that what you call a divine intervention?" she asked.

"It's what you call a marriage proposal," he replied.

She couldn't believe her good fortune. A Prescott married to a preacher. *That* had to be the greatest miracle of all.

He laughed at the expression on her face. "Let's go home to our little girl."

Taking her by the hand, he led her to their waiting horses.

Epilogue

It rained the day that Reverend Justin Wells married Sarah Prescott. It rained so hard that wedding guests sitting in the church had to hold umbrellas over their heads. Recent attempts to repair the roof failed to keep the water from seeping through rusty seams and holes left by popped nail heads.

Almost every vessel in Rocky Creek (including one that looked suspiciously like a chamber pot) had been strategically arranged to catch the drips from the leaky roof.

Justin stood at the front of the church between two overflowing soup pots, waiting for his bride. It seemed like he had been waiting for this moment forever, though it had only been a few weeks since Sarah agreed to marry him.

Nearby, baby Elizabeth slept in her carriage, commanding one of the few dry spots in the church.

Since it didn't seem right to perform his own wedding ceremony, Justin had asked Judge Fassbender to do the honors. The judge stood next to him, rainwater dripping off the top of his hat and settling in a puddle around his feet.

On cue, Ma positioned herself in front of the piano, lifted her hands to the yellowed keys, and began to play. Unable to read the notes on her rain-soaked music sheets, she played the only song committed to memory: "Mary Had a Little Lamb."

Fortunately, the piano was so out of tune and the plip-plopping sound of water so loud that only the most discerning ear recognized the song. That ear belonged to three-year-old Jesse Moreland, who promptly began to sing on the top of his lungs.

He was quickly admonished by his horrified mother. Once order was restored, all eyes turned to the back of the church.

Sarah stood at the doorway, and Justin's heart skipped a beat. She was dressed all in white. Her low, square neckline was edged in pleated lace as was the wraparound skirt and gently puffed sleeves. Her flame-red hair cascaded down her back in a riot of shiny curls. On her crown she wore a wreath of blue and white wildflowers.

Noticing the toes of her red boots showing beneath the satin hem of her skirt, Justin couldn't help but smile.

He winked at her and she smiled back. Like a woman chasing a chicken, she then stomped down the aisle, skirting around puddles and high-stepping over dishpans in her haste to reach him.

Breaking every rule in the *The Bazar Book of Decorum* and without the least bit of hesitation, she threw her arms around Justin's neck. Her brazen behavior brought scandalized gasps from beneath the dripping umbrellas.

"Not yet," he whispered, hands at her waist.

The judge waited for Sarah to disengage herself from Justin and cleared his throat. As if he feared they would all be washed away before the exchange of vows, he rushed through the preliminaries quickly. In his haste, he apparently forgot the usual custom of letting the groom go first. Instead, he turned to the bride.

"Do you, Sarah Jane Prescott, take this man, Justin Bradley Wells, to be your lawfully wedded husband?"

"Yes, yes, yes!" Sarah declared, throwing her arms around Justin once again.

"Not yet," Justin said, gently removing her arms.

Fassbender stared at her like a scolding parent before turning his attention to Justin. "Do you, Justin Bradley Wells, take this woman, Sarah Jane Prescott, to be your lawfully wedded wife?"

Justin, sensing that Sarah was about

to throw herself at him again, shook his head at her and reminded her softly, "Not yet."

Sarah stared at him, a look of dismay on her face. Even Judge Fassbender looked taken aback. Murmurs rose from the crowd.

Mrs. Hitchcock gasped from the front row, the water-drenched feathers of her hat drooping in front of her face. "Oh my, oh my."

The other members of the Rocky Creek Quilting Bee looked equally dismayed.

In a moment of confusion, Ma began to play another rousing rendition of "Mary Had a Little Lamb," much to little Jesse's delight.

The instant the music stopped, Timber Joe stood and pointed his rifle straight at Justin. "Hold it right there, Reverend. You're not going AWOL on your wedding day. Not if I have anything to say about it."

"AWOL? What in the world?" Realizing with sudden horror how his words had been misinterpreted, Justin quickly made amends. "I meant . . . I do, I do, I do. I do take Sarah Prescott to be my lawfully wedded wife." And so there would be no further misunderstanding, he repeated himself again. He then dug into his pocket for the gold ring ordered from the Montgomery Ward catalog and slipped it around her finger.

"I thank God every day for bringing you and Elizabeth into my life. And I promise to love and cherish you from this day forward."

A collective sigh greeted Justin's declaration of love, and Timber Joe backed away, bowing to the audience as if he, alone, saved the day.

The judge dumped the water off his hat and replaced it before adding with great flourish, "I now pronounce you husband and wife."

Justin never thought to hear more beautiful words. Finally ready for Sarah's eager embrace, he waited, but Sarah didn't move. If anything, she looked uncharacteristically demure, even with the raindrops dripping off her nose.

"Sarah . . . now," he said with a grin.

This time, when she flung herself at him, the wedding guests burst into applause.

Reading Group Guide

1. What made Sarah initially decide to stay with Justin, and how did those reasons change during the course of the journey?
2. Justin had no weapons and no knowledge of the Wild West. Yet Sarah felt safe with him. Why?
3. Justin always took the path of least resistance and didn't even fight the false charges lodged against him in Boston. By nature a peaceful man, what happened during the journey that brought out his fighting spirit?
4. How did finding baby Elizabeth change Sarah? How did it change Justin? How did it change their relationship?
5. Justin's favorite hymn was "Amazing Grace." Why do you think he identified so strongly

with the words of that traditional hymn?

6. Sarah said the West didn't change a person; it simply made you more of who you were. What did she mean by that?

7. During the course of the journey to Texas, Justin was forced to grow and change in ways he never imagined. God tested him as both a Christian and a man. Name a time in your life when God put you and your faith to the test.

8. What drew Sarah to the Lost and Found church?

9. Sarah was told by the pastor of Lost and Found to follow God's signs. Describe a time in your life when you felt God leading the way.

10. Sarah believed in God, but she was afraid to put her trust in Him. Yet she took a big chance in going back to Rocky Creek. What part did her faith play in that decision?

11. When did Sarah's opinion of her brother George change, and how did it affect her? Was there ever a time that you disapproved of a loved one's actions? How did this affect your relationship?

12. Justin said that God always sends someone to help in time of need. Name a time in your life when one of God's "angels" helped you. Were you aware of God's help at the time?

13. During the course of the story, Sarah learned that God loves you even if you aren't perfect and "don't know no four-footed words." How has your relationship with God changed through the years?

14. Justin knew how to minister to people in Boston, but he questioned his ability to help the folks in Rocky Creek. Sarah told him all he needed was his faith. Has there ever been a time that you doubted your ability to do something? What

part did your faith play in over-coming your fears?

15. Rocky Creek is a wild frontier town where revenge passes as justice and God is an after-thought. In what ways does the condition of the town (and church) mirror the spiritual de-cay of Rocky Creek's citizens?

16. Justin questioned God's rea-sons for sending him to Texas. When did he finally understand why God sent him there?

17. How were the folks in Rocky Creek different from those in Boston? How were they simi-lar?

18. Justin didn't want to leave Boston and the church he loved. But by following God's plan, he gained so much more than he lost. Can you think of something bad that happened to you that later turned out to be a blessing in disguise?

Acknowledgments

Reverend Justin Wells is a firm believer that God sends the right people into our lives when we most need them. God has truly sent the most extraordinary and caring people my way at just the right time. Here are but a few for which I am most grateful:

My agent, Natasha Kern, who can't be praised enough for her wisdom, knowledge, insight, and encouragement. Some people show you stars, others lead you to them and she led me to my wonderful editor Natalie Hanemann, who shared my vision for the book and helped to make it what it is today.

Jennifer Stair whose eye for details has made this author look good. Jennifer Deshler, Katie Bond and the entire Thomas Nelson family for their hard work, support, and good humor.

My dear friend, Lee Duran, who has not only helped me through some very dark times, but has the thankless task of reading my first drafts. Her amazing ability to look at my work and say "it stinks" while making it sound like I just won the Pulitzer is truly a gift.

I'm also grateful to Chelley Kitzmiller who first suggested I try my hand at writing an inspirational novel and has since forgiven me for calling her idea crazy.

My family, especially my husband, who had learned to live with all the challenges of a writer's life. To Darin Keith, Robyn, Natsuko, Daniel, Warren, Summer, Brian, Danny, Courtney, and Bryanna who make it all worthwhile.

Pastor Jeff Cheadle whose weekly sermons continue to inspire and help me grow in my Christian faith.

My many, many friends who add such richness to my life and who inspire many of the eccentricities in my books (and have the good grace not to recognize themselves in print).

My readers who give me more joy than I could ever give to them. Please join me in the fall of 2010 for the next novel in the Rocky Creek Romance series.

Nothing pleases me more than to hear from readers. You can write to me at the following postal address: P.O. Box 630288, Simi Valley, CA 93063.